ONCE UPON A *Family Tree*

ONCE UPON A *Family Tree*

MICHELLE DE LEON

A STREBOR BOOKS INTERNATIONAL LLC PUBLICATION
DISTRIBUTED BY SIMON & SCHUSTER, INC.

Published by

Strebor Books International LLC
P.O. Box 1370
Bowie, MD 20718
http://www.streborbooks.com

LCCN 200311576
ISBN 1-59309-028-5

Distributed by Simon & Schuster, Inc.
1230 Avenue of the Americas
New York, NY 10020
1-800-223-2336

Cover painting: André Harris

First Printing October 2004
Manufactured and Printed in the United States

10 9 8 7 6 5 4 3 2 1

DEDICATION

I dedicate this book to all my family and friends near and far.
Especially Calandra and Angela.

ACKNOWLEDGMENTS

I acknowledge God in all that I do because it's for His glory. And He has truly blessed me by surrounding me with real friends and family who support my efforts at all times. I especially give thanks to my Strebor cohorts: Zane, Charmaine and everyone who plays a part in making it happen.

I thank Brenda Woods, Kim Azille, Thomas Green and Archie Williams for their wisdom, assistance and career advice. I also thank all the readers who have taken the time to give me their feelings and thoughts. You are so very appreciated.

I thank my church family: Victory Baptist Church of Stone Mountain, GA. "We've gotten through another week and the devil has failed again!"

I thank the loves of my life: Joseph, Jasmine and Kierstin. I've got your backs forever.

CHAPTER 1

BOOM-BOOM-BOOM BA-BOOM-BOOM!

The place was jumping; the bass was thumping. Bodies mingled covered with sweat. In the pungently pissy corridors, bodies were covered with kisses and hickeys. Wanna-be men, rubbing up some what-you-thinkin'-of women in the project stairways. How romantic.

Yolie was oblivious to all that. Her hands worked the turntables furiously. She had the crowd in the palm of her hand. They all were familiar to her. The buildings of the Roosevelt Houses were like a small town. Everyone knew each other and their business. Yolie had received many invitations into the hallways, but she had other things on her mind. Giving the neighborhood something to gossip about wasn't on the agenda.

She had the center jamming to Busta Rhymes, P-Diddy, EPMD. Yolie got her props. She could rock a jam (even though she was "a girl").

"Damn, Yo. It's about to jump off in here!"

"We about to raise the roof in this mug!"

Hundreds of hands were pushing up an imaginary roof. Everyone was "FUBUed" down. With a little Tommy thrown in for good measure. Borinquas and Morenos. Yolara belonged to both. She looked to the back and saw her half-sister, Egypt.

Yolie didn't have anything against Egypt. They shared the same father, Meshach Burkette. He wasn't a faithful husband (Yolie's mother, Caridad, was evidence of that), but he was a dedicated father who loved his daughters.

Yolie often felt bad that she couldn't have a real relationship with Egypt, but she couldn't blame her. She was the "legitimate" one who couldn't stand Yolie, the "love child." Egypt glanced at Yolie for a second and then turned to some guy she was with.

"What's up, Yo?" a voice yelled above the music.

Yolie turned around to see BulletProof. Now with a name like that you just knew what was what.

"What's up, B.P.?" Yolie said to him.

"You seen Kaliq? The nigga said he was gonna be here."

"I haven't seen him yet," she answered.

"How's that butter pican Rican doing? Yo moms is da bomb. She got it going on, no joke," BulletProof exclaimed.

Yolie was used to the guys acting up over her mother. Caridad was a beautiful woman. She was her mother, but also her best friend. Cari had made a lot of mistakes, but her heart was always in the right place. It often led her to the wrong place, but her motto was "que sera, que sera" (what will be, will be).

"Mommy is all right. Is Kaliq still picking the boys up this weekend?"

"You know my cousin don't miss no opportunity to spend time with his shorties, bee."

"He is a good father. Me and Mommy do our best with the twins, but they need their dad."

"I can't say if I woulda been better off with my pops around, but it woulda been nice to have a choice."

BulletProof had lost his father a long time ago. The saying goes you don't see too many old drug dealers. BulletProof should heed that, but he was just "caught up."

"I'm tired of hollering over this music. Let's go over there," Yolie suggested. She brought the crowd under control by throwing on a slow jam. Mary J. singing about "A Dream."

"You know my cousin is feeling you, right?"

Yolie could feel a blush come across her face. "B.P., you know me and Kaliq together would just be too tacky. He is my little brother's father."

"Yeah, but him and yo moms ain't never had nothing together, but that one time. Yo moms is fine and all, but I told him you the one he should be hittin'. I ain't with that older woman taboo shit."

Yolie was saved from having to respond to that comment when a fight broke out. She saw the flash of metal just as someone grabbed her by the arm. People were making a mad dash for the exits. Yolie had just made it out the door as the first shots rang out. She had thought it was Bullet Proof who had grabbed her, but she looked up to find Kaliq was the one with the firm grip on her arm.

"Let's get out of here," he said.

"I can't leave my equipment in there."

"All right, but we're waiting out here until we see what's what," he told her.

"Damn, can't even throw a party without some shit going down," Yolie complained.

"That's why I hate Brooklyn. Do or die Bed-Stuy. I'm not trying to take Travis and Trevor away from your mother, but I wish she'd move out of these projects."

She often wished the same thing, but it wasn't easy. Cops finally arrived at the scene. Of course, no one admitted to seeing anything of importance. An argument had taken place that led to shooting. Same old, same old. Once the excitement died down, Kaliq helped Yolie take her stuff upstairs.

The apartment was dark when she opened the door. "I guess everyone's knocked out."

"I'm surprised Cari slept through all that commotion," Kaliq commented.

"Mommy can sleep through anything. I know she did some overtime before her tour today. I call that post office a plantation. You know she works a mandatory six days on them stupid machines."

"I'll get more construction work when the weather gets warmer. I'll be able to help out with the kids even more then," he said while fidgeting.

"You want something to drink?" Yolie offered as she kicked off her platform sneakers.

"No thanks. Actually, I got to get going. I only stopped by the center to pick up something from Dennis, a.k.a. BulletProof," he explained still fidgeting.

"What's the matter?" Yolie giggled.

"I gotta go bad," he answered.

"Why didn't you say so? You know the way to the bathroom."

He followed her to the bathroom. Her room was right across from it. She sat on her bed and started to pull her socks off. In her dresser mirror she could see Kaliq hadn't closed the door completely. Yolie tried not to peek through the door. Kaliq was tall and muscularly slim. His dark good looks reminded her of that R&B singer, Brian McKnight. She averted her eyes as she saw the light go out.

"Thanks," he said. "Tell Cari I'm still taking the boys Saturday."

"All right. Thanks for the help, Kaliq." She walked him to the door and said good night. Lying across her bed, Yolie thought about what Bullet Proof had said (who would have thought his real name was Dennis!) She didn't know if she should believe that Kaliq liked her. For that matter, should she even want him to? That would be one for the *Jerry Springer* show.

"I'd like you to meet our next guest, Yolara. Yolara has a secret she'd like to reveal today on our show," Jerry would say.

"Yes, Jerry. I'm in love with my mother's one-night stand."

(Ooohs and aaahs from the audience)

"If there was no love relationship between the two, what's to stand in your way?"

"Well, you see, that one time resulted in my five-year-old twin brothers, Travis and Trevor."

(More ooohs and aaahs from the audience)

"How do you think this man feels about you?"

"I have no idea. His cousin did say he was attracted to me, but…"

"Well, let's bring him out and see what he has to say. Here's Kaliq."

Kaliq emerges from backstage with Caridad right at his heels.

"My daughter is NOT going to go out with my sons' father. No way. What kind of sick shit is that? All in the family? First the mother, then the daughter!" Cari yells at Kaliq, smacking him in the head. Everyone breaks out into a fight. The crowd goes wild. (Yolie knew her mother would never hit anyone, but it made the daydream funnier.)

She pulled off her stripped nylon Adidas warm-ups, but left her Phat Farm T-shirt on. Yolie was glad she had gotten her pay for dee-jaying the party upfront. She did pretty well for herself. She was saving up for college expenses. With her father, Meshach, being a bus operator and Caridad working for the Postal Service, financial aid would be a joke; they earned too much to qualify. They were good jobs, but they hardly made you rich. Caridad had heard there was some kind of benefit the P.O. had to help employees put their kids through college. Yolie wasn't sure how things would work out from her father's end of the bargain, but she had every confidence that he would come through for her.

Yolie's mind was so wound up, that she was having a hard time falling asleep. Her thoughts wandered back to Kaliq. She could recall a time when he was one of her least favorite people. When Cari told her she was pregnant, Yolie was twelve years old; a kid who was still clinging to the hope that her parents were somehow going to come together. She had no basis for that, but it was a dream that she felt was ruined by Kaliq's presence.

Yolie remembered giving Kaliq a hard way to go whenever he came over to the house. He took it in stride and tried to win her over despite her teenage tantrums. As she got older, her girlfriends started to comment on how fine they thought her brothers' father was. At first, she thought they all were crazy, but eventually she came to the same conclusion. One day Kaliq had offered to baby-sit the boys at Cari's house while she went to an appointment. Yolie was fourteen and the twins were a little too much for her to handle on her own, so Kaliq wanted to help out. It was a blistering hot day and the babies were cranky and uncomfortable.

"Why don't we run a bath with cool water and let them chill out in there for a while?" Kaliq had suggested.

"I'll get their bath toys."

It had definitely done the trick. Yolie and Kaliq were soaked by the time the kids were ready for their naps.

"So, what do you want to do now?" Yolie asked.

She could tell he was only trying to be nice. "Uh, I don't know. What do you feel like doing?

"We could hook up the PlayStation," Yolie said while running off to get the CDs.

They competed against each other fiercely for a whole "NBA Live" season. The two played and pigged out until Yolie fell asleep on the couch. With everyone in the house asleep, Kaliq flicked through the rest of her CDs to see what else was worth playing. He had just popped a game in when someone started knocking on the door. Kaliq had recognized Meshach through the peephole and opened the door for him.

"Hey, what's up, man? Is Cari here?" Meshach had asked, but stopped short when he looked past Kaliq and saw his daughter sprawled out on the couch. Kaliq could feel the tension build immediately. He knew there was about to be trouble. Meshach marched over to the couch and shook his sleeping child.

"Yolara, where is your mother?"

Rubbing her eyes, it took Yolie a moment to get her bearings. "Hi, Daddy. Mommy is out. Kaliq came over to help me watch the babies."

"Why couldn't you take the boys to your house and watch them?" Meshach asked Kaliq suspiciously.

"Mr. Burkette, I was just trying to help Cari out. These are my children. If they were gonna be more comfortable here, then here is where I was gonna be." Kaliq tried to speak to him respectfully, but Yolie could see it was a strain. She wondered what her father had thought was going on.

"I just don't think it's appropriate for you to be here alone with my daughter."

"We were playing 'NBA Live.' Everything is cool," Kaliq tried to reassure him, annoyed that it was necessary to do so.

"What time did your mother say she would be back?"

"She had to go into Manhattan. Who knows how long that's gonna take," Yolie answered her father. He glanced at his watch. Since he was in his uniform, she knew he was about to head out to the depot.

"Tell Cari I will call her tonight." He contemplated telling Yolie to come ride the bus with him until her mother returned.

"Okay, Daddy," Yolie told Meshach as she hugged him.

"Kaliq, walk me to the door." Kaliq sighed as he followed the man. "Just watch yourself all right. If I hear any shit…"

"Mr. Burkette, I don't know what you trying to say."

"I'm trying to say that you'd better not be trying anything with my child."

"That's ill. I'm here to do right by my kids, just like you, Mr. Burkette."

Meshach did not look convinced, but he let it drop for the time being. That night Yolie recalled there was a big battle over the phone. She could only hear her mother's side of the conversation, but that was enough.

"Burk, you cannot tell me who to have up in my house. He is my sons' father and he is welcomed here anytime. More welcomed than you if you want to know the truth about it."

Back then Yolie would cry in her room whenever her parents got into it. She heard Cari say that Meshach had no business being jealous of Kaliq. He hadn't wanted her, so why should he care who she was dealing with now? This made Yolie's feelings for Kaliq uncertain again. Sure, she had developed a crush on him, but was he really the cause of her parent's breakup or not? Ultimately, she realized he wasn't. No matter *whom* Cari was seeing, Meshach's reaction was the same.

Yolie finally began to drift off, wondering what new drama was in store.

CHAPTER 2

Meshach Burkette was a little preoccupied that morning. His mind was hardly on the current ranting and ravings of his wife, Olive. He didn't doubt she was going on about something she wanted, but he hadn't managed to get. Olive was under the mistaken impression that he gave a damn. Yeah, there was a time when he did. Growing up, they were inseparable so it was a natural course of events that they should marry. Then a strange thing happened. Complete transformation.

"*Come on over here and give me what you good for,*" he'd tease.

"*Now, Meshach, you know we ain't got no time for that. You know we due to meet the Covingtons at B. Smith's for brunch today.*"

"*The who to have what? Babe, you know I ain't trying to spend my RDO with some uptight siddity friends of YOURS,*" Meshach complained.

"*Well, I guess you don't really want any of this stuff after all,*" she countered.

She sauntered over to his lap and stroked him playfully between his legs. Just as he was about to return the favor, she'd jumped up and ordered him to be ready in an hour.

Yes, he had Olive tuned out. He saw his escape when Egypt entered the kitchen. "Hey there, Egee Bird. What it look like?"

"Mornin', Daddy," Egypt greeted her father.

"You didn't hang too late last night, did you?" he asked.

"I don't know why you had to go to some PJ party anyway. You know wherever there's a center party there's trouble," Olive interjected.

"As a matter of fact, there was some beef last night. Two niggas…I mean brothers, got into it and somebody started shooting." Egypt quickly corrected herself when she saw the daggers her mother shot her way at the term *nigga*.

Meshach immediately thought about Yolara. "What? Did anybody get hurt?"

"No, you pretty much know the drill. Once some loud talking gets started, you gets to steppin'," she assured him.

"That's it. You're not going to any more of those things. Do you hear me?" Olive stated.

"It's not like it used to be. You do need to be careful out here, Egee."

"Well, hey I use good judgment. That girl Yolie, she's the one that needs to exercise some good sense," Egee said expectantly.

Meshach often wondered if his oldest girl knew that she had a half-sister out there. There were a few times when he caught a certain look in her eye. Nothing would please him more than to have his two girls interact as family, but he wasn't ready to deal with the shit that would ricochet off too many fans.

"I'm gonna have a smoke out on the porch," Meshach announced.

He gazed up the street wondering how things had gotten so out of hand in his house. He worked like a dog to make the mortgage every month, but what was the use of it all? Olive was not the woman he loved anymore. She was too busy trying to be something she wasn't. Complaining about project parties when she had come from the worst building they had ever erected in Brownsville. He was proud of her at first. She had moved up pretty fast at her office. She was a manager's assistant at DuValier's (a Swiss luxury watch outfit). Once the company invited her to attend the annual shareholders meeting in Switzerland that was all she wrote. Olive had become straight-up bourgeois overnight. He was surprised she hadn't left him and his "quaint" little Flatbush home.

Damn, he missed Cari. She was real all the time. Every inch; every nuance. He could still recall the first time they had met.

"Excuse me, miss, but you want to drop your fare in the box, please," Meshach had asked her.

"I'm sorry, mister, but they didn't have my bus pass ready at school. I'll bring money tomorrow, all right," she informed him with a mischievous gleam in her eye.

"That'll work for tomorrow, but that don't solve your problem today. You wanna step off my bus, please."

"You got to be kidding me. Ain't it against the law to throw a kid off the bus or something?"

"No, but it's against the law to evade the fare," he reminded her while throwing open the door.

For the rest of that school year they played a kind of cat and mouse game. He knew he was borrowing trouble, but hey, Caridad Flores was worth it. He'd been married just over a year and already Olive was pregnant with Egypt. He was obligated to his family, but Cari was like an itch that when you scratched it the relief was unbearable.

"Hey, Burk (the name his co-workers called him), you know I'm graduating this year. You wanna be my prom date?" Cari had joked with him. That day she rode the line with him until clearing time. A lot of the guys at the depot had some action on the side. There were all kinds of bus groupies. Chicks who'd attach themselves to an operator and take *him* for a ride.

"Yo, man. You letting that little Puerto Rican princess lead you around by the nose. Brother, she ain't even letting you get any. Man, if you know like we know, you'd take her to the last stop. Heh, heh, heh."

And he was stupid enough to follow that misguided piece of advice. One day she rode the line with him again and he felt it was time to make his move.

"Are we gonna get together tomorrow, Burk?" Caridad had asked him. She stretched herself across the first row of seats.

"Sure, what would you like to do?" Meshach inquired.

"I don't know. Tomorrow's a half-day. Why don't we go down to Coney Island. Or better yet, let's check out the Village."

He hated to disappoint her, but there was no way he could do all of that. A momentary twinge of guilt hit him as he thought about the appointment he had with Olive's doctor. She was having a difficult pregnancy and they were going to see a specialist.

"Why don't we have lunch?" he suggested.

"Come on, man. We always go out for lunch. There are two other meals during the day, you know," Cari complained. "We don't spend any real time together at all." She tossed her long brunette hair over her shoulder, exposing a long graceful neck.

Meshach knew he was more than likely asking for trouble, but he got up from the driver's seat and sat beside her. "Cari, you know I'd be with you more if I could. Baby, you know I'm still married." He felt akin to a heel even mentioning it.

"You don't have to remind me," she answered while stroking his face. "But you know how I feel about you, right?"

He was fully aware of her feelings and his own. Meshach sat her in his lap. It was dark out and no one was on the street. He'd already turned out the lights on the bus. It was a cool spring night, but to Meshach the heat was unbearable. Cari was young, giving, and smart. He often imagined how it would be if they could take their "thing" further. Olive wasn't his friend anymore; she was just his spouse. He and Cari discussed issues and told jokes. He was older, but not so much so that he couldn't relate to being a high school senior.

"What's more important is that you know how I feel about you," he replied. He lifted her onto his lap. He forced his greedy hands to take their time as he ran them up her back. A small sound emerged from her. Meshach reached around to palm her breasts. She wasn't buxom by any means, but they were delicious nonetheless as he turned her around so he could place one in his mouth. She seemed a little apprehensive at first.

"What if someone sees us, Burk?"

He answered with a gentle tug of her nipple. His hands sought to know her even better. He caressed her everywhere he could reach. He was surprised at his own guttural sounds. It had been so long since he had felt this. It made him angry when Olive's face threatened to ruin this secret moment. He tried to drive it away by kissing Cari as deeply as physics would allow. A sweet taste that he had sampled many times, but at that very moment felt like sustenance. She returned the kiss with an equal force that threatened to bring the moment to an abrupt end. However, they kept on. Growing bolder, Cari undid his zipper. She played with his manhood the way a child handles some new discovery. He could tell that she wanted to take her time, but time was of the essence. He deftly moved her cotton panties to the side, then Meshach raised her up onto himself. He met her eyes, wondering if he were crazy all the while. The look of wonderment on her face was so endearing to him that he knew that instant that he loved this girl. Meshach buried his face in her bosom as he guided himself into her. She jerked slightly, maybe surprised at how quickly they were moving on. She then wrapped her arms about his neck and shoulders.

"Don't hurt me, Burk," she whispered.

He could feel her every drop. There was a resistance that was both painful and exhilarating. Cari began to grip him even tighter as she tried to meet his upward thrusts with downward ones of her own. Meshach thought he would lose his mind with every rhythmic stroke. He breathed her name as she did his. When he had finally filled her up with all of himself, it was more than he could stand. He quickly took her mouth again to stifle the screams that threatened to alert all of DeKalb Avenue.

Cari fell against him seemingly exhausted. In a moment of sheer male bravado, Meshach thought her tear-filled eyes were signs of pleasure.

"Hey, hey. What's this?" he asked her, still holding her in his lap.

"Nothing. I'm just being stupid," she answered, wiping her face with the back of her hand.

"As much as I'd like to stay here, well not here…, but with *you* all night, a brother's got to get this bus back to the depot." He gently lifted her up off his lap. They had created quite a mess. "Let me get you something; hold on."

He searched his bag for some tissue or a handkerchief. He took her face into his hands. Tears still streamed down her face.

"It didn't hurt so much really. I just wanted so much to be with you," she told him quietly.

It wasn't until Meshach went to tidy up himself that he noticed the red drops left behind on the white cloth.

"What the hell…? Cari, are you okay? Did I…" Meshach left the question hanging in the air. "*Don't hurt me, Burk.*" That's what she had said.

"Cari," he hesitated, "This wasn't your first time, was it?"

She didn't answer right away as she straightened her clothes. "I think we should go now."

Dumbfounded, Meshach returned to the driver's seat and started the bus. He had driven several blocks before he pulled the bus over. They were nowhere near the depot. He went back over to Cari and took her up in his arms again.

"I'm so sorry, baby. You deserved better than that," Meshach consoled her this time, wiping away tears of his own.

***

Meshach was brought back to the present when he heard the front door open.

"Daddy, you know Ma's gonna get at you," Egypt teased her father.

"Damn, can't a black man get no peace?" he teased back.

"What were you supposed to do today, huh?"

"Egee Bird, if you don't remind me, I'm gonna spend the next two weeks in the doghouse."

"You're supposed to get Ma's car tuned up so she can take it to that spa she and her cronies are headed to this weekend."

"Shit, is that this weekend? I'm gonna have to take it over to Paco. He would do the best work for the cheapest price."

"Want me to go with you?" Egypt offered.

"Nah, ain't necessary. Besides, I know all you really want to do is see that boy from Roosevelt. Telling you, you better watch your back over there."

"Yeah, OK," she responded halfheartedly. "See ya later, Daddy."

"Check ya later, Egee."

As Egypt watched her father head for the Camry parked in the driveway, she knew just as sure as she knew her own name that Meshach didn't want her tagging along because he was gonna go see the other one.

CHAPTER 3

Caridad and her boys were dancing across the living room to the blaring music. This was their weekend ritual. They'd have a pancake breakfast with all the works. Cari would help them read the Sunday comics and explain the jokes to them. Then she'd throw on some old disco tunes and they'd have a ball.

"Helloooooo!" Yolie called out. "Did you little people save me any grub?"

"I saved you two, Yolie, but Travis ate all the syrup!"

"Did not. You ate up the rest of it!"

"And good morning to you, too." Cari smiled at her daughter.

"You know they had some more drama down at the center last night?" Yolie told her mother as she scooped up the last strip of bacon before the twins noticed it.

"Yolie, nobody got hurt, did they?" her mother asked with concern.

"No, but you get tired of the same old shit. I'm a damn good deejay if I do say so myself. They ought to give us hazard pay or something."

"Yeah, well, take it up with the union," Cari joked.

"Speaking of unions and all that kind of stuff…"

"I know what you're gonna say. Yes, I'm looking into that information about college tuition," she reassured Yolie.

"I know I'm getting to be a nag about it, but I don't want to miss any opportunities."

"Believe me, baby, I don't want you to miss any either." Cari grabbed Yolie by the hand and twirled her around the "dance floor."

The twins ran off to their room to play some more. Yolie helped her mother pick up after them.

"I saw Kaliq last night," Yolie said.

"That man is so busy, I'm surprised he made time to go to a party," Cari said as she brushed at a spot on Trevor's jeans.

"Well, he was really only there to drop off something for B.P. Did you know that his real name is Dennis?"

Cari laughed. "Figures."

"Mommy, do you think…?"

"Do I think what, *mi hija*?"

"Never mind. He told me to tell you that he'd be over on Saturday to pick up Trav and Trev."

Caridad sincerely doubted that that's what was on Yolie's mind. She knew her child well. Miss Yolara had developed a little crush on Kaliq. That was a strange turn of events, but that seemed to be Cari's life story.

"Do you want anything in particular for dinner tonight?"

Before Yolie could answer, there was a knock at the door. She stepped over an army of small soldiers to get to it. Through the peephole she saw Meshach.

She hastily unlocked the door and slid the chain off. "Daddy, what's up?"

Meshach caught his younger daughter as she jumped into his arms. He had just seen her last week, but this was the greeting he always had waiting for him.

"I came to examine your head myself," he told her as he kissed her cheek.

"Huh? Have you been getting too close to the bus fumes again?" Yolie kidded him in return.

"All right now. For real, what's this shit about you almost getting shot up last night?"

"Well, that's a gross exaggeration," Yolie answered, motioning him to sit on the couch.

Cari emerged from the kitchen. "Hey, Burk. I thought I heard your voice. How are you?"

"I lost ten years off my life when I heard about that shootout at the center," he told Cari. "Don't you think these 'functions' are getting out of hand?"

"Life around here in general is getting out of hand. It's not as bad as it was, but you know how Roosevelt is, Burk."

"Yeah, I know and that's why I don't think it's a good idea for her to do these parties," Meshach reasoned, his voice rising involuntarily.

"You know Yolie is well-known and well-liked around here. Everybody on this block got her back," Cari countered with a small rise in volume of her own.

"Um, excuse me, but I'm still right here," Yolie said.

"You know I don't think it's being responsible on your part to allow her to…"

"Oh no, don't even go there, Meshach Burkette!" Cari retorted.

"Okay, I'm outta here if y'all don't stop," Yolie informed her parents. "I know I'm still your little girl and all that, but I could get hurt just crossing the street…"

"Yeah, that's comforting," Meshach interrupted.

"How did you find out about last night anyway?"

Meshach instantly put on the brakes. He was never comfortable talking about Egypt to Yolie. It was almost like he tried to pretend she didn't exist for Yolie's benefit. He loved them equally, but he was afraid his youngest child would harbor some resentment towards him if he mentioned life at home with Egypt.

"You don't have to tell me. I saw her there," Yolie answered her own question. "Do you jump on her case about hanging out in shoot-'em-up territory, too?"

"Of course, I caution her about the streets. Egypt's nearly twenty-one. I can't make her not go somewhere," Meshach told her sheepishly. "Besides, she'll be heading off to Spelman soon…"

"What? Egypt's going to Atlanta?" Yolie asked, obviously stunned.

"She wants to transfer down there. You know we got people down that way…"

"No, I don't know you got people down that way," Yolie interrupted him again. "Would you excuse me?"

Before Meshach could protest, she was off to her bedroom.

"Dammit, why did I have to say anything?" he chastised himself under his breath.

"Don't put all the blame on yourself, Burk. I knew what we'd be in for when I told you I wanted to keep our baby. I came to terms with it, but Yolie is another story. We were just talking about college tuition."

"You know I'm gonna help out with that, Cari."

"But Burk, it's not just the money. She's never been able to do the whole family thing with you. I believe she thinks Egypt is your top priority because she's always lived with you."

"Cari, you know that's not true. I care for both my girls the same."

"I know that, Burk, but as a kid that's how she felt."

Meshach walked over to the window. He leaned his forehead against the cool glass. "I never meant to hurt her, Cari."

"We know, Burk. I should have played my cards a little differently, too."

With his back turned he didn't see Cari reach out to him, stopping short. Honestly, she didn't mean for him to. Cari had made up her mind that Meshach Burkette was someone she couldn't afford to have in her life anymore. At least not the way he had been.

"She'll cool down, babe. I'll tell her to call you later," Cari said softly.

When Meshach turned around he saw the same young girl he'd fallen for. Her hair was shorter, but still flowed prettily around her face. She also had lightened it so it was now a blondish brown. Three children had enhanced her figure, not ruined it. She was just a beautiful woman. She used to be his woman.

"I got to have the car looked at. I'll probably be in the neighborhood for the next few hours. Tell Yolie to beep me if she wants me to come back up here before I head back to Flatbush."

"No problem. Talk to you later," she said to him as she walked him out. They both knew the habit of kissing each other goodbye had been a hard one to break, but it just seemed so natural for so long.

After an awkward moment at the door, Meshach went to wait for the elevator.

CHAPTER 4

Kaliq had slept in that morning. Between work and school, he was completely worn out. He was nearly finished with his B.A. He had always dreamed of becoming an architect. Even as a kid he could appreciate the beauty of the brownstones on his block. His family had owned the house he lived in for years. However, his folks did what most old folks did when they retired. Moved down South. Kaliq knew his mother would go upside his head if she ever heard him refer to her as old folks. They had just worked hard all their lives so they could afford to retire and leave New York while they were still young enough to enjoy life. They also wanted to see their children well provided for. Kaliq's three older sisters were all married and scattered to the four winds, so he had kept the brownstone.

B.P. was his roommate—a decision he was already regretting. He loved his cousin, but Lord knows BulletProof had made some bad choices throughout his life. Kaliq didn't pretend to be any type of role model, but he had hoped hanging out with him would give B.P. some other ideas.

Kaliq felt he had enough responsibility trying to raise his two sons. Fatherhood had come as a complete and total shock to the then eighteen-year-old high school senior. He had a future that now included not one, but two children. Kaliq hadn't told his parents about the situation until after they were already moved down South. He knew they would have prolonged going, and he was already at odds about what to do without their well-meaning interference. He hadn't dreamed Cari would want to keep the babies after their one night together.

"Kaliq?" he remembered her saying. "I know I sort of came on to you. No, I definitely came on to you. It wasn't the smartest thing I could have done. Not to put you down or anything…"

"Cari, what are you tryin' to say?"

"There's no other way but to come and tell you. I'm pregnant, Kaliq."

"But, shit…I mean, how? I mean, I know how, but…"

"I know it's a surprise. No one was more shocked than I was. You don't have to *do* anything. I mean to say that I feel as if I took advantage of you. You shouldn't have to shoulder any responsibility if you don't want to," she quietly informed him, finally taking a seat on his couch.

"I can handle my end, but what exactly do you plan on doing?" he asked hesitantly.

"Man, I honestly don't know, but I can't blame this baby anymore for my behavior than I blame you. You know I was trippin' 'cause Yolara's father's been treatin' me like sloppy seconds. I couldn't take it anymore. I've been in love with that man since I was in high school. When I finally ask him to put me and Yolie first, he said he 'couldn't just up and leave his marriage.' I'm like what the hell you talkin' about. In my book, you up and left your marriage when you first had me. I know you probably don't want to hear all of this."

In Kaliq's mind he wished she had said all of this sooner; but then he had to be honest with himself. The day she had offered herself to him, he hadn't asked any questions; horny idiot that he was.

"Let me ask you this. Why me?"

She turned to him and stroked the side of his face. "I've watched a lot of the guys end up playing for the wrong team. Maybe it was a subconscious sort of thing, but I felt I could trust you. It's like I was on some sort of stupid mission, but I had sense enough to pick you. You know we all pretty much know everyone's business. Your parents did well bringing y'all up. Besides, it wasn't as if I was lookin' for a sperm donor. You're a fucking handsome guy."

They had started kicking it at a block party. His boys had silently urged him on when they had noticed Cari come up to him. She was slightly intoxicated, but not enough to *not* know what she was doing. Her suggestions were subtle, but not to be mistaken. A few of the older folks began clucking their tongues as if they were witnessing a lioness moving in for the kill.

Once it had finally gotten dark, she invited him up to her apartment.

"Have a seat. Do you want a Malta?" she had offered.

"Yeah, that would be all right," he managed to answer, not quite believing his luck. He wasn't a virgin by any means, but he wasn't a player either. This older woman thing was a new and exciting experience.

"You can put on some music if you like," Cari said as she handed him the bottle of cold Malta.

He knew enough to throw on the *Quiet Storm*. An evening of slow jams was definitely called for.

"Where's your kid?" he somehow remembered to ask.

"She's staying with her godmother out in Sheepshead. You hungry?"

"Nah, I'm all right." Kaliq started to feel a little uncomfortable all of a sudden. He could feel his body reacting to her nearness. Cari was totally sexy. Not in that cheap obvious way, but all the fellas was "riding her bra strap," as they used to say. He hoped he wasn't getting in over his head. Then he cursed himself for acting like a fool. She had only invited him up to…to what?

"Do you mind if I lay my head on your lap, Kaliq?" she asked while doing it at the same time.

"Sure," he said, realizing at the last moment that she'd be able to feel his "situation."

Cari didn't say anything about that; she just kind of rambled on. "You got a girl, Kaliq?"

"No," he answered, awkwardly putting his arms around her.

"Can I be your girl tonight?" she inquired, shifting her body so she could look up into his face. In the dark he hadn't noticed Cari's eyes were glistening. In response, he bent over to kiss her shyly on her mouth. They never left the couch. They joined together in her living room with some song he had never heard playing in the background.

A couple of months had passed before she told him the news. They had remained friendly with each other, but nothing had ever happened between them again. His boys had pressed him for information, but he never told them anything. He wasn't sure what to make of their brief encounter, but he was aware that she hadn't meant for it to happen again. Then one day she dropped the bomb.

"Kaliq, I realize I didn't have to mention it to you at all, but I'm not that kind of woman. I'm sure you're wondering just what kind of woman I am, but I wouldn't do that to you or my...our baby."

"I take that to mean you want to keep it?" Kaliq asked, desperately not wanting to sound like the scared kid he was.

"Yeah, that's what I mean. Like I said, you don't have to be involved if you don't want to. I didn't handle that situation well at all and I'm sorry," she said to him with deep sincerity.

What was he supposed to say? Don't sweat it?

"My parents didn't raise me to sidestep my part in a mistake. Not that our kid is a mistake, but..."

"Kaliq, I know what you mean." She heaved a great sigh and started towards the door.

"Where are you going?' he asked. "You just gonna leave just like that?"

"Kaliq, I feel foolish enough. Please just let me go. We have a lot of time to deal with this mess, but for now I just want to get some air," she answered as she continued towards the door.

"What makes you want to have this kid, Cari?"

"I know how it feels not to be wanted. This baby may not have been conceived in the best way, but it's a part of me. And besides Yolie, me is all I have."

With that she closed the door.

***

Kaliq rolled over and looked at the digital clock on his nightstand. He finally dragged himself out of bed and headed towards the kitchen. His stomach had been growling, but he'd been too tired to do anything about it.

B.P. and his boys had taken control of his living room. He didn't think to say *their* living room, because his cousin saw himself as more of a guest than a roommate. He knew the house was paid for, so he felt there was no need to offer any rent. Besides, Kaliq knew how BulletProof made his money and he didn't want anything to do with it anyway.

"What up, dogs?" Kaliq asked groggily.

A dull chorus of "Kaliq" greeted him back. They were wrapped up in a Jets game. Kaliq was just about to go straight into the kitchen when he stopped himself. He knew he must've been losing his natural mind. He slowly turned back to the group scattered about the room and couldn't believe what he was seeing.

"Yo, Dennis! Can I speak with you for a second over here?"

B.P. backed his way into the kitchen so he wouldn't miss the play that could earn the Jets the first down they so desperately needed. When he was within arm's reach, Kaliq snatched him into the room.

"Yo, cuz. What's the matter with you?" B.P. asked, snatching his arm back. He knew it was serious when Kaliq called him Dennis.

"What the hell you doing cleaning those guns in my house?" Kaliq demanded to know. He kept his voice down because this was a family thing. Those cats out there were in no shape or form family to him. One no-good was enough to deal with.

"Why you buggin', man? We ain't havin' no target practice or some shit like that. You've got to maintain your stuff…"

"Yo, 'cuz', don't try to play me, man. I've told you before I don't want that shit up in here. You're a grown man. What you do is your business. Travis and Trevor are my business. If they needed to come over here unexpectedly, I don't want to have to explain to them…"

"All right, I get it. Damn, man. You know I ain't tryin' to disrespect you or nothin'. You my peeps and those little shorties my peeps. I tell the guys to clear out with that shit, OK?"

"Thank you. I'd appreciate that," Kaliq told his cousin as he reached into the freezer to see what he had to eat.

"You do good with them kids. Especially since you got more than you bargained for. I can remember when they came out to the waiting room and told you you had twins. You liked to pee in your pants, son," B.P. reminisced, laughing uncontrollably.

"Ha, ha. All I know is that after all that craziness, I'm blessed to have my sons. It was touch and go for a while with Cari's delivery."

"Yeah, man. She came through it like a trooper. But I want to know when you gonna hit those other skins?" B.P. teased.

"What the hell you talking about?" Kaliq inquired as he settled on a frozen pizza.

"Yolie, man. You know you dyin' to hit that," B.P. said as he licked his fingers.

"You are a sick person."

"Yeah, a'aight. Tell me you don't get a woody thinking about Yolie," B.P. countered, snatching a Sunny D. from the fridge.

"I'm not getting into this conversation with you again. Besides, you got some business to take care of," Kaliq said, pointing towards the living room.

"Okay, we out," B.P. said as he slapped his cousin on the back.

With the house to himself, Kaliq could enjoy some peace and quiet. He looked at the frozen pizza and opted for a salad he'd thrown together yesterday instead. If he was going to stay ahead of the game with school, work and the kids, he had to take better care of himself. After he finished his lunch, he changed into his ball gear and headed out to the courts down the street.

It was a bright afternoon. The weather was a little on the cool side, but it was still pleasant. The council was in full effect. Mother Layton from Friendly Baptist stopped him to ask about his parents. He knew she was in constant contact with his mother, but he played along. It was her way of letting him know that he was keeping an eye out. Needless, to say his mother had not been thrilled when she found out Cari was pregnant.

"What kind of hussy is she to allow herself to get knocked up by a teenage boy? She's a grown woman; she ought to know better," she'd fumed.

"Come on, Dessa. Kaliq ain't no little kid. He played an equal part in this here thing. Now, we know Cari ain't bad people. I can't tell you what possessed her, but we all done been possessed at one time or another. You know we wasn't married yet when we had Ariyan," his father had said.

"Oh, Lord! Kaliq Nichols, you ain't planning on marrying that woman, are you?"

That's how it went for several months. They came back to New York a week before Cari's due date. They weren't keen on the idea, but they had adjusted somewhat. They had gone with him down to Brooklyn Hospital when he got the call that Cari was in labor. He hadn't asked to be in the delivery room and Cari hadn't invited him. She wanted him to be nearby, though. She was good about including him in all the planning. He even attended the baby shower. He wasn't sure what to expect from that. At first, her friends just openly stared at him. He couldn't make out what they were whispering, but their sudden smiles had made him nervous. Apparently, they were plotting to dress him up as part of some hokey baby shower ritual. He objected at first, but then he decided that if he was going to be down, he had to be down all the way. It turned out to be worth it to see Cari laugh. She had gotten so big; she was always uncomfortable.

At the hospital, it had been a long day. Cari's labor seemed as if it would last forever. When Yolie's godmother, Idalia, finally came out to give them the news, Mr. Nichols barely caught his only son before he hit the floor. Idalia told them that the *twins* were being taken to ICU.

Cari had looked small and frail when Kaliq went in to see her.

"Did you see them, Kaliq?" she groaned.

"They are beautiful, Cari. How are you feeling?" He realized it was probably a stupid question.

"Right now, I feel very lucky. They made it. I made it. We weren't so sure what was gonna happen there for a minute."

She winced as he tried to sit alongside her bedside. "I'm sorry."

"It's OK, Daddy." She grinned at him.

In an instant she was asleep. His beautiful Cari. She wasn't really his, but in a way she was. He knew they wouldn't be anything more than friends, and that was fine with him. Yet, their relationship would always go beyond friendship because of the two lives they had created together.

He had caught a lot of flack over it, as he knew she had, too. At that moment, all he could do was give praise that they were all still alive.

All the courts were full; mostly little kids trying to be like Mike. At the far court he noticed some girl shooting hoops by herself. It wasn't until he got a little closer that he realized it was Yolie.

"You go ahead, Rebecca Lobo," he called out.

"Can't you read the jersey? It's Theresa Weatherspoon, thank you," she greeted him, grazing his cheek with a kiss.

"How about a little one on one?"

"I don't want to embarrass you out here, son," Yolie chided as she spun her official WNBA ball on one finger.

"I'll take my chances," he declared, snatching the ball from her.

He hadn't expected her to be much competition, but she came close to whipping his butt. Her moves were graceful, yet forceful. "Oh, come on. That was a flagrant foul," he complained.

She laughed while taking the ball to the hole. "Yeah, right. Let's go to the videotape."

"I'll let you have that one," he told her as he raised himself up off the ground.

"You ain't letting me have nothing. I'm taking it, son," she teased him as she deftly dribbled the ball between her legs.

"First, the deejay thing; now hoops. Are you sure you're a girl?" he kidded her.

"I resent that remark. See, now I'm gonna have to take back my offer of a cool drink."

"Can't take a joke? I'm about to die from thirst," he said as he dragged her off the court. "Have you heard anything else about what went down last night?"

"No, not yet. But my father came over this morning trippin' over it. I understand his point, but sometimes I feel like he only steps in when it's time to do the Daddy thing."

"From what you've told me, he doesn't sound like such a bad father," Kaliq said, not completely meaning it. He had his own ideas about the man.

"No, he's not really. But it's like I'm the dirty little secret. You claim Trav and Trev outright. Daddy's got to see me on the sneak tip. Eighteen years of that gets real tired, you know?"

"Yeah, I can see what you mean," he agreed, handing her a Mistic juice.

"I love my father and I know he loves me, but I just feel like 'my sister,' Egypt, will always get the most of being his daughter while I get what's left over," Yolie explained to him downing the drink in a few gulps. The drink felt good; it was an unusually warm January day.

Kaliq found her to be just as beautiful as Cari. She was a tawny brown-skinned girl with jet-black hair. She was developing what promised to be a very shapely figure. The combination of African-American and Puerto-Rican American gave her an exotic look. She was one of the guys, but very much a woman, too.

"I found out she's going to Atlanta to continue her college education. Here I am wondering how I'm going to get into a CUNY school..."

"Hey, I go to a CUNY school," Kaliq interrupted, feigning offense.

"You know what I mean. There's no way we could afford for me to go away if I wanted to," she continued.

"Do you want to go away?"

She stared into his eyes for what seemed like a moment too long, then answered, "Sometimes I'm not sure of what I want."

They finished their drinks in silence. There was a strange vibe going back and forth between them. Neither wanted to question it out loud.

"How about another game?" Kaliq finally asked.

"No, thanks. I need to get upstairs and finish my paper that's due tomorrow. I just came down here to blow off some steam. But I'll let you get a rematch," she taunted.

"I don't recall you winning that game, miss."

"Now, Kaliq. Take it like a man," she told him, waving good-bye. As they walked away they both willed each other not to turn around and look back.

5

C ari was running late as usual. Her ability to sleep so heavily could really be a problem. She almost never heard her alarm go off. If Yolie didn't come in to get her up she'd never make it. She rolled over and looked at her digital clock. She convinced herself that she could afford another five minutes in bed. Cari grasped her pillow between her legs. She absentmindedly groaned as the friction she was causing with the pillow brought up physical stirrings she hadn't felt in a while. Cari heaved a great sigh and decided it was time to get up after all.

The kitchen had been tidied up earlier by Yolie. Cari knew her daughter was a true blessing. Cari's own family was scattered from corner to corner; some were in P.R., others in Florida. Her children were her world. She sat down to pour herself some juice and thought about what she would plan for them this weekend. She then remembered that Kaliq was going to have the twins; maybe she'd plan a girls' night out with Yolara. Her first-born was graduating from high school soon. She didn't want to miss any opportunities to be with her. Cari tried hard to be everything her kids needed. Their fathers were good to them, but she was their real life. She dragged herself into the shower after her second glass of Tropicana.

Cari methodically blended the water to the exact temperature. Her body was still tight and toned. She worked regularly to maintain her figure. She was only thirty-eight, but three children could do serious damage if you weren't careful.

The hot water pulsating against her felt like heaven, but she knew she was already pressing her luck time-wise. She hastily rinsed the suds away and stepped out the shower.

She jumped into a pair of Yolie's denim overalls with a Gap tee underneath. Her light blue Reeboks and matching Yankees jacket were thrown on next and she was out the door.

By the time she'd reached the large post office on Eighth Avenue in Manhattan, Cari felt as if she'd already worked her eight-hour tour.

Her hanging partners were gathered around the time clock.

"Girl, you like living life dangerously. You always just making it up in here!"

"Did some fine thing hold you hostage this morning?"

"Please, you know it ain't no one but me and my pillow when I get up in the morning," Cari jokingly reminded her co-workers.

"Yeah, I know what you mean. My baby's daddy comes over when he can't get none from no one else. And me with my horny self welcomes him with open legs!"

They had a good laugh over that and then slyly dispersed when they noticed a supervisor looking in their direction. Cari made her way over to the barcode machine she usually worked. From a distance she could see Rue was already prepping the mail.

"Hey, what's up, Cari?" Rue asked as she jogged the mail before letting it fly through the machine.

"The same old stuff. We've got a lot of mail to do, I see," Cari responded as she put labels into their appropriate trays.

"You know how that goes. I'm sort of glad. If I can keep my mind on this shit, I won't have to dwell on the crap I'm having to deal with now," Rue said, brushing her hand through her short chestnut-colored hair.

"What kind of drama are you living out now?" Cari questioned her friend. "You're like those novellas that my mother used to watch all the time."

"You know my on again-off again girlfriend has decided that it should be off permanently," Rue informed her as she slung the mail onto the machine.

"She always says that, Rue. What makes this time any different?"

"Petra's going to relocate with her company to Massachusetts. She says that it's over for good. I offered to try to get a transfer to Boston, but she said she doesn't want me following her. Can you believe that shit?" Rue complained.

"I've been there and done that. I wasted so much time with Burk although I loved him. I tried to tell myself that if I hung in there, he would come around. He never did and after thirteen years I finally got tired of waiting. We had times together that were special. Even after I had Yolara, we still had our thing, but I wanted a real family for my little girl. As much as he loved us, he wouldn't leave his legitimate family. It had me pissed for a long time. That's why I slept with Kaliq in the first place. I wanted to strike out at him. I didn't think Kaliq would be affected; it was meant to be a one-night stand only."

"So why did you keep the babies?"

Cari reached for another tray of mail. "I love kids and I didn't think it was fair to end the pregnancy because of my stupidity."

"Yeah, but…"

"I heard it all back then. I'd given nearly fifteen years of my life to a man that was never going to be all mine. The baby was half me and me was good enough at that point," Cari explained.

"That's all well and good, but right now I feel like getting plastered," Rue grumbled.

"Do you want to hang out tonight? We all haven't done that in a while."

"I don't feel like a crowd. Besides, I don't want the whole building to know my business," Rue answered as she stopped the machine to free some mail that had gotten jammed.

"Well, just you and me can go for a drink if you want."

Rue secretly enjoyed the idea of an evening with Cari. She had developed a crush on her friend. She realized it during one of her and Petra's off times. Today she was dressed in some baggy overalls, but Rue remembered the first time she had seen Cari rock a mini skirt. She was the sexiest woman she'd ever met. She had a wild innocence if that made any sense. Her long sandy-colored hair was a complete turn-on. Rue was distraught over her breakup with Petra, but a night out with Cari was a calming thought.

"All right; that sounds cool to me," Rue agreed.

They spent the rest of the tour confiding in each other. After work, they walked down Eighth Avenue to a little bar. It was after midnight when they sat down at a table. The dark and smoky room was alive with thumping club music.

"It's kind of loud in here, Rue," Cari shouted across the table.

Rue didn't particularly care. She downed one rum and Coke and ordered another. "You wanna dance, Cari?"

"Sure, let's go," Cari said as she sipped the last of her piña colada.

The small crowd danced in a fury. It was as if everyone were trying to wrench a multitude of troubles from their bodies. Cari and Rue laughed as they banged into each other. They were by no means drunk, but the music had an intoxicating effect.

They had danced to several songs when the beats began to slow down. Cari had turned to go back to the table, but Rue gently restrained her. Mariah Carey's "I Still Believe" was playing.

"I'd like to dance with you some more if that's okay," Rue said into Cari's ear.

Cari didn't feel she had any real reason to say no. She had known from the very beginning that Rue was into women. She was comfortable with that. She even suspected that Rue had a thing for her. Rue never pursued it and she was truly a good friend to Cari. She offered good advice and was fun to hang out with.

Cari remained on the dance floor with Rue. She stepped into her arms and laid her head on Rue's shoulder. Rue had a clean, fresh scent. Cari could smell the apple shampoo she used. Rue was a very ample woman. She's what you would call a handsome woman. She had dark hair and even darker eyes. Her features worked well with her creamy complexion. She sported a red and black plaid shirt with a red tank beneath it. Her black jeans clung nicely to her round behind. Cari had to admit it did feel nice to have someone wrapped around her again. True, it was only a dance, but you appreciate whatever contact you get when it's been so long.

"Check out those two dykes," some jerk called out.

"Yeah, but that Puerto Rican one is kinda hot," the other chimed in.

Cari was incensed at their behavior. She decided to give them something to look at. She pulled Rue closer and kissed her hard. Rue was taken aback for a split second, then she joined in wholeheartedly. She put her hands in Cari's hair and tilted her head back so she could kiss her neck.

"Can we watch you get it on?" the men whooped.

The women smiled deviously at them and finally returned to their table.

"Rue, I'm sorry, but I had to do something."

"Do you see me complaining?" Rue teased.

"You're not a bad kisser."

"So now you've had your first lesbo encounter," Rue said, signaling for another drink.

"Who said that was my first kiss with a woman? Back in the day we used to experiment with all kind of things. It's fine, but give me a dick." Cari laughed.

"Oh yeah. Look where just two dicks in particular got you!"

Cari laughed again. After they finished their drinks they paid the bill and left. The night was cool, but the streets were still alive with people hanging out.

"Say, why don't you come back to my place? It's too late to go back to Brooklyn now anyway. I also don't like that you travel this time of night on the train by yourself," Rue said.

Cari hoped she hadn't led her friend on with her antics on the dance floor. She had a point about the lateness of the hour, but she didn't think it was wise to go back to her place.

"I don't think so, Rue. I should go home."

"Come on, Cari. I won't bite unless you want me to," Rue said playfully.

Cari was tired and didn't look forward to the train ride back to Brooklyn. "All right, but let me call Yolie to let her know I'll be staying in the city tonight."

Rue could not believe her luck as she watched Cari walk over to a nearby pay phone. She would never have dreamed of coming on to Cari. Cari hadn't exactly come on to her either, but it was closer than Rue thought she'd ever get.

Cari hung up the phone. "Well, lead the way."

The two caught a bus down into the village. They walked the remaining few blocks to Rue's neighborhood. The smell of burnt debris stunned them as soon as they turned the corner. Several bystanders still crowded the streets. You could tell the fire had been put out some time ago, but the agony of devastation was still fresh.

"Oh my God. Shit! What happened?" Rue searched the block for a familiar face. People were sadly shaking their heads in disbelief. Others shifted through the rubble hoping to save someone's memento or a child's favorite toy. Cari ran to catch up to Rue as her friend rushed into what was left of her building.

Once inside the damage didn't seem too extensive. They cautiously made their way up to Rue's third-floor apartment. There was a lot of smoke and water, but nothing seemed burnt.

"Look at this, Cari. It's going to take forever to get this place back together again," Rue moaned, angry tears filling her eyes. Most of the windows had been broken. The bureau and the nightstands were all waterlogged. Her clothing and intimates were soaked and smelled of smoke. A mirror that had hung on the wall was shattered in pieces at the foot of the bed. The carpet squished as Rue bent down to reach under the bed. She pulled a small wooden chest from beneath it. She used a small key to open it and check its contents. From Cari's viewpoint, the papers stored inside seemed to be fine.

"Oh, Rue, I'm sorry. Baby, maybe we should go back to Brooklyn after all. We can deal with this tomorrow," Cari tried to coax her. However, Rue wouldn't leave until she found out what had happened. They were told that Mrs. Lansky had fallen asleep with a cigarette. She was stinking drunk as usual and hadn't realized what was going on right away. She had horrible burns, but she was still alive.

Cari helped Rue gather together what she could and led her back down to the street. They walked in silence to the subway station. Cari knew she was suffering, but she was at a loss for words. Rue was drained. First there was Petra's desertion and now her apartment was ruined. Everything was so waterlogged, she couldn't see salvaging much. She paced the platform as they waited for a train to pull into the station. Cari sat quietly holding Rue's belongings. Down the platform she noticed a man staring at them. Cari was a little uneasy riding the train at three in the morning. Rue finally noticed the man, too.

"What the fuck you looking at, huh?" Rue demanded.

"Baby, not here. I know you're upset, but let's not add another tragedy to this evening, okay?" Cari begged as she grabbed Rue's arm.

"Why, Cari? Why? I don't deserve this shit," Rue cried. Cari was a little startled when Rue punched the pillar. She wrapped her arms around her weeping friend. Fifteen minutes later, the train finally pulled up. A homeless man was laid out the whole length of a bench. There was no one else in the car. Cari and Rue huddled together at the other end of the car. Rue wanted more than anything to feel Cari's lips on hers again. She didn't want to take advantage of the situation. Rue was certain Cari would have allowed her to out of sympathy. Instead, Rue just closed her eyes and let the rocking of the train lull her. Cari watched for any trouble, but it was just the three of them the entire train ride. The man hadn't stirred at all. When they pulled into their stop, Cari dragged Rue from the seat before the doors closed. "Welcome to Bed-Stuy."

CHAPTER 6

Olive was a little perturbed with her boss. The same boss who didn't know a quarter of what she knew about anything. He was always coming to her with questions and taking credit for the answers. He hadn't ordered enough diamonds from Belgium. However, he had managed to buy too much gold from Italy. Olive swore she wished she had a rich white daddy, too. It was obvious that was the only way Brett Kravitz had gotten his position.

He stayed in the office long enough to make it look like he was dedicated to the success of the company, but fifteen minutes after old Ben Kravitz left for the day, his good-for-nothing son was out the door, too. Before he slithered to the elevator, he had said to her, "Ollie (a pet name he had for her that she absolutely abhorred), you handle that Belgian bitch so well. I know you can have the diamond situation cleared up in no time." With that he was gone.

Olive did stay behind to finish up some work of her own. She felt it was a matter of time before old Ben realized little Brett was not going to work out after all. She was hoping that the CEO would finally recognize her full worth and offer her the position like he should have in the first place.

She rubbed her eyes after an hour at her computer. She picked up the picture of Meshach and Egypt she had on her large cherry wood desk. Olive often stopped to wonder what had happened to her marriage. She didn't like to admit failure, but her union with Meshach had turned out to be just that—a failure. She had loved that boy with reckless abandon. In a way she still did. However, she hadn't grown very fond of the man he had become. He was complacent with his job as a bus operator. He had gotten the job right on time. Olive had just found out she was carrying Egypt. She had hoped that it would have been a temporary thing or at the very least he would have moved up within the Transit Authority. He didn't even have aspirations of becoming a dispatcher. Olive realized that it was a decent living, and the years he had done a lot of overtime had helped them buy the house. Olive had bigger dreams than a house in Flatbush. She had hoped Meshach would reach higher, too.

She had grown to resent him a little more each year. She had finished her business degree when Egypt was old enough to go to day care. She had interned with DuValier and they were so pleased with her potential that they had offered her a job when she graduated. It took a lot of work to get where she was now and she had no intentions of stopping. Meshach had always encouraged her, but she was outgrowing him. She only stayed because of Egypt (or so she convinced herself). What did she need a man for anyway? All her sisters were divorced. Maybe that's why she stayed. Olive wanted to succeed where others had failed.

She quickly finished up what she was working on. Why did she always have to be the last to leave? She could have taken the subway home, but she always opted for the express bus. She could unwind and read her reports in peace.

Tonight she thought about Egypt's future. She was so happy that she'd be attending Spelman. Olive could care less what she chose to major in. Her child had big plans for herself.

Olive had only wanted one child. Meshach had wanted to try for a boy, but what could he do? Once in a while, she wondered why he had stayed in the marriage himself. He didn't seem attentive anymore. She knew she was still a good-looking woman. They occasionally had sex, but it was nothing to write home about. Sometimes Olive wondered if he cheated. She doubted it since he chose to stay married to her as well. Soon Olive had drifted off to sleep, but her mind was never at rest.

***

Meshach had decided to do some work around the house. It would be good therapy. He wasn't happy at all. He tackled the garage first. It was his least favorite place to have to clean, but it would be good for letting off some steam. He'd been thinking about Cari and Yolie a great deal. Both his children were going off to college soon. He wouldn't have to protect Egypt's feelings anymore. Meshach dreamt of being able to be out in the open with Cari and his youngest daughter. He realized Egypt would be upset, but she was not a little girl any longer. She was a woman embarking on a new life. He didn't deem it necessary to drop any bombshells until she was safely in Atlanta, though.

There was a load of junk he hadn't seen in years hidden in the garage. Toys, old sports equipment, his fishing rod, etc. Hidden way back on a high shelf he had even found an old small pistol he used to carry when he drove the night bus. In Brooklyn, if you knew what was what, you didn't work the hawk without a loaded piece. Meshach wondered if he should keep the gun inside the house. He already had another gun upstairs. The house up the block had been broken into last month. It couldn't hurt to have some extra protection. He and Olive had decided to get ADT—one of the few things they agreed on these days.

Meshach carried the weapon up to his bedroom. He had kept the gun cleaning kit in the armoire. As he was about to get started, his cell phone rang. "Hello."

"Daddy? It's me."

Meshach's mood instantly improved when he heard Yolie's voice. "How are you doing, sweetie?"

"I'm okay. Studying and all that good stuff," she answered.

"That's a breeze for my baby girl. You get your looks from your mother, but your brains are all my doing," he joked.

"Funny, she says the same thing about you!" After a long pause Yolie continued. "Daddy, I'm sorry I blew up at you the other day."

"Honey, that's all right. I understand. I know you get a little pissed at me from time to time and I can't blame you. I just want you to know that

I have always tried to do my best when it comes to taking care of you. I'm sure you think I fall short a lot of the time," Meshach admitted to her.

"It's not that you fall short…no, I take that back. Sometimes I just can't stand our situation. I wanted you to be around all the time. I don't like feeling like I'm an afterthought."

"You and Egypt share my heart equally. I know this isn't the most ideal arrangement, but…"

"Daddy, you don't have to say anything else about it. I don't want to get mad at you all over again. Mommy's birthday is coming up. Got any plans?"

"Yolara, you know your mother hasn't accepted any gifts from me in years," Meshach answered a little disgusted with the admission.

"You giving up so easy?"

"Easy? Are we talking about the same Caridad Flores? Your mother was too through with me a long time ago. I'll always love your mother. She gave me you. And she's hot as hell." Meshach laughed. He rolled over to other side of the bed to pick up the cloth he had dropped. He looked up and saw Olive's reflection in the mirror.

"Meshach, what the hell is going on?"

"Damn, Olive. What are you doing sneaking up on me?"

"Never mind that shit. Who you talking to, huh?"

"I'll have to talk to you tomorrow, sweetheart," he said into the phone before turning his attention back to his wife. "Let's not act like you didn't get the gist of my conversation, Olive."

"You've been cheating on me that long, Meshach? And got the nerve to call from my house!"

He wasn't going to get into whose house it was. "I never meant for you to find out this way, but yes. Olive, you know we've been having problems now. It don't excuse what I did all the way, but…"

"It don't excuse what you did none of the way, you lying bastard," she screamed as she reached for something to throw. He caught her hands before she had a chance to grab anything. She hauled off and spit in his face. "You no-good motherfucker!"

He let her yell and shout, but he warned Olive not to spit in his face again. "And what you gonna do? Hit me? Yeah, that would be the icing on this shitcake you baking right here."

"Shit, woman. You haven't exactly been the model wife. I would have jumped for joy if this was the other way around."

"So why didn't you get the hell out a long time ago," she hissed.

"Don't flatter yourself. I stayed for Egypt."

"Please—she don't need to see up close and personal how much of a dog her father is. I really don't believe this shit."

"What's not to believe? You ain't fucking me on the regular, so what the hell."

"That's what it's all about for you, Meshach? Your little spic girlfriend can do it better?"

They were so caught up in their argument, neither had noticed Egypt. "What is going on? The whole neighborhood is gonna be up in here soon."

"Go ahead and tell her, Meshach. Tell her how she ain't the only child after all."

At that moment, Meshach wanted desperately to strike her. "Don't bring her into this, Olive."

"Why shouldn't she know? You say she is the only reason you stayed. You're such a man, fess up to your daughter."

"No, don't. I ain't trying to be a party to this crap. Go on and kill each other. Maybe then y'all both will be satisfied and happy." Egypt backed out the bedroom and let her parents resume the battle.

"Ugh, you're such a selfish bitch, I swear!" Meshach growled.

"Well, I ain't your bitch no more."

An hour later the shouting and accusations finally stopped. Meshach agreed to spend the night out. He reminded her that it was his house, too, and he wasn't just going to give it up just like that. He also said he didn't think it was wise to stay there while he had a loaded gun in his possession. It had gotten really ugly. Meshach knew he was basically at fault, but Olive attacked every single grain of his character.

After he had finally gone, Olive went down into the den. She was exhausted. Secretly, she wondered why she was so upset. She should have been glad to be rid of him. Wasn't she just complaining to herself how little they had left between them? In her arrogance, she never would have imagined Meshach would have been carrying on an affair all this time. Perhaps it wasn't just having a woman on the side, but a daughter as well, an entirely separate family. Apparently, this Caridad person didn't want him either based on what she had overheard. Well, she could have him at last for all Olive cared. So what, Meshach had been her first and only? She was still a young woman; she'd find comfort in some other man. Someone who hadn't known her when she was a chubby teen. Someone who didn't know she went wild for Patti LaBelle. Someone who didn't know she was afraid to be by herself in a dark house.

"Oh, Lord. My man is gone," Olive wailed.

CHAPTER 7

Yolara sat at the kitchen table slicing green peppers. She had promised Cari that she would make pepper steak for her to take to lunch. To be nice, she had made enough for Rue to take as well. The jury was still out when it came to Rue. Yolie supposed she had no genuine reason not to like the woman, but she didn't get a warm fuzzy feeling over her either. Yolie tried not to show it to either of them. She had known Cari had a co-worker she considered a good friend. Yolie had also known this friend was a lesbian. That fact didn't bother her until she saw with her own two eyes that this woman lusted after her mother.

Yolie wasn't sure if her mother was aware or not, but how could she miss the vibes that Rue constantly threw off. In the beginning, Yolie had felt sorry for the woman. It was awful what had happened to her apartment. Four weeks ago.

Rue had more than made herself at home. Cari didn't seem to mind. Rue had started off by spending nights on the couch. A month later they had moved a daybed into Cari's room. It seemed as if the two had spent every waking moment together. They worked together, they hung out together and apparently they were all going to live together.

Yolie washed and seasoned the steaks. She heard a key in the door. Yolie expected to see Cari coming through the door. It was Rue.

"What's up, Yolie?" Rue greeted her as she tossed her knapsack into the chair.

"Everything's everything. Where's Mommy?"

"I don't know. I'm not her shadow 24 hours a day," Rue answered playfully.

"Could have fooled me," Yolie muttered.

Rue pretended not to hear the remark. "I'm not looking forward to work today. But I am looking forward to those steaks Cari was bragging about," she said, coming up behind Yolie.

Yolie tried to step to the side as nonchalantly as possible. Rue ignored that, too. "I didn't know you had a key, Rue?"

"Yeah, Cari thought it would be easier. You're in and out a lot. If she's not here, at least I can still get to my things if I have to."

"When will your place be ready for you to move back into?"

"You're not very subtle, Yo."

"I wasn't dissing you or anything. I was just wondering. I know me and Mommy must be cramping your style. I'm sure you're used to romancing the girlies on your own turf." Yolie giggled. "I'm only joking with you, Rue. But you must be missing your own space."

"Not really. I've been on my own for a long time. I'm enjoying this time with your mother. And you kids."

Just then Cari burst in with Travis and Trevor. "What an ordeal that was! Next time I'm taking you guys shopping one at a time," Cari playfully warned her boys.

"Can we go try on our jerseys again?" Travis wanted to know.

"Yeah please, Mommy?" Trevor chimed in.

"I don't know. I don't remember seeing your room cleaned up like you two had promised."

"Ah, man. Come on, Trev. We know what that means." The two trotted off to their room. They started off fine, but their attention was soon stolen by the WB. Afternoon cartoons had that effect on them.

"I am worn out. Work is gonna be a lot of fun today," Cari said sarcastically.

"I was just saying the same thing to Yolie," Rue said. "I need some Pamprin or Midol or something. Do you need anything while I'm out? I need to deal with these shitty cramps before we go to work."

"Nah, thanks. Just gonna stretch out on the couch for a few."

"How about you, Yolie?" Rue asked the girl.

"I'm all right."

"OK, be right back then."

Yolie waited until she heard the elevator. "OK, do you mind telling me what's going on with you and Miss Man? Midol? I didn't know dudes were finally getting periods!"

"Yolara Flores-Burkette. I know you ain't gay bashing," Cari asked, more than a little surprised at her daughter's attitude.

"It's not her sexual preference I'm concerned with. It's her Cari preference that's got me a little hyped."

"What are you talking about?"

"Mommy, you can't tell me you don't see that Rue has a crush on you. The woman practically starts dripping every time you walk into the room," Yolie told her mother frankly.

"Well, that's a nice way to talk to your mother," Cari responded lightly.

"You think this is funny? Ma, I'm telling you this chick has got it bad…" Yolie managed to say before her mother cut her off.

"Yolie, come here," Cari requested, patting the sofa.

Yolie went and sat beside her mother. "Mommy, you know the way is free and clear for you and Daddy now. Why are you wasting your time with Rue?"

"First of all, there is nothing free and clear about me and Burk. Baby, I know you've always wanted us to be a family. For a long time that's what I wanted for all of us, too. I came to terms with the fact that that was not going to be. And it still isn't going to be. Rue has nothing to do with it. A part of me will always love your father, but I am *not* running to his beck and call after all these years. The only reason he and his wife are separated now is completely by accident," Cari tried to explain to her daughter.

Yolie sat on the couch with her mouth poked out. "I guess I'll never have my turn at this family business, huh?"

"What are you talking about? I'm your family; Burk is your family; Travis and Trevor are your family," Cari protested.

"You know what I mean. Besides, I'm eighteen now. Can't miss what I never had, right? All these crooked branches on our family tree," Yolie declared with a forced smile.

Cari gathered her child up into her arms. "*Mi hija*, if I could have made it some other way just for you, I would have." She kissed Yolie's forehead.

"Got to go check your steaks. If one is burned I'll make sure to save that one for Rue," Yolie chided.

Cari tossed a throw pillow at her as she jetted towards the kitchen.

Rue took her time walking back from the Rite Aid. She realized she was falling hard for Cari. Rue knew Cari wouldn't purposely lead her on, but she could swear that at times she was getting signals from her. Sometimes she caught Cari looking at her at work. She would try to play it off, but they both knew she had been caught. Rue was reluctant to bring it up. She didn't want to jeopardize what they did have if she were wrong. But damn, it was getting more and more difficult to keep her mouth shut. Rue also realized that Yolie was wise to her as well. She genuinely liked the girl, but she knew the kid wanted her mommy and daddy together. What a big baby.

Sometimes, Rue wondered about Petra. She had really tried to make it work. Petra had been special to her. No, she wasn't her first relationship, but she was the only one who had amounted to more than just a fling. Rue had high standards; she wasn't going to settle for less. She understood that Petra had legitimate gripes. Rue was not always easy to live with.

"*Get away from me, you bitch!*" *Petra had screamed.*

"*Petra, I'm so sorry. Honey, you know I didn't mean it,*" *Rue cried as she rushed to the woman's side.*

"*Do not touch me again. Look what you did to my face!*"

Rue forced Petra's hand away so she could look at what she had done. "*Jesus, I swear I didn't mean to.*"

"*Fuck you! I'm going to take that transfer and if I see you in Boston, I swear I will get a restraining order. I'm sick of your shit, Rue. You need help. But I'm not dying to help you get it.*" *Petra grabbed her coat and raced from the apartment they had shared together.*

Rue fought the tears that threatened to fall. All of a sudden, she felt disgusted with herself. When she reached the corner, she threw the Midol in the trash before crossing the street.

CHAPTER 8

"This house is equally mine!" Olive was screaming for the umpteenth time. Honestly, Egypt was getting tired of hearing it.

"Ma, calm down."

"Let me tell you something, Egee. When you get your career going and start making your own money, make sure you buy your own home before you get married. And do *not* put nothing in that nigga's name!"

Egypt didn't chastise her mother for being hypocritical in her use of the "n" word. She really didn't understand why she was so upset. Since she was a little girl she wondered why her parents even bothered. It was obvious they weren't madly in love with each other. By the time she was older she doubted they even liked each other.

Egypt admired her mother's ambition and her accomplishments, but at times her marriage seemed to take a back seat to her career. She never once felt neglected by either her father or her mother, but she knew something was lacking. Then there were times she felt she shouldn't complain. None of her friends lived with both of their parents.

"He said her name was Caridad. She *must* be some hottie spic," Olive spat out. Egypt decided slang did not suit her mother at all.

"Ma, all you ever did was complain about Daddy anyway. Why are you so angry now?"

Olive threw herself down on the plum-colored leather sectional. She didn't know how to explain it to her daughter either. It occurred to her that Egypt had never witnessed a loving relationship between Meshach and herself. "He was my husband. We had a life together."

"Sure, but what kind of life was it really? You two only tolerated each other for my sake. You should be happy you don't have to pretend anymore."

Olive was shocked at her child's observation. "That's not completely true. I loved your father."

"So when and why did you stop?"

"Who said I stopped," the woman whispered.

"Ma, come on, is it no wonder he turned to some other woman? There were times I wondered if you had something going on the side, too."

"How long did you know about this woman and her kid?"

"Are you trying to tell me you didn't suspect? Then again with a progress report stuck up under your nose all the time, maybe you didn't," Egypt scolded. She hadn't meant for it to sound so mean, but her mother needed to be told about herself.

Olive didn't respond. She gazed at all the memories that were collected in that room. Memories that could have been happier ones if they had only tried. She believed they clung to a past that was carefree and magical. Somehow they had let go of the magic.

"Egypt, I'm sorry we…" Olive started, then realized her girl had already left the room.

Egypt was sitting in the silver Volkswagen Bug her parents had gotten her as a graduation present. She wanted to go see her father. He had rented a place near Flatbush Depot. Meshach was no great cook; perhaps they'd grab a bite at Kings Plaza. She adjusted her gold-wired frames on her face and checked her tiny twists. Her hair was taking forever to dred. She popped in Lauryn Hill and backed out the driveway.

***

Yolara was excited about spending time at her father's place. She had never visited his house. She knew where it was. Sometimes she would walk past it whenever she was in Flatbush. Yolie would fantasize about belonging there. Now, she was gonna hang out with her father in a place where they didn't have to hide their relationship from someone who could tell his wife.

"So what's on the agenda, Daddy?"

"I picked up some videos and a couple of jerk chicken dinners before I came to get you."

"I hope you got some good ones. These days if you don't catch a flick as soon as it comes out, you don't get to see it at all. Thank God they come out on video quick now. What did you get?"

"Classics. *Cooley High*, *Sparkle* and *Claudine*," Meshach told her proudly.

"You're kidding, right?" She could tell by his expression he wasn't. "Dang, I left my Afro wig at the crib." She laughed.

"Girl, you don't know what you're missing."

"Got an eight-track player in your new bachelor pad, too?" Yolie asked.

"You ain't funny. But I do have two turntables from *my* old deejaying days. Now you can see how it's really done," he told his daughter.

"What? You'd better step aside, son," Yolie bragged. They laughed and joked all the way to his place.

They had stuffed themselves with jerk chicken, roti, rice and peas. After dinner, the two settled down in front of the television with a couple of bottles of Ting and several chunks of bread pudding. *Sparkle* was the first tape they were going to watch when the doorbell rang. Meshach held his full stomach as he raised himself from the floor to answer the bell. His heart skipped a beat when he looked through the peephole and saw Egypt standing there.

Slowly he opened the door for her. "Hey there, Egee Bird. Come in."

Egypt saw Yolie as soon as she crossed the threshold. She felt her stomach drop. She wasn't about to let this girl run her from her father's apartment.

"Hello, Yolara," Egypt said softly.

"How are you, Egee?"

Meshach was stunned. "You two know each other?"

"They always think we're the last to know," Egypt said to Yolara. "Daddy, as big as Brooklyn is, it's a small world after all. I don't know Yolara personally, but I've known who she was for a long time."

"I'd know Egypt anywhere from all the pictures you showed me.

Besides, she goes out with one of the guys from Roosevelt," Yolie added.

His daughters seemed composed, but Meshach was a little thrown. He had often wondered if Egypt knew. She was a bright, perceptive young woman. They were only two years a part; it figured they might run in some of the same circles. He knew they had both been at that party, but he would have never guessed Egypt knew all along.

"Have a seat, Egee. Do you want anything? A piece of bread pudding?"

"Okay, I'll just work it off tomorrow." Egypt really didn't feel like being cordial to this girl. She didn't blame her for the breakup of her parents; that was going to be a done deal eventually anyway. What she didn't want to relinquish was her only-child status. Of course, she hadn't been an only child for eighteen years, but it didn't count if it was on the down low.

They watched the movie in relative silence. Yolara spoke up when Meshach went to put *Cooley High* into the VCR. "Why is it you never blew the whistle on my parents?" Yolie inquired of her sister.

At first Egypt looked at her like she was crazy. "What would you have done? I knew it would come up sooner or later. Daddy seemed to prefer later so I didn't rock the boat."

Meshach was surprised at Egypt. He knew she could have a sharp tongue like her mother when agitated. He knew this had to be killing her, but she tried her best not to let it show.

Yolara, on the other hand, could feel her half-sister's hostility as if it were tangible. She wanted to have a real discussion with this girl she shared a father with, but she could see that it would be slow-going if it went at all.

Meshach felt a tug in his chest. He didn't want to force the two on each other. He hoped like Yolie that they could all have a relationship together. That was going to be up to Egypt more or less. Midway through *Claudine*, Egypt announced she had to be going. "I've got a thing with Stefan to go to tonight."

Meshach was about to suggest that she take her sister home since she was going that way. As if she read his mind, Egypt abruptly added, "I'm not meeting him in Bed-Stuy. I'm picking him up from his job in downtown Brooklyn. Goodnight, Daddy. Later, Yolara."

Meshach walked his daughter to the door. "Thanks for coming over, Egee Bird. I've been wanting to see you more than I have." He bent down to kiss his child.

"Well, you know where to find me. G'night," Egypt replied before taking the stairs two at a time.

"Okay, Pop. You can breathe now."

CHAPTER 9

Kaliq was nervous about the blind date the fellas had set up for him. He had agreed that he needed to get out more often. Lately, his life consisted of school and work. He never complained about the time he spent with his sons, but he wanted his life to be full and complete. His homies figured he needed some female companionship. Naturally, B.P. was still playing cupid between him and Yolie, but as he said, "Don't mean you can't be getting some from another honey in the between time."

Kaliq wasn't only trying to make a good impression with his date; he felt he deserved a hot night out on the town as well. What could be hotter than Toni Braxton on Broadway? He had scored some discount tickets. She would be leaving the show soon, so they were making a big "catch her while you can" media thing. Besides, he sort of enjoyed *Beauty and the Beast* when he had watched the Disney version with the kids.

Kaliq had chosen his navy pin-striped jacket and his solid navy dress slacks. He didn't really care for ties so he just wore his stark white silk shirt open at the neck. He broke out his favorite pair of black Giorgio Brutini shoes. They still looked good although he'd had them a long time.

The guys hadn't said anything about her personality so he assumed that meant she was attractive. Everyone knew a "nice personality" was the kiss of death. Kaliq hadn't wanted her to feel uncomfortable so he suggested they meet at a public place in the city. He certainly didn't want this girl knowing where he lived, just in case.

Kaliq grabbed his smoke-gray trench coat and was out the door. He arrived in the city relatively early. He didn't mind; he liked walking the streets of Manhattan. He got off on pretending that he was the architect of some important edifice. He also enjoyed critiquing the buildings he saw.

He arrived at the designated meeting place five minutes early. The fountain in front of the hotel had colored lights surrounding the water. The effect was very pretty. Kaliq once again wondered what this girl would look like when someone came up and tapped his shoulder.

"Excuse me, but are you Kaliq Nichols?" she had asked hesitantly. Kaliq was in total shock. This woman was gorgeous. Blind dates *never* looked like this. "Are you Jeneill? Hello, how did you know it was me?" Kaliq asked as he shook her hand.

"Well, I was told you looked like Brian McKnight," she admitted coyly. *Well, no one told me you looked like Dominique Simone, B.P.'s favorite porn star*, Kaliq thought to himself. "Would you like a drink or something before we head for the theater?"

"That would be nice, thank you," Jeneill answered, taking his arm when he offered it. Things were starting to look up.

They had one Long Island Iced Tea each and shared an appetizer before heading for the theater. Their conversation was easy, not forced. Jeneill turned out to be a theater major; that was why she was so excited about seeing the show. Kaliq thought she would look sensational on stage or screen.

They decided on dinner at the Motown Café because she had never been there before. "So, Jeneill, what kind of food do you like?" Kaliq asked when the waitress had finally brought their menus.

"What do you suggest? It all looks so good. I like how they name each special after a Motown artist. Remind me to pick out something from the souvenir shop," she answered as she tossed her hair over her shoulder. The waitress tried not to roll her eyes.

"I don't know if you'd like it, but I had the Southern fried steak the last time I was here. But whatever you try, you've got to order the sweet potato French fries."

Jeneill took his advice and gave the fried steak a shot. Kaliq opted for the catch of the day. They ordered virgin drinks in cups fashioned to look like old microphones. While they waited for their food to arrive, they walked around the restaurant to admire all the memorabilia. Suits worn by the Four Tops and Boyz II Men. Pictures and statues adorned the well-known eatery. Record titles with their dates were posted all around the booths. Overhead, an announcer introduced the act that had taken the small stage in the center of the room. Five guys in sequin-lapeled black suits belted out their version of "Ain't Too Proud To Beg."

Kaliq and Jeneill sang along with the talent that performed for the diners. "They are pretty good," she said while bopping to the music.

"You should see the two that do Marvin and Tammy," Kaliq told her. "I'm just afraid that giant record spinning over our heads is gonna fall."

Jeneill looked up and saw a large-scale replica of an old Motown 45 spinning slowly above them. "That is just too smooth. I'm having a nice time, Kaliq, really." She went on to rave about the food when it had arrived, too. Kaliq offered dessert, but Jeneill said she was stuffed.

They agreed they would tell their friends to see Toni before she left the production. "Are you tired yet? I know a little jazz joint that would be nice to chill at for a while," Kaliq said to his date.

"Hey, call me the Energizer bunny. I'm game if you are."

They held hands at the little jazz joint they went to after dinner. It was nothing more than a hole in the wall, but it had charm and atmosphere. Kaliq's father had told him about the place a long time ago. He hadn't been there before, but he decided to take a chance on it. He knew his father would not steer him wrong when it came to jazz.

"We have got to get together again soon. Next time I'll treat." She grinned at him as she sipped her cappuccino.

"Just name the time and place."

There was a small dance floor where couples did the ritual slow grind. And finally they shared a kiss. Kaliq was wondering what her reaction would be when he mentioned he was the father of five-year-old twins. He was very upfront about his children. If a woman was going to like him or be with him, they had to know that he was a package deal. He wasn't going to force the kids on anybody. "You have very, very nice lips, Miss Waters. But I've got to bring our evening to a close. I've got plans tomorrow with my kids. It's hard work keeping five-year-old twins entertained." He waited expectantly for her reaction.

"You're kidding," Jeneill exclaimed. "When can I meet them?"

Kaliq breathed a barely noticeable sigh of relief. He followed and watched this beautiful woman as she sashayed down the street—her fur-collared suede coat rising with the night wind. She winked at him from over her shoulder. *Yes, there was a God.*

"You have got to come to one of my plays. I'd like to see some of your work, too. I'm sure you have some awesome sketches. Architects rake in big bucks. You're going to be living large one of these days, Kaliq."

He hoped she wasn't all about money. So many of the girls he knew were blinded by floating dollar signs. "Well, if it all works out. What about you? Is stage work what you prefer?" he asked as they fought the wind to get to the subway station.

"I just love acting, period. I'll do a dog food commercial if it will lead to my so-called big break," Jeneill joked. "You don't have to ride with me all the way to Harlem. I know you live in the opposite direction."

That was a test if Kaliq ever heard one. "Now what do I look like letting you ride the train by yourself. Girl, what was in that cappuccino you had?" he teased as he took her hand again. He didn't want to appear too forward so he didn't attempt to kiss her again until he had walked her to the impressive Harlem walk up she lived in with her family.

"Thanks again for the lovely evening, Kaliq. I would invite you in, but my parents would have a fit. You know what I mean," she said as she fished for her key.

"I completely understand; believe me," he answered. When she found her keys, he handed her her bag of Motown souvenirs.

"Thanks for the cup and the cap, too," she added before surprising him with a deeper kiss. "Goodnight. Call me tomorrow."

He promised her retreating figure he would. "I've got to go on blind dates more often," Kaliq said to himself.

CHAPTER 10

ari felt horrible. The flu was kicking her butt hard. If she had
known her symptoms would worsen, she never would have left
home at all. She ached down to the marrow of her bones. Lifting
the heavy trays of mail took some effort. Rue noticed the flushed look on
Cari's face. "Are you all right?"

"Not really. I could just drop right about now."

"You should go home. It's not worth it to kill yourself in this place," Rue
suggested, her brow knitted with concern.

"I'm not looking forward to that long train ride into Brooklyn. Maybe
if I hang around I can get a ride from one of the guys that leaves earlier."

"No," Rue said hastily, "Why don't you just take it easy? I'll do the bulk
of the work and we can go home together."

"I can't let you work this machine by yourself," Cari disagreed, setting
down a heavy tray of mail with a thump.

"It's not like I haven't done it before. You know how this place is when
they're short-handed. They could care less. At least this would be of my
own doing."

Cari was too tired to argue about it anymore. She just played it off
whenever a supervisor happened to walk by. She and Rue were regulars
who didn't get hassled by supervision very often. They did their job suffi-
ciently enough. Besides, the powers that be were too busy harassing the
casuals.

By the time they broke for dinner, Cari was feeling even worse.

"I can't take it. I'm gonna tell them to let me go now."

Rue didn't know how else to get her to stay. "I'll go with you."

"Come on, Rue, don't be ridiculous. I can…"

"Well, at least let me give you cab money," Rue offered.

"Are you kidding? To Bed-Stuy? You must be the sick one," Cari joked.

After a lengthy debate, Cari got a ride from Gibb, one of the mechanics. He was quitting early, so he offered to give her a lift on his way to Bushwick.

"I'll make tracks to get back to Brooklyn when I'm off," Rue assured her.

"I'll be fine. You worry too much, for real."

Rue didn't take her eyes from Cari until she couldn't see her anymore. She knew she was being obvious, but Rue wanted Cari to know exactly how she felt about her. Rue had decided that she had nothing to lose in going for it. She was certain that Cari wouldn't flip out when Rue admitted her feelings toward her. Even if she turned her down, Rue knew their friendship wouldn't suffer. That's why she loved Cari. She was an accepting person. Rue hadn't encountered too many like her. Needless to say, her German, Irish, Polish relatives were not thrilled to have a lesbian as one of their own. Rue had learned to not care (or so she had convinced herself).

She went back to the letter-sorting machine. She started to run the mail through. Rue was on automatic and didn't realize when Garcia came over to be her partner.

"Cari gonna be all right?" he said, dragging over another cart of mail.

"Don't worry; I'll take care of her," Rue muttered to herself.

***

Cari was exhausted. She barely managed to get her clothes off and the radio on. She ran a hot bath and put in her favorite dewberry bath beads. Yolie had bought her a gift basket from the Body Shop. She felt as if she needed a little pampering. She also lit a scented candle and set it by the tub. The steaming water was delicious. Cari submerged herself into its depths. The stereo was set on Jammin' 105. The Isleys were singing "For the Love of You." The tune immediately reminded Cari of Meshach.

She was so naïve when she had first met him. It was a condition that had not worn off with time. They had flirted shamelessly while he drove the bus. At first it was just a way of unnerving him because he had tossed her off the bus. Of course, that hadn't worked and she found out soon enough that she was attracted to him. She would meet him at the depot after his run. Sometimes they would go to the Country Kitchen. They would stuff themselves with soul food. Other times, she would have him take her to a movie or something. Meshach was a little uneasy with their relationship in the beginning. He had taken it hard when he realized he had unknowingly taken her virginity. Cari had worried that he was only spending time with her because he felt guilty. It had taken months for her to believe he was falling in love with her.

As time went on, they became closer. Cari had never asked him to leave Olive, not even when she had gotten pregnant. Naturally, she would have been ecstatic, but if she had to ask it would not have been the same.

Her parents didn't express any surprise at her situation. Her mother was just glad that Cari had chosen someone who could provide for the baby. It wasn't until Yolara had reached her teenage years that Cari began to feel that she and Meshach were depriving their child. When Yolie was little she would ask why Meshach didn't live with them. Cari would come up with all sorts of excuses. In the meantime, Meshach would constantly complain about Olive. Finally, she asked him why didn't he choose them over her. Apparently, he hadn't expected to hear that question after thirteen years. He hemmed and hawed about finances and joint properties. Cari was devastated. It took all the strength she could muster to end it with him. Meshach was not happy at all.

"Why do we have to stop seeing each other?" he had wanted to know.

"Burk, I have never asked you for anything for myself. Never. This is for our daughter. I don't see why you can't give our family a chance. You're always talking about the mess you live in now..."

"Cari, I've explained to you why…"

"No, you've given me a load of shit and expect me to swallow it," Cari shouted.

"Why did you have to get Yolie started in the first place?"

"Started with what? Wanting to see her father out in the open instead of on the sneak tip? I've got news for you, sweetheart; that has always been what she's wanted."

He tried to take her into his arms, but she shoved him away. "Do you think I think so little of myself to let you keep doing this? Then again, why shouldn't you think that? I'm not going to do this anymore, Burk. I'm not gonna deprive Yolie of her relationship with you, but ours is over."

They were brave words, yet that same evening she had her one-night stand with Kaliq. Cari dated occasionally. The single scene was a pitiful one in the nineties. No one she had gone out with was about much. Either they were into game playing or were too needy. Often they were good-looking, but didn't have anything going on upstairs. It was very frustrating. She didn't want to be alone, yet she wasn't going to settle just so she could say she had a man.

Cari added more hot water to the bath. Her mind began to wander again. She found herself thinking about Rue. She knew she was playing a dangerous game as far as Rue was concerned. Cari didn't know exactly what she felt for the woman. They had become friends instantly when they both started at the post office. They shared secrets and opinions. They hung out sometimes. Usually, when Rue was involved in a relationship, they didn't see each other as often. Cari admired the woman's dedication to whomever she was seeing at the moment. In many ways, Cari was curious as to how it would be with another woman. Rue Tenney was attentive, intelligent and actually a handsome woman. She was not mannish as her father would have said, but Rue was unashamedly gay. Cari knew that she wasn't encouraging her, however, she wasn't discouraging her either. During moments of complete honesty, Cari had to admit she was willing to explore the possibilities.

The bath was only a small comfort. She blew out the candle and drained the tub. Cari decided it was time to get doped up with flu medication. She knew Yolie could fend for herself and the boys were spending the night with Kaliq. She wrapped her body in a big bulky terrycloth robe and fell into bed.

***

Rue was tired and edgy. Garcia had turned out to be a gossipy bore. And they say women are bad! He knew everything there was to know about everyone in the post office. She had taken several bathroom breaks just to get away from the man. Rue just wanted to go home. She had taken to thinking of Cari's place as home. She had been back to her apartment a few times. There was still a good deal of work that needed to be done, but Rue was not in a hurry. As long as she was welcomed, she would continue to stay with Cari.

Sometimes Rue felt a little guilty. She had been so attached to Petra that at times she wondered about how quickly she had fallen for Cari. Petra was a moody girl. She had just recently come out when Rue had met her, but she was not happy about it. It had taken Rue a long time to get the girl to feel comfortable in her own skin. That was the reason why their relationship had been off and on. When Petra decided it was not okay to be gay, it was off. When she missed Rue and couldn't possibly live without her, it was on.

It could be tedious, Rue had to admit, but she cared deeply for the melancholy redhead. She recalled their final blowup.

"Pet, where were you today?" Rue had asked.

"Out and about, Rue. You know my schedule. Never a spare moment for much else but work," she answered casually.

"I don't know about that. I could have sworn I saw you earlier today."

"Love, I doubt it. Besides if you had, why wouldn't you have said something?"

Rue pulled the girl onto her lap. "Petra, you don't have to lie. As a matter of fact, I would prefer you not to insult my intelligence with your sloppy lies."

"Rue, what are you talking about?" she asked nervously. She tried to move Rue's hands from her body. Her lover would not relax her grip.

"Are you going to tell me why I saw you kissing that man in front of Uno's today?" Rue growled as she snatched Petra by her hair.

"Rue, stop it. You're hurting me!"

"Don't you think it hurts me to see you with a man? With anyone for that matter? I've been good to you, Petra. I don't deserve this shitty treatment," Rue continued, as she shoved the girl to the floor.

"Rue, you know how it is with us," Petra said with fear.

"I know that I'm not taking this from you," Rue declared as she kicked the frantic girl in the face. Petra started screaming. As if a switch had been flicked, Rue was immediately on her knees beside the girl.

"Petra, are you all right?" Rue asked contritely. She panicked as she realized what she had actually done. Petra was hysterical. No words would calm her down. The same day she packed her things and moved out. Rue didn't understand what had come over her. She had loved Petra. Maybe the idea of her being unfaithful while Rue herself was totally committed had just pushed her to a limit. She had to get a grip on herself. It was inexcusable. She was fortunate that Petra hadn't pressed charges as she had threatened. It occurred to Rue that perhaps she hadn't been completely fair to her former lover. True, she had never cheated, but she had always nursed a small crush on Cari. The whole thing was causing Rue to get a migraine. She just couldn't wait to get to Brooklyn so she could enjoy a relaxing evening with Cari.

Rue let herself into the apartment. It was late when she finally reached Bed-Stuy. She knew the twins were staying with their father. The answering machine was flashing. There was a single message from Yolie letting her mother know she was going to stay over at Idalia's. Rue could not believe her luck. She quietly walked across the room. Cari's bedroom door was ajar. Rue stood in the doorway several minutes watching Cari sleep. Finally, she moved towards her to feel her forehead. Cari was a little warm. Rue opened her robe with care. Her body was magnificent. Cari was at least six years older than she was. Her skin was naturally lightly tanned. It took every ounce of control Rue possessed not to rush the moment.

She decided to disrobe and lie next to Cari. She knew her friend was a heavy sleeper so she felt confident that she wouldn't wake up suddenly. Rue lightly traced Cari's breast with her finger. The contact seemed electric to her. She gently brushed Cari's lips with her own. She moved to the tip of her nose, then her eyelids. It wasn't until Rue started to nibble on her earlobe that Cari began to stir.

"Rue?" she asked sleepily.

Rue continued to work on her ear. It was a spot that had always driven Cari crazy and Rue was lucky enough to have chosen it. Cari was torn between stopping her and wanting more. While Rue's tongue played with her ear, her hands gently kneaded her breasts. It caused a strange sensation, but not an unpleasant one, Cari decided. It had been a long time, but she was not going to use that as an excuse. She wanted Rue to do this to her. As if she sensed Cari's thoughts, Rue boldly placed her fingers on Cari's thighs. She slowly parted her legs and nestled herself between them. She treated Cari with a deep, sensual kiss that lasted a full minute, but seemed like an eternity. Cari felt a little dizzy. It was overwhelming. Seizing the moment, Rue went on exploring with her mouth. She moved down to her neck and shoulders. Cari arched herself as Rue bit her nipple. She giggled out loud as she passed her navel. However, she lay perfectly still as she realized where Rue was headed next. She grew excited at the thought and all of a sudden she felt like she was floating. Rue was immediately intoxicated. The sweetness of Cari was better than she had expected. She wanted to absorb her very essence. She was pleased with the rhythmic thrusting of Cari's hips. Rue grasped both Cari's hands as she anticipated her climax. It had been a while for both of them and it was over in an instant.

"Rue, I don't know what to say," Cari admitted breathlessly.

Rue placed her index finger over Cari's mouth. She reached for the comforter that was hanging precariously over the side of the bed. She wrapped herself around Cari and covered them both.

CHAPTER 11

K aliq was distracted. The professor's booming voice carried to
the rear of the lecture hall where Kaliq was seated. Earth science
was not his favorite topic, but he needed it to fulfill his course
requirements. He was thinking about after class when he would meet
Jeneill. She was performing in a play that evening. The theater department was putting on a drama in one of the studios of the NAC Building
of City College. Kaliq truly enjoyed attending the school. He wondered
how he had never noticed Jeneill on campus before.

They had gone out several times. He enjoyed her company. She was
a talented girl who could carry on a good conversation. Of course, her
favorite thing to talk about was acting, but Kaliq didn't mind. It was
refreshing to see someone so dedicated to their dreams. Jeneill had big
dreams. He was flattered when she had invited him to see her perform.

Finally the hour was over and he could escape the boredom. Kaliq had
little tolerance for anything besides architecture, but he knew these
classes were a necessity. Kaliq spotted Jeneill standing in front of the
administration building. Good God; she was a gorgeous woman. Her
long brunette hair (not all hers, she had admitted) hung halfway down her
back. Her light brown eyes (ah, not real either) were a perfect comple-
ment to her oval-shaped face.

Jeneill also had curves for days. Kaliq hadn't thought too much about
dating in recent months. He knew he had some feelings for Yolie that he

had never really dealt with, but that was a situation he didn't want to touch.

"Hey, Kaliq," Jeneill greeted him with a brief peck on the cheek. "These are my friends, Marco and Blaine."

Kaliq said hello to Jeneill's castmates. He immediately realized Marco would not be competition. He was full-blown gay. Blaine was a petite little blond with a huge smile. "So when does the curtain go up?"

"We're heading over to the dressing rooms now," she told him as she looped her arm in his.

They chatted for a little while until it was time for them to change into their costumes. Kaliq had heard that the theater department put on some very good plays. He enjoyed things like that, but he hadn't indulged in too many outside interests in a long time. He felt it was time that he developed a social life again. He knew he pushed himself too hard at times. However, it was important that his sons have a father they could be proud of.

He recognized a few of the students seated in the audience, but none that he knew personally. The head of the department came out and welcomed everyone and introduced the play. Jeneill was in the very first scene. She was dressed in rags. No trace of the beautiful girl he knew remained. Her makeup made her appear old. Her hair was gathered up and wrapped in a scarf. Even her voice had made a transformation when she spoke her first lines.

The play had turned out to be a very moving story about a homeless woman. Jeneill was outstanding; they all were actually. Kaliq made his way to the backstage area. "That was something. You all were on the money."

"I'm glad you liked it," Jeneill told him modestly.

"Seriously, it was really good. What are you guys planning to do now?"

"Well, we were gonna go into the city. Hang out a little bit. I didn't commit to it because I thought maybe…"

Kaliq cut her off. "If you aren't committed, would you like to go out with me tonight?"

Jeneill tried to hide the relief from her face. "I'd like that a lot, Kaliq."

He decided that he would bring her to Brooklyn. He told her he would treat her to Junior's famous cheesecake.

"Are you trying to fatten me up, Mr. Nichols?"

"Cheesecake would not be my weapon of choice, Ms. Waters."

They took the number one train to 96th Street, then transferred to the number two. Junior's was at the last stop, Flatbush Avenue. The well-known restaurant and bakery was packed as usual, but they squeezed in. Kaliq ordered the strawberry-covered cheesecake, while Jeneill favored the blueberry. They ate their desserts and laughed a lot. Afterwards, they went walking. "Since we're in Brooklyn, why don't we go back to your place?" Jeneill suggested.

"Okay, we could do that if you want."

They hopped a bus to take them into Bed-Stuy. It was turning cold out, so they quickened their steps. They nearly collided into BulletProof as they turned the corner.

"What up, cuz?" B.P. asked, looking directly at Jeneill.

"Hey, what's up? Jeneill, this is my cousin, Dennis," Kaliq introduced.

"How are you doing, Dennis?"

"Not as fine as you."

"Where are you headed? We were about to go in," Kaliq questioned, hoping B.P. would catch the hint.

"I was about to go inside myself. Now that the NBA is back in business, I've got to get my fix. I missed the game, so I've got to catch the rewind."

The three of them stepped inside the house. Kaliq switched on the lights. "This is a nice house you've got," Jeneill praised.

"Thank you. Please have a seat. Would you like something else to drink?"

"Sure, whatever you've got."

"Would you like something with a kick to it?" B.P. offered.

Kaliq shot his cousin a nasty look which B.P. ignored. "Well, maybe some wine," Jeneill answered.

"How about Riunite?"

"That's fine. Thank you."

Kaliq did not like the direction this evening was going. He wasn't sure if inviting her to his bedroom was appropriate, so they all sat in the living room watching the Knicks game. Jeneill didn't seem to mind, but he knew she wasn't really into the game.

"So cuz tells me you do plays and shit," B.P. said.

"Yeah, something like that." She smiled. "So what kind of shit do you do?"

B.P. laughed and turned back to the game. Kaliq was glad his cousin chose not to answer that one. The Knicks went into halftime. "Hey, cuz, I forgot to tell you Yolie called. She wants you to call her back tonight."

Jeneill gave Kaliq a casual glance. "Yolie is my sons' sister. She's probably calling for her mother," Kaliq explained.

"When am I going to get to meet your boys? That picture you showed me was too cute."

"This is your weekend, right? Maybe you can hook something up," B.P. prodded.

"I can't this weekend, but I'll make it my business for your next one," Jeneill answered.

"Why? What's up?" B.P. continued.

"Damn, Dennis, mind your own," Kaliq said, getting further annoyed with his cousin.

"If you must know, Mr. Man, I've got my sistas retreat this weekend," Jeneill told him good-naturedly.

Kaliq called B.P. into the kitchen. "Yo, what are you doing, man?"

"What?"

"You know damn well what, motherfucker."

"Do you realize homegirl looks like Dominique Simone? Boy, I'd tear that back out!"

"No, I hadn't noticed," Kaliq lied. "You are deliberately trying to mess up my groove here."

"Kaliq, I don't know who you tryin' to fool. You know as well as I do that you've had the hots for Yolie since she was sixteen years old."

"And who the hell are you? Ghetto Cupid? You don't know shit about what I feel for her and I'd appreciate it if you'd make yourself scarce."

"Yeah, whatever, man. Just let me know how the pussy is, a'ight." B.P. chuckled.

Jeneill stood up as the two entered the living room. "It's getting late. I should be heading back uptown."

"Nah, it's too late. I know my cousin ain't gonna let you travel by yourself and I also know he probably don't feel like riding up there neither. Why don't you just crash here? I'm about to be out anyway."

Jeneill looked skeptical at first, then she said that would be fine with her. "I've got to get up early, though."

Kaliq was a little surprised. "Oh, okay. I'll straighten up my room for you. If Dennis is gonna be out all night, I'll take his."

B.P. looked at his cousin with sheer disbelief. "All righty then. It's been a pleasure. Hope to see you again soon," he said to Jeneill with a sly grin.

"Well, likewise, Dennis."

They went into his room after B.P. left. Kaliq began to pick up discarded laundry from the floor. "I'm sorry about him."

"For what? Your cousin is just real."

"A little too real sometimes. I don't want you to feel like you were tricked into staying here tonight."

"It's really okay, Kaliq. I was sort of hoping you would suggest it yourself."

Right about then Kaliq was feeling like a big punk. He was very attracted to Jeneill. He was just a little gun-shy since Cari. Who's to say that couldn't happen again despite contraception? He already felt he was depriving his children. He had a good relationship with Cari, but they weren't a family in the traditional sense of the word. These days, who was?

Jeneill came up behind him and wrapped her arms around him. She smelled of raspberry and mint. The scent rose up off her skin like a vapor. She loosened her long hair from its clip. With her tongue she began to caress his neck. She reached around and felt between his legs. Kaliq could sense she was on a mission. As he began to react to her touch, he heard her give a small moan. He turned her around so he could kiss her. She greeted his tongue hungrily. They eased themselves onto the bed. He managed to slide her blouse off without interrupting their flow. She slid off the bed to kneel before him. She fussed with his pants until they came undone. She stroked him gingerly causing him to feel near explosion. He was about to raise her up when the phone rang. "Shit, who is that?"

"There's only one way to find out," she informed him as she lifted the phone from its cradle.

"Hello?" he said with a hint of irritation.

"Kaliq? Hi, it's me. Did 'Bullethead' tell you I called?" Yolie chimed from the other end.

"Yeah, he did. What's up?" he asked. Jeneill looked up into his eyes as she freed his manhood from his paisley boxers.

"Well, Travis and Trevor have been invited to a birthday thing at the Discovery Zone Saturday. Mommy wanted to know if you had some other plans that couldn't be changed. They are really looking forward to it, but she told them we'd have to check with you first."

"Hey, whatever they want to do is cool. It's their weekend, too," he said, hoping his voice didn't sound too strained as he felt Jeneill take him into her mouth.

"I'm gonna tag with y'all since my girl is bringing her daughter, too. So how's everything? Let me know when I can drop by City. I still want you to show me around the school. If you still want to that is."

Jeneill motioned for him to keep talking. She actually was enjoying the tortured look on his face.

"I can do that. I've been waiting for you to set up a date."

"We can figure it out Saturday. Can't wait to see you…I mean to see you with the boys," Yolie stammered.

"I can't wait to see you, too." As he said that, Jeneill bit down on him.

"All right. I'll let you get back to whatever you were doing. Talk to you later. Goodnight."

"Goodnight, Yo." The words were barely out before he erupted all over Jeneill's grinning face.

"Now that is out the way, we can have a little fun," she teased.

CHAPTER 12

"Hurry up in there, Cari. We're going to be late," Rue called from the bedroom.

"Look, you can't rush perfection," she answered back.

"If you don't hurry up, there isn't going to be anything to look perfect for. The reception will be over."

"Just because it doesn't take you that long, doesn't mean the rest of us have that same luxury."

Rue stepped into the bathroom where Cari was applying her makeup. This was their first time going out as a couple publicly. They knew their co-workers were pretty much in tune with what was going on between them. However, they had chosen not to advertise it.

"Why not. I'm sure those nosy shitheads at the post office have figured it out anyway. Besides, if we were still only friends we'd probably go together anyhow. What's the difference?"

Cari knew what the difference would be. Her feelings for Rue were still a mystery. She had always cared deeply for her. Yet Cari had never contemplated getting involved with a woman before. She didn't see anything wrong with it; she just never figured she'd be in the situation herself. Cari just felt drawn to Rue. She was loving and fun. Her mood could be dark sometimes, but she was so open to affection that Cari felt needed and wanted. Love was love. She couldn't deny that she always loved Rue anyway; what would be the harm in exploring new possibilities?

She stood at the sink in her new Victoria's Secret apparel. Rue was pleased to see her lover's beautiful body adorned in the pretty apricot-colored underwear. Her breasts were full and inviting. Her legs were well sculpted from the workout Cari gave them. She especially loved to see them in garters and stockings. She was about to reach out and touch her when the boys bum-rushed the bathroom.

"Mommy, I've got to pee," Travis announced.

"I've got to do number two," Trevor added.

"Okay, slow down. Trav, you do your business first so your brother can have the seat to himself," their mother instructed.

Rue backed out the bathroom and nearly collided into Yolie.

"Sorry, Rue. Are you guys almost ready?"

Rue searched Yolie's face for any betrayal of ill will. There wasn't any, but she was pretty sure the girl wasn't totally happy with the circumstances either.

"We could have been ready if your mother wasn't such a slowpoke."

"All right, out of my way. All I have to do is put on my clothes now." Cari pushed her way between the two.

"Finally we're getting somewhere," Rue said as she closed the door behind them.

"Baby, you don't have to close the door," Cari said as she debated which perfume to use.

"I know, but as cool as Yolie is I didn't want her to see me do this," Rue told her as she kissed Cari passionately. Cari lost her breath for a second. When Rue finally pulled away, she found Cari's hands working to unbutton Rue's black jacket.

"I think we've got some time after all."

Yolie could hear the sounds of kissing and giggling through the door. She heaved a small sigh and went to see what her brothers were up to. Before she reached them, there was a light knocking at the door. She ran to get it and saw Kaliq as she peered through the peephole.

"As much noise as your sons make, you need to knock a little harder than that!" she joked as she greeted him with a kiss on the cheek.

"Let me know if they step out of line," he said as he stepped into the apartment. "I'll tighten their little asses up."

"Believe me, they know how far to go. They got three butt kickings to get through between Mommy, you and me."

They made their way back to the boys' room. Cari came out of the bedroom dressed in a two-piece ivory number that was to die for. Kaliq gave a low whistle as he pecked her on the forehead. "Lookin' good, mamacita."

Rue came out adjusting her clothes. "Hello."

"Kaliq, this is my…friend, Rue. Rue, this is the boys' father, Kaliq."

"How are you?" Rue asked, as she possessively wound her arm around Cari's waist.

"I'm pretty good. Just gearing up to be worn out at Discovery Zone," he replied as he shook Rue's free hand.

"Speaking of which, we'd better get out of here. Come on, guys. It's time to go," Yolie called.

The two were dressed and ready to go. They raced each other to the door, but had to go back when Cari reminded them they didn't kiss her goodbye.

"Have fun and be careful," Cari warned.

"Yeah, same to you," Yolie joked.

Once they were out in the hallway, Kaliq pulled Yolara to the side. "What was that?"

"Oh, you mean Love, American Style? I don't know what kind of trip my mother's on. Rue is all right, sorta kinda, but this whole new development is bugging me out."

"When did this happen? I thought Cari was seeing that guy…"

"Please, you know Mommy. She barely gives a person a chance before she decides it's a no-go. That's why I don't get how 'this' came about. I had no idea she was into lesbians. And to be honest, I don't really think she is. She's the kind of person who just loves people—period. Maybe she figured she shouldn't knock it until she tried it," Yolie concluded.

"That's her business. I don't have a problem with anyone as long as they aren't mistreating my kids," he said as they boarded the funky elevator. They squeezed in to make room for a guy and his pit bull. Yolie pressed herself up against Kaliq. He could sense her fear. The dog gave a low growl as he sensed it, too.

"He don't bite," the guy reassured them. Yolie did not look convinced.

As they reached the lobby and safety, the boys ran ahead. "Wait for us!" Kaliq called to them.

From their window, Rue watched the four of them go up the street. "So that's the infamous Kaliq. He ain't bad-looking. I see why you…"

"Don't even go there. He's a good father and a loyal friend. Can't ask for more than that," Cari interrupted. "All right, let's be out."

They arrived at the reception a half an hour late. However, the bride and groom hadn't shown up yet. The word was that the limo caught a flat on the way from the church. When Cari and Rue entered the hall, they saw some of their friends waving at them from the other side of the room.

"Well, it's about time you two showed up!" Pam shouted above the music. The dance floor vibrated as people were grooving to a Ricky Martin tune.

"Blame it on glamour puss over here," Rue told them.

"That outfit is slamming, though," Zoe commented.

"Yes, she wears it very well," Rue agreed as she pulled Cari close.

"I'm gonna check out the bar. You coming, Rue?" Cari asked.

"I'm right behind you."

"Where else would she be?" Pam said snidely to Zoe.

"What's with this Ellen and Anne thing they got going? I thought Cari was strictly dickly."

"Girl, the way she's been dogged out by Yolie's father, it's no wonder she done turned to fish fillet."

"Ain't no man could do me that wrong. Bumping uglies wouldn't do a thing for me. I need penetration from the *real* thing."

"Humph, I ain't got nothing against Rue, but she think she *is* the real thing. She's pretty. I don't know why she got to act so mannish."

Cari and Rue mingled with some of the other guests. Cari could see when it slowly dawned on people that she was *with* Rue. Rue would make sure they got the message with an affectionate gesture that went beyond friendship. That didn't stop some of the men from asking her to dance.

She wanted to, but Rue knitted her brow every time some man requested a spin on the floor.

There was a commotion by the entrance. Apparently, the newlyweds had finally made it. The crowd stood up and cheered. Before the couple could be spotted there was a parade of bridesmaids and groomsmen that seemed to go on forever. Finally, they saw Garcia and his wife as they stepped into the room. They looked deliriously happy. Cari had stopped wondering if she would ever have a big wedding herself one day.

After a hundred toasts, the couple was able at last to make the rounds. "Hey, I'm glad you all could make it!" Garcia beamed.

"Congratulations, Gee. May God bless you," Pam offered.

Everyone held up a glass in agreement. "Thank you. This is Ariana, my wife."

She was a lovely petite young woman. Her gown was gorgeous. "Please, everyone dance; enjoy yourselves."

A handsome dark-skinned Puerto Rican man joined them. "Everyone, this is my brother, Ignacio. He came in from P.R. just for the wedding. He's never been to the States. Can't speak a word of English," Garcia informed them.

However, an interpreter was not necessary when it became apparent that Ignacio wanted to dance with Cari. A beautiful ballad had just begun. Cari took his outstretched hand and followed him to the dance floor.

Pam and Zoe gave each other knowing glances as they watched the steam rise off Rue.

The night was drawing to an end. Rue tried hard to keep her attitude in check. She rationalized that it was only a dance, but she didn't like the way Ignacio (or any other man for that matter) stared at Cari. Cari said she wanted to make one more trip to the bathroom before they left. She excused herself from the table and headed for the powder room. Rue was visibly chomping at the bit. Half a minute later, she excused herself from the table and went towards the restrooms.

"Well, that didn't take long, did it?" Zoe told her girlfriend.

"Uh-humm," Pam answered.

Cari was about to enter a stall when she looked up and saw Rue's reflection in the mirror. "Had to go, too?"

"No, I was just making sure Lover Boy hadn't followed you in here."

"You don't have a bit of sense," Cari joked as she shut the door. "It turned out to be a really nice party."

"Yeah, that outfit of yours sure was a hit," Rue grumbled.

"Well, that's why you buy it. You don't get your money's worth if no one notices it."

"Oh, people noticed it all right. Half your tits are hanging out of it."

"Ha, you didn't seem to mind that before we left the house," Cari kidded. She was a little surprised to see the stern look on Rue's face. "What's the matter, Baby?"

"I just don't like when people look at you like predators," Rue stated with her arms folded across her chest.

"Baby, I wouldn't mind if people looked at you. It's a compliment when others appreciate your good taste."

"Bull shit. That man would like to fuck the shit out of you. Is that what you want, too?"

"To get the shit fucked out of me? Yeah, but not by him," Cari reasoned. She nearly lost her balance as Rue pushed her back into the bathroom stall. She hiked Cari's skirt up above her waist. With an abruptness that startled Cari even more, Rue forced her fingers underneath the lace panties. She smeared Cari's lipstick on both their faces with a rough kiss. The more Cari tried to shove her away, the more aggressive Rue became. She'd finally managed to get inside Cari despite her protests. "Get off! What is the matter with you? Stop!"

Rue was lost. Cari eventually managed to push her off and Rue stumbled back almost to the sink. At that moment, some of the other guests came into the bathroom. Cari closed the door to the stall so she could pull herself together. The older women had puzzled looks on their faces. Rue turned to the sink and started to run the water. She had really gone too far. "Cari, I'll be back at the table."

Cari didn't respond. She waited for the powder room to clear out. She went to the lobby to claim her coat and left.

CHAPTER 13

Kaliq and Yolie were exhausted after their day at the Discovery Zone. They were climbing and sliding on the equipment like a couple of big kids themselves. The boys were getting a little whiny because they had reached their limit, too. Yolie went with them back to the brownstone.

Travis and Trevor immediately fell off to sleep as soon as they hit the couch. Yolie dumped their overnight bag on the floor. Kaliq saw the red light blinking on his answering machine. He pressed the play button. The first message was from his boy, Todd. Jeneill was the second message. The third was a hang-up, but the last message was from his mother.

"Kal, this is mom. We need you to call us as soon as you get this message okay, son? Love you."

Kaliq had a bad feeling in the pit of his stomach. He had to try the number again when he made a mistake in his haste. The phone rang five times before he heard his father's voice. "Hello?"

"Daddy, it's me. What happened?"

"Calm down, Kaliq. It's your grandmama, Nana Zee. Her heart's giving out, son. The doctors say it don't look good. They are advising us that if any family members want to see her before she's gone, they need to come now."

Kaliq was stunned. He couldn't believe his grandmother was dying. There was no one in the world like his Nana Zee. Zora Abernathy. She was his mother's mother. Nana had to be more than eighty years old. All the children loved going down South to spend the summer with her.

Sometimes she'd come up to New York, but she really didn't enjoy the city at all. But she'd do it for her babies.

"How is Mama?" Kaliq asked his father, Nathan.

"You know your mama. She putting up a good front for your aunts and uncles. Can you make it down here, son?"

"I'll have to work some things out, but I'll be down there as soon as I can. Hopefully, in a couple of days."

"That would be good if you can arrange it," Nathan said.

"Is Mama there?"

"No, she down at the hospital. But I'll tell her to call you back tonight, okay?" Nathan promised. "I don't want to run up your bill so I'll holler at you later."

"I don't care about the damn bill, Daddy."

"Don't swear, Kaliq. And don't give me any shit. Bye now."

Kaliq replaced the phone on its hook. Yolie came up to him. "Didn't sound like good news." She gently rubbed his back. He told her about his grandmother's condition.

"Do you think Cari would give me a hard time if I asked her to let me take the boys down there for a week? Nana Zee never got to see the twins in person and this might be her last chance," Kaliq told her as he accepted Yolie's hug.

"I can't speak for her, but I'm pretty sure she'd suggest it herself. We can call her later. I can hang out for a while if you want."

He plopped down on to the floor. She didn't say anything for a time. Kaliq was fighting back tears. He watched his sons sleeping on the couch. They were fraternal twins who shared both their parents' traits. Travis liked to draw already, just like his dad. Trevor was loving and friendly just like his mother. He loved his children with a vengeance. "I can't be too late, Yolie."

"You won't be. Nana sounds like a woman who's not going to give up without a fight. And she'd definitely wait for you," Yolie tried to assure him. "I've never been down South. It's probably like Puerto Rico. Countrified as it wanna be."

"I thought Puerto Rico had big-time cities," Kaliq said, trying to shake his mood.

"It does, but my people aren't from them. We be mountain folks. I know my father is from South Carolina. Of course, I've never been there, especially not with him."

"Don't you have winter recess or something now?" Kaliq asked.

"Yeah. I'm too glad. Senior year can stress you out."

"Why don't you drive down with me? I'm not going to be able to afford to fly on this short notice. I know your father helped you get your license. I can rent a car and we'd take turns driving. Besides, it would be easier to deal with the kids if I had someone traveling with me."

"I'd like that. Mommy just might be down with that, too. How come you don't ask B.P., though?"

"Five-year-old twins are enough. I don't need to add a twenty-year-old baby to the mix."

Yolie helped him get the boys undressed and ready for bed. After the Discovery Zone, they had hung out at the Promenade. There was a breathtaking view of Manhattan along its boardwalk. Yolie remembered the old woman who had said they made a beautiful family. They knew what she had assumed, but it was too complicated to explain to someone who was "old school." They just accepted her compliment graciously and walked on. They had stopped off to buy some ice cream for later. Kaliq went to the refrigerator to fix them a couple of bowls. They were stretched out on the floor looking at some sketches Kaliq was working on, when B.P. burst in.

"Hey, Yolie what's up?" he greeted her by pulling her hair.

"You stupid," she said, feigning anger. Her swing had just missed him.

"I got a call from Mama and Dad. Nana Zee is in the hospital. She's probably not gonna make it, cuz."

B.P. got quiet for a long moment. "Damn, man, that's fucked up. Nana Zee is da bomb. She and you the only ones that really treat me like anything. Everyone else either just tolerates me or straight disses me. Man, this shit ain't fair."

"I know, Dennis, but she's old, man. Her heart is tired. I don't want to see her go," Kaliq answered.

"Well, I ain't gonna see her go. I want to remember my girl the way she was. You know they don't never fix you to look like yourself when you lying in that box," B.P. commented.

"I'm going to take the boys down to meet her. I just hope we're not too late. Yolie wants to come, too."

"Yeah, her Pops ain't gonna be too happy about that one," B.P. teased halfheartedly.

It was a thought that hadn't occurred to Yolie, but she didn't care. Her family needed her. These were her brothers' relatives, but they had always been accepting of her, too. Now that Meshach and Olive were separated, she saw more of her father, but he hadn't mentioned meeting anyone else on his side of the family. This was an opportunity she didn't want to pass up. Deep in her heart she realized that Kaliq was a big part of her wanting to do this. She loved that someone had mistaken them for a couple. She couldn't let go of this silly daydream she had of them being together. Yolie wasn't too sure of the logistics, but she wasn't going to lie to herself.

"So what you gonna tell Dominique Simone?" B.P. asked his cousin.

Kaliq once again shot him the look reserved just for him. "I'm going to tell her the truth."

"Yeah, that shit's gonna go over real well. I'm about to jump into the shower. Yolie, I'll catch you later."

"Goodnight, Dennis."

"Hey, he's the only one I let get away with that shit; calling me Dennis," B.P. called over his shoulder.

Yolie raised herself up off the floor and took her bowl into the kitchen. Kaliq followed her in. "Thank you for hanging out, Yolie."

"For you, anytime. I'll let Mommy know what the situation is and call you in the morning."

"I'll get my jacket so I can walk you back," Kaliq said. He knocked on the bathroom door. The water wasn't running yet, so he knew his cousin could hear him. "Dennis, I'm going to walk Yolie home. The twins are sleeping in my room. Keep an eye out."

"You got it, cuz," he hollered back.

They discussed the details of their trip as they walked back to her building. "I hope Cari agrees."

"Don't worry. I just hope I don't get any flack from Daddy," she admitted.

"I wouldn't let anything happen to you."

"I know that," Yolie answered softly. She reached up to kiss his cheek. "Talk to you tomorrow, Kaliq."

He had waited with her for the elevator. As the door closed, he wished he had ridden up with her. These projects were a mess. Anything could happen from point A to point B. He hung around for a couple of minutes to make sure everything was all right.

Yolie let herself into the dark apartment. She nearly broke her leg trying to get to the window. She saw Kaliq's tall dark figure going back the way they had come. She rubbed her shin where she had bumped it into the coffee table. "Yolie, you are so stupid," she said aloud to herself.

As she switched on the light, she heard the key in the door. Cari stormed into the apartment looking like she was looking for someone to kill.

"Mommy, what's the matter?" Yolie questioned with concern. "Where's Rue?"

Cari had to take a couple of deep breaths before she answered. "The reception was beautiful. We were having a good time. And then Rue just lost her fucking mind." Cari then told her daughter basically what had happened.

"That's strange, Mommy. I have to tell you I don't always have a good feeling about Rue."

"She's a good person, but she has let past relationships cloud her judgment. She thinks I'm gonna do something to hurt her, I guess. Yolie, I am new to this kind of relationship, but that has nothing to do with the fact that I have always respected her."

"Mommy, what is up with you and this relationship anyway? We talk about everything and I don't remember you mentioning you were gay," Yolie finally asked.

"Honestly, Yolara, I don't know how to answer that. I've found women attractive before. I think we all do. Women can openly admire each other. But when I saw that Rue had feelings for me, something urged me to go for it. It's the perfect thing. A woman knows what you want and need because she feels the same things you do. And it was nice to have someone genuinely care about me. A lot of the guys I was talking to weren't about anything. They weren't particularly interested in my viewpoints or desires. I saw a chance to be with someone I've always liked anyway. Is that so wrong?"

"In some ways no and in some ways yes," Yolie concluded. "Man or woman, she had no cause to overreact like that. If you two can't fix that, you don't need to be together at all."

Mother and daughter sat and talked for a long while. Yolie told Cari what was going on with Kaliq and about his request to take the boys to Georgia.

"That would be all right with me. I'll call him myself to express my condolences. I'm tired, *mi hija*. I'm going to bed now." Cari kissed her child on the forehead and went off to her room.

Yolie washed up and went to bed also. About an hour later, Rue came home. She knew Yolie was in her room. She could see the light from the television from beneath her door. Cari's bedroom door was closed as well. Rue slowly tried the knob. She half expected the door to be locked. It wasn't. The room was dark, but she could see Cari's form lying across the bed. She didn't want to wake her by turning on the light. Rue just slipped off her jacket and pants and tried to get in the bed beside her. She was careful not to touch her either. Rue had spent the rest of the evening in a bar. She had cursed herself all night. She couldn't deal with any more drama so she tried not to disturb Cari. There would be plenty of time for that in the morning.

Cari, however, wasn't asleep. She saw every move Rue had made. She was still very angry with her, but she wasn't up for a confrontation either. "If you ever touch me like that again, you will have to leave my house. Do we understand each other?"

Rue was a little startled by Cari's voice in the dark. "Yes, it's understood."

CHAPTER 14

Meshach was taking Egypt to get her car serviced. It was an unwritten rule that this was his job. Of course, he didn't mind doing it for her. He wanted Egee to be as safe as possible out on the road. She was due any minute. They were going to pick up some things at Sears after they were finished at the mechanic's. Meshach missed her terribly. She was about to be off to Spelman in the fall and he wanted to spend as much time with her as he could. He would have loved for his two daughters to get along as true sisters, but he could see that wasn't going to happen. He knew Yolara was willing, but Egee was not able. Not now anyway. He wasn't going to force the issue. He knew his oldest child harbored enough bad feelings as it was.

He almost didn't hear the doorbell above the vacuum. He let Egypt in. "What's up, Egee?" he asked as he hugged her.

"Everything is all right. How's bachelor life?" she asked coyly.

"I miss our house. I miss you."

"Do you miss Ma?" she asked as she stepped into the living room.

"I miss the woman your mother used to be," he told her. "You probably don't remember, but there was a time when we were happy with each other. But I don't want to talk about that now. I'm still steaming over the fact that I'm responsible for mortgage payments on a house that I don't even live in anymore."

"Yeah, she told me she wants to talk to you about getting your name off the deed or whatever. She's bugging, Dad. I love Ma, but she can work the last nerve of your last nerve," Egypt confided.

"Can she really handle a mortgage by herself? Did y'all hit Lotto and forget to tell me," Meshach joked.

"Please, I wish. She finally got that position as head of her department. The president's son messed up one time too many. They probably aren't paying her what they would be paying some white guy, but they know she does her job extremely well and she'd be willing to take less even though this new salary is lovely. I think she could swing the house with no problem."

Meshach had mixed emotions about that. They went into that house together. Why should she be the one to keep it? He could handle the payments himself. He hated living in an apartment again. He wasn't going to dwell on that right then.

Meshach and Egypt spent a couple of hours at the mechanic's shop. Afterwards, they headed over to Kings Plaza. The mall was crowded, but they made it into Sears. They browsed as they looked for the automotive department. Meshach noticed Egypt look over his shoulder.

"Hello, Burk."

He turned around to face Caridad. She was loaded down with bags. She was decked out in a deep-brown leather pea coat and matching riding boots. Her pants were the clinging kind. Her hair was gathered up in a ponytail that hung from the top of her head. She looked delectable. Egypt looked from one to the other.

"Hey, how are you, Cari? This is my daughter, Egypt. Egee, this is Yolie's mom," he said, introducing the two awkwardly.

Egypt seemed as if she was going to ignore the introduction at first. Meshach saw the cloud that passed over her face. "Hello, how are you?" It took some effort but she managed.

"I'm pretty good, thank you. Just picking up some things for the kids. Yolie and the twins are going down South."

"Oh, really. Who do you know down South?" Meshach asked immediately suspicious.

"Kaliq's grandmother is terminal and doesn't have much time left. He wants her to see his children before it's too late. Yolie said she'd like to go with them."

"They flying down there?"

"No," she answered, prepared for the attitude that she knew was coming. "On such short notice all he can do is rent a car and drive."

"And who is she going to be staying with? They are not going to shack up in some hotel?"

"Burk, Kaliq's parents have a house down there. You know the Nichols are good people."

"I know no such thing," he snapped.

"Well, I'm telling you they are. Travis and Trevor's grandparents are loving, respectful people. They think the world of Yolara and so does Kaliq," she tried to assure him without getting loud.

"That's exactly who I'm worried about. This Kaliq isn't all of that now, is he?"

"Why, because I turned to him after you dumped me?"

"Okay, this is my cue. Daddy I will see you later," Egypt said, turning to go.

"No, sweetheart, wait," Meshach begged as he caught her by the arm.

"I apologize, Egypt. I didn't want to start nothing, but hey…," she said to the girl with sincere remorse.

"We will discuss this further before she goes anywhere," Meshach told Cari.

"I don't see where there is anything to talk about. She's eighteen years old. She didn't have to ask me anything." Cari nodded at Egypt and headed off towards the nearest exit.

"That was nice," Egypt said sarcastically.

"I'm sorry, Egee Bird. You girls are my world. I'm just not comfortable with certain things."

"Let's just get the stuff," she said as she walked towards Sears' automotive department.

Meshach couldn't help but turn and look for Cari's retreating form. She was gone. He fumed. Yolie hadn't asked him anything. His afternoon with Egypt was pretty much ruined. They didn't talk much after the encounter.

Egypt dropped her father back at his place. They kissed each other goodbye, but he saw the hurt in her eyes. Once she was gone, Meshach went back out to his car and headed for Bed-Stuy.

He pulled into the parking lot that divided the two towering project buildings. He figured he had beaten Cari back. He wanted to talk to Yolie without her interference first. He waited anxiously for the elevator to come down. He considered for a moment that he was overreacting. But Cari had made his blood boil in more ways than one. He stepped aside to let the people stepping off the elevator get by. The elevator stopped on every floor on its way to the sixth. He could smell something good cooking from somebody's apartment. He used the knocker to bang on Cari's door.

"Who is it?" an unfamiliar voice called from inside.

"Is Yolara home?"

"I repeat, who is it?"

"This is her father, Meshach Burkette," he answered with annoyance. He heard the locks turn at last. The woman who opened the door was dressed in gray sweats and a white tank. Her body glistened with perspiration.

"Come in. Yolie and or Cari should be back in a minute," she told Meshach.

He felt her checking him out while his back was turned. "I'm sorry. I didn't get your name."

"Because I didn't give it. I'm Rue Tenney. Please sit down."

She walked over to the television to switch off the Billy Blanks Tae Bo tape she obviously had been working out to.

"Can I get you anything?" Rue asked over her shoulder as she went into the kitchen.

"No, thank you."

They both looked towards the door as they heard the jangle of keys. Cari struggled with the door and her packages. Rue rushed over to help her out. "Hey, Baby," she said as she planted an unmistakably passionate kiss on her lips.

"Damn, Kings Plaza was packed," Cari started. She stopped in her tracks when she saw Meshach sitting in her E-Z chair. "Did you make a bee line for my house or what?"

"I told you I wanted to discuss this trip with you," he said haltingly, not quite believing his eyes. *Shit, something else no one had bothered to tell me about.*

Rue made no move to give them any privacy. Cari didn't request any.

"What is the big deal, Burk? They are going to see a dying woman! They won't even be gone a week. There is no school; it's winter recess or whatever they're calling it this year."

Meshach couldn't think straight. This butch had just kissed his Cari.

"I agree with Cari and Yolie. They…," Rue began.

"Um, excuse me, but this is our child. I don't mean to be rude, sir. What the fuck is going on here anyway?" Meshach shouted.

"Who the hell you talking to like that?" Rue yelled back, moving towards him.

"Rue, don't," Cari intervened. She stepped in between the two of them.

"You better watch yourself, boy," Rue said with venom.

"Boy? I'll show you a boy, bitch."

Cari thought she was going to lose it. "I said shut up. The both of you."

"So, you swinging that way now, Cari?" Meshach shot at her.

"Your shit drove her to another woman, homie. If you would have treated her better, she'd be sucking your dick instead of mine."

Meshach had to stop himself. The two women had no idea he was packing his gun. He never came to Bed-Stuy without it. If he didn't get a hold of himself in the next instant, his girls would be visiting him upstate. "This is the way you bringing up our child?"

"You know, Burk, your opinion doesn't mean much to me anymore. I understand Yolie is our shared responsibility, but you've got to understand she's not a baby anymore. I raised her right. My private life is my private business. Yolara respects our being together and that's enough for me. So would you please leave now? We can continue to be cool; it's up to you," Cari lectured.

Meshach was shocked. He just shook his head and stormed out the door.

"He has a hell of a nerve," Rue protested. "You sure can pick 'em. What did you ever see in that asshole?"

"Please, Rue. My head is killing me now. I spent nearly half my lifetime loving that man. I don't feel like talking about it now," she said while rubbing her temples.

"You wish you were still with him?" Rue asked darkly.

"Not that again," Cari pleaded.

Rue knew not to go too far. Instead she went into the kitchen and brought out some water and two Tylenol gelcaps. "Let's just forget it," she urged as she massaged Cari's neck and shoulders. Cari closed her eyes as Rue's hands worked her over. "Let's just forget all about him."

CHAPTER 15

Egypt was mentally tired. The last person she expected to see was Caridad Flores. She couldn't wait to go to Atlanta. Her mother liked to pretend she wasn't missing her father. Sometimes she felt like telling her he'd still be there if she hadn't treated him like shit. Yeah, sometimes she just wanted to scream it into her face. Olive wanted everything her way. It was *her* master plan, not God's. If things didn't go how she wanted them to, then they just weren't going to go at all. Egypt loved her mother, but she was not blind to her faults.

She could hear the stereo going full blast as she approached the house. Olive was sitting at the dining room table sorting bills.

"Hey, Egee. You got a cigarette on you?"

"I thought you quit," Egypt asked her mother as she sifted through her bag searching for a loose cigarette.

"I had but DuValier's has made me revert back to this nasty habit," she complained.

"It's not easy at the top, huh?" Egypt said.

"Ha ha. You ain't funny, miss," Olive retorted as she lit the offered cig. "Did your father take care of your car?"

"Yeah, we covered everything. You'll never guess who I met today."

"My head is too full to make it work that hard. Who?"

"Cari."

"Not exactly what I wanted to hear, Egee. I know you blame me for

Meshach's indiscretion. I'm not the one who stepped out," Olive argued grimly.

"I never said all of that, did I?"

"You don't have to say it," she said as she snubbed out the cigarette.

"If you weren't going to smoke it…"

"So what does the bitch look like?" Olive asked in spite of herself.

Egypt was almost sorry she brought it up. "She's a very good-looking woman. Did you think she wouldn't be?"

"That's not necessary, Egypt." Olive cringed.

"I'm sorry, Ma, but you're right. I do think you played a big part in what went down. I know how it is being your daughter I can't imagine being your husband. You're demanding, up tight, snobbish. There were many times when Daddy and I both just wanted to feel like we mattered a little more than your precious career."

"Well, I'm sorry you felt that way. I just needed to make a success of my life. I wanted more than what my family had growing up in the projects. Your father had the same aspirations himself once. I don't know what made him give up on being a doctor. He used to talk about it all the time when we were coming up. He did well in college in the beginning. Once it got too hot…"

"He got out of the kitchen," Egypt finished. "College isn't for everyone. Once he got with Transit he was satisfied. He enjoys his job and it makes good money."

"But imagine how much better our lives would be if he had become Dr. Meshach Burkette."

"Better for who? He is…was happy. You were the only one complaining. I'm going upstairs. Let me know when you're ready to eat dinner."

Olive watched her child ascend the stairs. She couldn't believe she had come out her face like that. Then again, she was absolutely right. Olive couldn't believe how much she was missing her husband. She knew he had ruined the marriage, but she didn't want to think how it could have been different if she had tended to it better herself.

"What am I saying? The bastard cheated on me," Olive said aloud.

She glanced down at her bills and shoved them aside. She turned off the stereo as well. She looked up at the dining room wall and saw a framed photograph of her graduation picture. Olive remembered the day Meshach snapped the picture. She had just completed her bachelor's. She had graduated cum laude with a degree in business from Baruch College. It was soon after that she found out she was pregnant with Egypt. Those were some lean years. As soon as Egypt was toilet trained and could go to a day care center, Olive had set out to find a job. Meshach supported her decision. He had wanted them to get a house and he knew it would be easier with the two of them working at it. Besides, he knew his wife well. She wouldn't have been able to stomach being home all the time. She needed to be a success.

"No one wants me, Meshach," Olive would come home crying. "They expect me to be experienced. How can I be experienced if no one will hire me?"

"You graduated near the top of your class. If they don't recognize your potential, it's their loss. Someone out there has sense. You just haven't found them yet."

The following week she had gotten an interview with DuValier's as a manager's assistant. She was afraid to get excited when they had called her back for a second interview. It was Meshach who had told her the good news. "You got the job, baby! The watch company you told me about called today asking if you could start Monday."

The work had been menial in the beginning, but it was a foot in the door. Days when she had felt discouraged, Meshach would make her feel like a woman with a well -placed kiss or a sexy gesture.

"Ummm, you trying to kill me woman?" he purred.

"I got a lot of things to work out," she teased in return.

"Work 'em out, baby. That's what I'm here for."

The lovemaking had been primal at times, but always satisfying.

Olive would trace his finely chiseled face. He was a warm cocoa color. His short dark hair had a slight wave to it. His build was thick and muscular. Olive could remember when he was a skinny kid growing up on DeKalb

Avenue. He had come into his own and she had craved him with a passion. Her own tea with milk complexion and full figure would change very little over the years. They were still a handsome couple. Or were.

Olive thought about the fights and arguments that had taken over their marriage. She thought about the dwindling sex life. She cursed the indifference that had blanketed their whole relationship. Drained, she went up to her bedroom. She stared at her reflection in the mirror. Olive wanted to be with Meshach again. The way they had begun. Logistically, she knew it was too late, but what could it hurt to talk about it? She searched her closet for something eye-catching but casual to put on. She ran a comb through her slick new hair cut. She scrubbed the old make up away and applied more natural colors. She snatched up her purse and headed for the door before she could lose her nerve.

"Egee, I'm going out for a bit. You don't have to wait for me to eat," she called out to her daughter.

Before Egypt could respond, Olive was out the door.

CHAPTER 16

Yolie was busy packing her suitcase. She could hear the boys arguing next door. There was a big debate over which toys they would bring for the road trip. It would be nice getting out of the city. She'd been South to visit relatives in Florida, but this would be her first time in Georgia. Her father had mentioned they had kin in Atlanta, but she had no idea how far that was from Wynetta. According to Kaliq it was a small town near Savannah.

"Are you about done with your bags?" Cari asked her as she entered the room.

"Almost. I don't want to drag too much stuff with me, but at the same time I don't want to get caught short either."

"I just wish this was a happier occasion. Is there any word on how Kaliq's grandmother is doing?" Cari inquired while she helped with the packing.

"So far there hasn't been a change. I hope we're not too late."

"I'll pray for her. Are you going to be all right?"

"I'll be okay. Hopefully, Kaliq won't fall apart."

"I don't worry about Kaliq. He has done a good job growing up. I feel like I might have forced him to grow up before his time. I told him he was under no obligation to raise these kids, but he sort of looked at me like I was crazy. I trust him with Travis and Trevor. And I'm trusting him with you," she added with a smirk.

"And what is that look for, Mommy?"

"Oh, *mi hija*. I am not blind or stupid. Love can be found in the strangest places, huh?" Cari grinned.

Rue stepped into the doorway. Yolie tried not to resent the intrusion. Did this woman have to be under foot all the time? Yolie was sure that Rue was more than happy to get her and her brothers out the house for a few days. She really tried to get along with Rue. They were civil and polite with each other, but they were nowhere near forming any sort of bond. It wasn't the gay thing. She figured her mom was entitled to explore whatever experience she wanted. Sure she had secretly hoped her parents would get together. What kid wouldn't? It was just that something did not sit right with her when it came to Rue.

"So how long do you think it will take you all to drive to Georgia?" Rue inquired, butting in on their conversation.

"Kaliq says it could take about sixteen hours," Yolie answered, zipping up her cosmetic bag.

"We used to take trips cross-country when I was growing up," Rue added.

"Really? You never told me that," Cari told her.

"Well, we've got a lifetime to find out all kind of things, babe."

Yolie turned her back so they wouldn't see her cross her eyes.

Cari went next door to finally settle the dispute between the twins.

"All right, you two. I tried to let you to come to some agreement on your own and it ain't working. I'm going to pack your stuff."

There was a chorus of aahs. Rue stepped up to grab Cari from behind. "What do you feel like doing tonight?"

"I don't know. Maybe catch a flick. What do you think?"

"Sounds good to me."

Yolie dove for the phone on its first ring. "Hello?"

"Yolie, it's me. Are you guys ready?" Kaliq asked.

"Yeah, we're all set. Are you coming over now?"

"I'm going to gas up and stuff like that. We should buy some stuff to take on the road with us. Those guys will want Mickey D's every time we pull over. It's cheaper and healthier to bring our own food," Kaliq advised.

"Sounds like a plan to me. Do you want to shop first?"

"We could do that. I'll swing by to get you. We'll run the errands. Then come back to get the kids," Kaliq told her. They finalized a couple more details and hung up.

Over at Kaliq's house, B.P. was getting into his John Madden PlayStation game. "So are you gonna take Yolie to a motel?" B.P. asked his cousin.

"This ain't no social event. Do I have to remind…"

"All right, damn. I know how serious it is. A brotha can't try to lighten a moment."

"I'm sorry, man. I'm just so anxious to get down there," Kaliq apologized as he gathered his bags. "You wanna help me get these things into the car."

They packed his duffel bag and one suitcase into the trunk. They both looked up to find Jeneill approaching them.

"Hi, Kaliq. I was hoping I'd catch you before you left," she said as she reached up to kiss his cheek.

"Jeneill, what are you doing out here? I told you last night when we spoke you didn't have to come out to Brooklyn," Kaliq said.

"I know, but this is a sad time and I figured you could use your friends around you."

It wasn't that he didn't want her around. Kaliq had too much going on at the moment to have to add Jeneill to the mix. "It's about time I met your kids anyway," she continued.

"I was just about to run some errands and then pick them up," Kaliq told her.

"Hey, you can put me to some good use. I'll help," Jeneill volunteered.

Kaliq very well couldn't say no after she had made the trip from Harlem. "All right. Let's go then."

B.P. gave his cousin the "you're in for it now" look. They hopped into the Saturn he had rented that morning.

Yolie was organizing which CDs and tapes she wanted to bring when she heard the knock at the door. She laughed at herself for checking her hair before she went out into the living room. Yolie stopped in her tracks when she saw the drop-dead gorgeous girl standing at Kaliq's side as her mother opened the door.

"Yolie, it's Kaliq," Cari said stupidly.

"What's up?" she greeted.

Kaliq introduced the two hoping he didn't sound foolish. "Yolara, this is my friend Jeneill. She came out to give us a hand. Jeneill, this is Yolara."

"Nice to meet you, Yolara," Jeneill said.

"You can call me Yolie. Nice to meet you, too."

"Let's get the food shopping out the way. We can get gas in Jersey. It's cheaper out there. You ready?" Both girls answered yes simultaneously.

Yolie followed them out. Her mother gave her a sympathetic smile.

Jeneill sat up front with Kaliq while Yolie tried not to sulk in the back. They made small talk on they way to the supermarket. Jeneill made certain Yolie understood that Kaliq was *her* man.

"Kaliq, honey, I wish I were making this trip with you."

Kaliq fidgeted in his seat. "I don't want to throw my entire family at you all at once. Besides, we still getting to know each other."

Yolie said a hooray to herself. "Kaliq, are we going to bring a cooler or something to carry drinks in?"

"Thanks for reminding me. I've got a cooler in the basement. Just have to remember to buy some ice."

They pulled into the parking lot. Jeneill immediately attached herself to Kaliq's side. She secretly gave Yolie the once-over. She cursed Yolie's startling good looks. And that damn long black hair of hers! She knew Kaliq considered this girl family, but woman's intuition told her that the feeling was not mutual. She then convinced herself that it was silly to worry. Yolie was a child, a good five years younger than Kaliq. Besides, how sick was their situation anyway? But damn, even his kids' mother looked good.

They picked up all kinds of sandwich fixings and snacks. They threw in some fruit for good measure. They also stocked up on juice boxes for the kids. Once the food and drinks were packed, they went back to Cari's to pick up the children.

"I just want to call my father before we hit the road," Yolie informed them. Meshach picked up after the second ring. "Hi, Daddy. We're about to leave now. Just wanted to say goodbye. Yes, I will. Why? Ah, come on,

Daddy. Is that really necessary?" Yolie huffed as she handed Kaliq the phone. "My father wants to talk to you."

Kaliq took the phone from her. "Hello, Mr. Burkette."

"Hey, Kaliq. I'm really sorry to hear about your grandmother," Meshach offered.

"Thank you. We're praying that the doctors are wrong."

"Well, you have my prayers, too." He paused. "You know I'll kill you if anything happens to my baby, don't you?"

"I'm fully aware of that, Mr. Burkette. I ain't ready to die yet," Kaliq reassured him. Yolie rolled her eyes. She took the phone back from Kaliq and bid her father farewell. They all said goodbye to Cari with hugs and kisses. The kids made their usual race to the elevator.

"Kaliq…" Jeneill poked him and nodded towards the kids.

"Boys, y'all ain't got no manners? Say hello to my friend, Jeneill."

The twins were instantly bashful, but they managed to mumble "hello" in unison. Kaliq hadn't planned on making any detours, but he told Jeneill he'd drop her off in Harlem. She'd readily agreed and they were on their way.

Jeneill lived in a five-story walk up near Harlem Hospital. Yolie and the kids stayed in the car as Kaliq walked her upstairs.

"Call me as soon as you get there. I want to know you arrived safely," Jeneill made him promise.

"Of course, I will. See you soon, Jay," he said as he hugged her.

As soon as Jeneill had left, Yolie jumped into the front seat. It still smelled like raspberries and mint. Yolie found liquid car freshener in the glove compartment and began to spray freely. When Kaliq returned to the car she looked at him and gave a half-giggle. "So that's the flavor of the month, huh."

"Okay, Yolie. Don't start none, won't be none." He turned the ignition and pointed the Saturn towards I-95.

CHAPTER 17

Olive wasn't sure if what she was about to do was a good idea or not, but she jumped into her Camry and headed for Meshach's place. Egypt had mentioned where his new apartment was soon after he moved. It had been an ugly scene that day she found out about Cari. She hadn't thought that she would ever find herself on her estranged husband's doorstep. Olive pulled up in front of Meshach's place and parked. She sat there for a good ten minutes before she got out. She could hear the television through the door. She rang the bell. Olive heard the covering of the peephole slide back. It was all she heard for several seconds. Meshach wore a puzzled expression when he finally opened the door. "Nothing's happened to Egypt, has it?"

"No, she's fine. May I come in?" she said with more courage than she felt.

Meshach started to make a wisecrack, but thought better of it. Instead, he stepped aside to allow her to come in. "What can I do for you, Olive?"

"That's a strange question. ain't it? Look, before we go at it again, I thought it might be a good idea to have a rational discussion before we took any official steps to end our union."

Meshach wasn't sure who this woman was, but he didn't recognize her as Olive Burkette. "What exactly does that mean, Olive?"

"Do you have anything to drink? A couple shots of whiskey might do the trick," she tried to joke.

"What's this all about?"

She sat down on the plaid loveseat without being asked. She felt silly, but there she was. "Meshach, I just want to know a few things. Why did you do it in the first place? Cheat, I mean?"

"What good will it do to rehash this?" Meshach said shamefacedly.

"You have to have had some reasoning behind it. Egypt seems to think it was mostly my fault. I suppose that's what you think, too?"

"Olive, I'm not going to go around pointing fingers again. We had problems but no one made me step out on you. I should have ended things before I moved on to someone else, but we had a life with Egypt that I just couldn't...," he managed before he was interrupted.

"I think you didn't want the same things out of life that I wanted," Olive observed.

"No, I guess not. I wanted my wife to be satisfied with the choices I made in regards to my life. No, I couldn't hack college. I have no regrets. I tried. Transit came along just in time. It's a steady, well-paying job. It's not a doctor's salary by far, but it has helped to keep a roof over our heads."

"But why can't we have more than that? I wanted us to move into Brooklyn Heights. I wanted to travel around Europe...," she tried to explain.

"Listen to yourself. These were things you wanted. Not necessarily things I wanted. When I took the bus operator's job, I was thinking about what I wanted for our family. Olive, those things you're talking about are nice. But that ain't the kind of life I want. Hanging out with a bunch of stuffy wannabes."

She was bushed already. He fixed her a glass of brandy. They went on talking, each being extra careful not to fly off the handle. "So where did you meet this woman?" Olive finally asked.

Meshach was about to object, but answered her question instead. "She used to ride my bus to school. She was a senior at Boys and Girls High School."

"So how old is your daughter by her?"

"Yolara was eighteen earlier this year. She'll be graduating from Brooklyn Tech this June."

"You always did want more children," she commented. "Are you and the mother together now?"

"No, strangely enough, she's done taken up with some woman—if you can call her that."

Olive tried not to laugh. "So does that mean there's a chance for us?" She was as stunned as Meshach when she said it.

"Maybe you need to lay off that brandy."

"I'm not drunk, Meshach. I might be crazy, but I'm not drunk. You used to tell me I was starting to change. I didn't think so, so I ignored you. Believe me, I don't know how to handle this affair you've been carrying on...By the way, were there any others?"

"No, there never was anyone else," he said quietly.

Olive wasn't sure if that was good or bad. Several women would have meant that the flings were meaningless. One woman probably meant that he really loved her. It broke her heart.

"I'm making an ass out of myself, ain't I?"

Meshach went to sit beside his wife. "No, I was the bigger fool, you could say. I just don't believe what I'm hearing. It took my cheating for you to realize that you wanted me?"

Olive didn't respond right away. "Yes, I suppose it did."

"Don't you think that says it all?"

Olive set her glass down on the coffee table. She gathered her coat and bag. "Well, I'm glad we hashed it all out anyway. I'll be seeing you, Meshach. Should we contact lawyers now or something?"

"I suppose that's our next logical step, but don't feel like it's got to be done tomorrow." He still couldn't digest their conversation.

She glanced around the small apartment. "I know you miss the house."

"I hear you want to make the house solely yours," he ventured. Meshach saw her cringe a little. "Never mind, Olive. Are you okay to drive home?"

"I'm all right, really. I had to do this and now it's done." She walked through the door as he opened it for her. As a spur of the moment decision, she took his face into her hands and gently kissed his lips. She didn't say anything else.

Meshach closed the door behind her. He could feel his eyes start to well up. "Damn, Olive. Damn."

CHAPTER 18

Kaliq was happy with the time they were making. He would call ahead for progress reports whenever they made a pit stop. The boys were a little restless when they were up, but they slept a good deal of the time. Yolie loved the opportunity to drive. She wasn't panicky or impatient. She did very well, which was a relief to Kaliq.

"I'm gonna miss out on some work this week. My construction gig isn't a sure thing all the time, so I've been making some extra cash typing term papers, and creating business and greeting cards with my computer," Kaliq said.

"Mommy says she wants to get me a computer for my graduation present. That would be da bomb. I could keep track of all kind of things. Look up stuff on the web about the music business. I want to get into record engineering or something like that. Maybe even produce."

They were listening to one of the mixed tapes she had created as they cruised down the highway. Her sense of style was very impressive. Yolie possessed a good ear.

They saw the umpteenth sign urging them to visit South of the Border. It was a popular rest area in South Carolina. "Once you see South of the Border, you know you don't have to much farther to go," Kaliq explained.

Yolie chuckled. "Yeah right. You've said that about a few places."

"I think we'll stop there. The kids might want to get a souvenir or something. They've got millions of those."

They drove the remaining miles to the Border. The kids automatically wanted to know where the bathroom was. After they browsed the shops and bought your basic ashtray, tee shirt and back-scratcher-type gifts, they went back to the car to fix themselves something to eat.

Kaliq found himself staring at Yolara. He remembered the threat her father had administered before they had left. Kaliq didn't have anything against her father, really, but he did think he had a lot of nerve. His parents, Nathan and Goddess (Dessa for short), had been married forever. They were happy with each other. They made it their business to keep their union blissful. That's not to say they didn't have their spats. But the mutual respect ran so deep that all was patched up and forgiven in record time. His mother's favorite motto was never go to bed angry. He watched Yolie fix the kids sandwiches and give them each a juice box. She loved her brothers and they were crazy about her. He had some sort of feelings for Jeneill but they were in their beginning stages. He wasn't about to rush into anything. Although he had been a little surprised at her showing up the way she had, it was really a nice gesture. Kaliq didn't want to hurt anyone. He had a feeling Yolie was going through some of the same emotions he had about their relationship.

"Are we almost there yet, Daddy?" Trevor asked.

"What is that? In the little kids handbook? You've got to ask that question a minimum of a thousand times on each and every trip," Kaliq mused.

"Well, are we?" Travis joined in.

"Yeah, we're getting closer."

"I can't wait to see Grandma Dessa's new house," Travis squealed.

"Grandpa Nate said he'd show me how to work the tractor," Trevor bragged.

"Well, let's get going then. Yolie, I'll take over for the final stretch."

"Aw, I was getting the hang," Yolie mocked.

"Believe me, you did pretty good," Kaliq complimented as he opened her door. "For a woman."

She scowled at him, but then broke into a smile. The kids made a game of counting cars of each color. Yolie began to nod off. Kaliq watched as the sun began to set. The South was a beautiful place. He didn't blame his parents for wanting to move back down. They were able to buy a lovely home for a lot less money than it would have cost them in New York. They were both able to retire early. That's what Kaliq hoped to do also. He didn't know what to expect in the future. He knew he'd never leave New York as long as his sons were there. He had no plans to try to get custody of them either. Cari was a great mother and they were happy. However, he had to admit he'd love to raise them in Georgia.

Once they entered the small town of Wynetta, it took Kaliq a few moments to get his bearings. He remembered the old abandoned slaughterhouse in the center of town. He made a few turns and found the area where several new homes had been built over the last few years. He spotted his father's conversion van parked in the driveway.

Goddess Nichols was out the door before her son could even put the car in park.

"Oh, I'm so glad y'all made it," she cried as she rushed over to the car.

Yolie slowly woke herself up and stretched. The twins had already tumbled out of the car. Yolie wiped the corner of her mouth as Mrs. Nichols came over to her side of the car. "Hello, Ms. Nichols," she greeted her warmly.

"You'd better get out here and give me a hug, girl."

Yolie stepped into the woman's warm embrace. She knew it had taken them some time to get used to the circumstances that bonded Kaliq and her mother. They were just concerned for their son. Once they got to know Cari, she was welcomed into the family. They weren't close really, but there was a genuine fondness.

"What a trip. The couple of times we've been to Florida, we always flew. But driving was pretty cool. I just feel a little knotted up," Yolie told her.

"Well, come on inside. Kaliq, you can bother with those bags later. Y'all hungry? I made barbecue ribs and cabbage. I've perfected the art of home-made biscuit baking and to top it off, I whipped together a banana pudding."

There was a chorus of "I want some" from the boys. Kaliq licked his lips. "I was just about to say I wasn't hungry, but suddenly that's all changed."

They went into the house. The weather was a lot warmer than it had been in New York. March could be unpredictable. Dessa commented on how just last week they had had a cold spell.

"I guess the news about Nana is still the same, huh?" Kaliq said.

"Doctors just don't know what to make of it. In the beginning, they said Mama wasn't gonna last too much longer. I think she's got other ideas 'cause she's still hanging in there," Dessa reported.

"But is she suffering any?" Kaliq questioned further.

"Well, that's what I'm concerned with. I don't want Mama to leave us but if she's gonna be in constant pain, I'd rather see her go on to a better place," Dessa said, trying to fight tears.

"Where's Daddy?"

"He went down to the lodge. The Masons had a meeting this evening. He said he'd hurry back as soon as it was over. Let me show you where you gonna sleep." She gave Yolie a tour of the house and showed her where she could put her things. Kaliq was going to share a room with the twins. They held off on dinner until Nathan arrived. Mr. Nichols was just as handsome as his son (or vice versa). He welcomed Yolie the same way his wife had. The boys bum-rushed him as soon as they saw a chance. They finally sat down at the dining room table. Glasses of sweet tea were passed all around. The food was beyond heavenly.

"If you ask me," Nathan began, "I think your grandmama's just waiting to see you."

"I hope I don't fall apart when I see her," Kaliq worried.

Yolie was seated beside him. She reached over to stroke his hand. He gazed into her eyes and gave a silent thanks. The Nichols exchanged knowing glances.

After dinner, Yolie whisked the boys away to give them a bath.

Nathan joined his son out on the porch. "So, you seeing anyone steady, Kaliq?"

"I'm talking to this girl named Jeneill. She's really nice and has got it going on all the way."

"And what did she have to say about you and Yolie?" Nathan probed.

"She knows our situation."

"And that would be what? That you are in love with that young lady?"

"You sound just like Dennis, Pop," Kaliq countered, purposely avoiding the question.

"You can deny it out loud all you want. But Stevie Wonder *and* Ray Charles can see how much you two mean to one another. Now, I ain't pushing you into anything. I'm just saying handle your business, son."

Kaliq stayed out on the porch after his father went back inside. He went around to the back of the house. He wanted to see the shed his father had built since he'd been there. On his way, Kaliq caught a glimpse of Yolie through the guest-room window.

She sat naked on the bed while she towel-dried her hair. Her lean body was still beaded with water in some places. Kaliq felt terrible for invading her privacy, but he couldn't pull himself away either. She reclined on the giant bed pillows. She seemed to just be staring at the ceiling. Slowly she began to massage herself—one hand to her breast, the other down below. Yolie hesitated for a brief moment and then began again. He could see her body moving ever so slightly in a rhythmic motion. Suddenly, she jumped up. Kaliq was afraid she had spotted him. However, she grasped one of the pillows and mounted it. Her movements became more frantic as she began to grind herself into the pillow. Kaliq was growing more ashamed by the moment, but he stood still. A moment later he could see her orgasm. Yolie shivered as she threw her face down into pillow. After a while, she reached over to retrieve a nightshirt from the chair beside the bed. Kaliq held his breath as she switched off the lamp. It was going to be a rough night.

He tried to rest, but his sleep was fitful. Kaliq thought he heard the click of the bedroom door. Yolie's body formed a silhouette in the doorway. She stepped in and closed the door behind her. "Hi. I couldn't sleep. Must be lying in a strange bed that's keeping me up."

All Kaliq could do was stare at her dumbly. Her hair hung loose around her shoulders. Her nightshirt barely covered the essentials. "Yolie, can I help you with something? It's late," he whispered loudly, surprised at his own harshness.

He could see she was a little taken aback. "I didn't mean to disturb you. I'll go back to the guest room."

"No, I'm sorry. I just had to...," he stuttered.

"You don't have to explain anything. I get it."

"What is it you think you get?" he tried to tease.

"More than you think," she assured him.

"It's just that we are in my parents' home and it's different here than back in New York."

"What does that mean, Kaliq?"

He was failing miserably. "Just that I know how free and open you and Cari are about things. This might not look bad in your eyes, but all I'd need is for my mother to..."

"What? Come by and catch me trying to seduce you or something?"

"Did I miss a beat? You know that I'm with Jeneill. Besides, me and you together just is ridiculous," Kaliq said.

"Yeah, you got that right. Don't flatter yourself by thinking I'd want your tired ass," she answered, hoping he wouldn't see the tears welling up in the semi-darkness.

"Was it a mistake for me to bring you down here, Yolie?"

"No, the mistake was mine." The two remained silent for a moment. Outside the door they could hear footsteps.

"All right now. It's time for everyone to retire to their own rooms," they heard Dessa call out.

"Well, was there anything else?"

Yolie stormed from the bedroom. She just managed to stop herself from slamming the door when she saw Mrs. Nichols closing her own. Yolie marveled at Kaliq's nerve. She allowed angry tears to fall.

Kaliq punched at his pillow. "What the hell is the matter with me?" He knew he had to make things right with Yolie. He had gotten out of hand with her. "It's gonna be a long week."

CHAPTER 19

BulletProof was spread out on the couch. He'd just finished his around-the-way dinner—chicken wings with pork fried rice. As usual he'd eaten too much. He had found one of the family photo albums sitting on the end table. Kaliq had dragged them out the day he got the call about Nana Zee. B.P. opened the book and flipped through its pages. He found a picture of his mother, Angel.

Angel had died when B.P. was in high school. She had always been frail and of poor health. Yet, she was a strong woman in other ways. B.P. knew there weren't any photos of his father in the book. No one had wanted Angel to get hooked up with the man. Carter Stokes had been a big-time hustler. If he couldn't achieve the desired results from one criminal means, then he'd pursue others. He was the hardest-working man on the block. He had gotten sent up once before B.P. was born. A parole violation got him put away the second time. By then, Angel was carrying their child.

She would praise Carter's good qualities. The family thought she had taken leave of her senses. She promised Carter that she was being faithful. He wanted to know the word on the street, but she had no idea what it was he needed to know. She'd write and send pictures. Dessa had told her sister that Carter was only using her. Angel would put together care packages as if Carter were just away at camp. She swore that when they were together, he wasn't like his street persona at all. No one really believed that. Angel was a sweet naïve girl who saw the good in every-one—whether it existed or not.

It had been a few days past B.P.'s fifth birthday when Angel received the news Carter had been killed by a corrections officer. She became totally distraught. Her family tried to console her, but she started spending all her time in church. Angel thought that if she prayed hard enough, God would forgive her man. She also prayed for their son, Dennis. She tried to paint a rosy picture for her son. However, all everyone said was they hoped Dennis wouldn't grow up to be a drug dealer like his father.

Growing up, B.P. did get involved with petty crimes. He hung with a bad crowd. One day he was in the wrong place at the wrong time. Some serious shit was going down and his boys needed backup. Needless to say, the episode ended in gunfire. Not a single bullet had touched him. Henceforth, the nickname BulletProof.

B.P. had always resisted the big-time stuff. He loved his mother and knew she'd be disappointed. His boys called him a punk, but they respected his decision. B.P. cut class almost every day. Angel would plead with him to finish high school at least. He agreed he would and then skip out the same day. He dropped out altogether when his mother got terminally ill. It had been her heart, just like Nana Zee. He hated watching his mother die. Where was the God she was always preaching about? Once they buried her, B.P. had no place to go. He didn't have a job so he couldn't keep their apartment. That's when Kaliq invited him to stay with him until he got himself together. That had been a year ago.

Kaliq had no real idea of what B.P. did. He had his suspicions, but B.P. never admitted much. He figured the less Kaliq knew the better. Besides, B.P. felt like he couldn't afford to get too close to anyone again. No one ever knew how devastated he was over his mother's death. They all assumed he was coldhearted like Carter Stokes. All except Kaliq and Nana Zee.

B.P. tossed aside the book when the phone began to ring. "Talk to me," he answered.

"Dennis? This is Jeneill."

"Hey, what's going on, baby?" B.P. asked, sitting up.

"That's what I called to find out. How is your grandmother doing, Dennis?"

"The last time Kaliq called he said she was about the same. No better; no worse."

"I was thinking about doing something special for him when he got back. Maybe cook him dinner over at your place."

B.P. wondered why he didn't have a dime piece like Jeneill jocking him hard like this. "I'm sure cuz would appreciate that."

"Well, I feel bad for him. And you. How are you doing, Dennis?"

"I'm all right. Just hangin' in." B.P. did some fast thinking. "Say, do you know how to cornrow hair, Jeneill?"

"Sure, why do you ask?"

"My braids are busted right about now and the girl who usually does them for me is out of town. Do you think you could stop by one day this week? Or maybe you can hook that dinner thing up for the day Kaliq's due back. Make it a surprise. What do you think?"

"Sure I could do that. I'll come over early to braid your hair and then start cooking," Jeneill agreed.

"Beautiful, beautiful. Let me get your number so I can call you when I know they are on their way back," B.P. innocently suggested.

"All right. You got a pen?"

After they hung up, B.P. couldn't believe his luck. He knew Kaliq didn't really want this girl. He acted like he did, and on some level he might've, but Jeneill was wasting her time. B.P. thought who would be better than himself to be there waiting in the wings.

CHAPTER 20

Kaliq had never been an early riser, but the smell of food cooking tapped his nostrils. He could hear all kind of activity going on around the house. The boys were tearing through the house, their grandfather calling behind them to slow down. Pots were clanging against pans in the kitchen. After he finished his business in the bathroom, Kaliq joined his mother and Yolie at the table.

"Well, it's about time, sleepyhead," Yolie announced, trying to act as if nothing were wrong.

Kaliq tried to clear the sight he had witnessed the night before from his mind. After their little spat, the image of her pleasuring herself continued to mess with him. "Hey, what can I say? A brother's tired."

"Please don't let that boy fool you. Most of the time he won't get out that bed until someone drags him out—whether he's sleep or not!" Dessa interjected, obviously choosing to forget the previous night's events as well.

"Leave it to your mother to tell all the bitness," Kaliq said. "It smells so good up in here."

"I'm gonna have to play some serious ball when we get back. I know I'm gonna gain a good fifty pounds down here. I helped your mother fry some fish. She's also got grits and corn muffins to go with them."

"We don't eat like this at home and it's a good thing," Kaliq stated as he reached for the apple juice.

"Soon as we finish breakfast, we'll head on out to the hospital," Dessa told her son as she set the table. Yolie went out to gather up the boys.

"Yolara's a fine young woman, Kaliq," Dessa continued as soon as Yolie was out of earshot.

"Not you, too," Kaliq moaned. "Last night was not what you might have thought, Mama."

"Oh, I know you two got better sense than that. Well, apparently you can't see the forest for the trees. Now I don't know how tangled our family tree branches are gonna get with you two hooked up, but…"

"Ma, don't you think she's a little young for what you're proposing?"

"Y'all don't have to rush into anything. There's plenty of time. Life is too short, baby. I thought Mama'd be around forever, but she's not. I don't want you to miss out on something special," Dessa explained to her youngest child. Then she changed the subject. "Your sisters have been calling every day. Ariyan and Chesny made it down last week because that's the only time they could get off from work. Reva is gonna try next week to bring the girls down. The hospital has given us permission to bring the children into the room."

"What are we gonna do, Ma?"

"Don't start me up," she whispered.

Nathan, Yolie and the twins finally made it to the kitchen. "I thought it would be nice to show Yolie where we grew up. Show her the real country life," Nathan suggested.

"It depends on how Mama's doing," Dessa answered. "Okay, did y'all wash them nasty hands of yours?"

After everyone had their fill of breakfast, they climbed into Nathan's van and started the five-mile trek to the hospital. Wynetta had grown by leaps and bounds in the past ten years. The hospital was virtually new, but the staff was topnotch.

The nurses welcomed everyone and invited them to come into the room. They cautioned the children to be on their best behavior and respect the needs of the other patients.

Zora Abernathy was a formidable figure even in her delicate state. She was hooked up to all sorts of machines. Her eyes were sharp and they brightened as soon as her family entered the room.

"Look who we brought with us today, Mama," Dessa boasted to her mother.

"How you doing, Nana?" Kaliq asked his grandmother.

"Lord, have his mercy; it's my baby. How you been, Sugar? Come give your Nana a hug." Zora grinned.

Kaliq cautiously embraced his grandmother. "Nana, this is Yolara and these are my sons," he said to her as he nudged the twins forward.

"How my great-grand babies? And Miss Yo Lara, nice to meet ya," Zora said as she motioned the children to come closer.

"I'm happy to meet you, too, Ms. Abernathy," Yolie said, touching the woman's cheek with a kiss.

"Ain't they instructed you to call me Nana Zee just like everyone else."

A short white man in a lab coat came into the room. He greeted the family and then proceeded to check Zora's vital signs. "Well, how you feeling today, Miss Zora?" he asked with a heavy drawl.

"Fair to middlin' as they say, Dr. Welles."

"I have to tell you that you've got us stumped. We're starting to see a steady improvement. We didn't want to get y'all's hopes up, so the first couple of days we didn't mention it. However, now we can say with certainty that you are on the mend, Miss Zora."

"Doctor, are you absolutely sure?" Dessa asked, afraid to believe it was true.

"Yes, ma'am. I'm happy to say I am," he said while Nathan nearly dislocated his arm shaking his hand. "I'm gonna allow y'all to stay a little while longer, but then we've got to let Miss Zora rest. Now that we've made some progress, we don't want to undermine it in any way."

They all nodded in agreement. Zora tried to sit up in the bed. "I told y'all I wasn't going nowhere."

They laughed and caught up with each other before the nurses reappeared to shoo them all away.

"We are gonna go to church tonight. We have to give thanks to the Lord that He saw fit to let us keep her a little while longer," Dessa urged.

"Church? It ain't Sunday," Trevor observed.

As promised, Nathan took them to the spot of town where he and Dessa had grown up. His childhood home had long been abandoned. He still owned the property, but had yet to do anything with it. He joked with Kaliq about his taking the land to move on. "You ain't funny, Pop."

The kids took off running down the dirt road that ran alongside the property. Yolie challenged them to a race (their favorite thing).

"Can we go into the woods, Yolie?" Travis wanted to know.

"I don't know, little brother. Looks kinda scary in there to me."

"I know I ain't going in there," Trevor said, folding his arms across his chest.

Nathan showed them other parts of town and they met a lot of folks that were related to them in one way or another. They saw the old one-room schoolhouse. They went for ice cream at the Dairy Queen. Nathan let Yolie try her hand at driving the big van.

The kids denied being tired, but fell asleep as soon as they got inside.

"I noticed a court up the street. How about a rematch, Kaliq?" she asked with a look of challenge.

"Oh, you want some of this?"

"No, the question is can you handle this," she retaliated.

"You kids go and have fun while those little demons are napping," Nathan said and his wife agreed.

They retrieved a basketball from the backyard and headed for the court. They did a few stretching exercises before they got going.

"Are you enjoying yourself?" Kaliq asked, dribbling the ball between his legs.

"I can enjoy it better now that we know Nana is gonna be okay," she answered, stealing the ball from him.

"I always liked spending summers down here."

"With the food they have down here, it's no wonder. I swear the food is thicker down here."

"Oh, no doubt," Kaliq agreed. He tried to drive the lane, but Yolie was right there in his face. "Careful now, don't foul me."

"Does Miss Unbeweavable play ball, too?" Yolie asked as she snatched the ball away again and followed through with a pretty lay-up.

It took Kaliq a moment to get what she was talking about. "You ain't right."

"She go to City?"

"Yeah, she's a theater major. She's cool people. Really." He felt as if he were stepping into a trap.

"I'm sure she is," Yolie concurred as she passed the ball to him with force.

"What about you? You must be talking to someone?"

"Not in a long time. The guys I meet aren't all that. They just want to get into your drawers. It's old already," she grunted as she missed a shot.

"Has anyone had any success in that department?" he cautiously asked.

"Well, I'm no virgin, but I'm no ho either. Actually, I've only been with one guy. He was too forceful. But, why would you want to know any of that?"

"You don't mean that he raped you?" Kaliq asked, dropping the ball.

"Aw, hell no!" she answered. "He just didn't have any patience. No foreplay; no nothing."

"What do you know about foreplay?"

"What do *you* know about it?" Yolie came back.

"If you were a little older…"

"Or not so 'free and open,'" she finished for him.

"Why do you have to start some mess? I apologized for my behavior last night. Damn."

"Oh, and I accept it with gratitude."

"You and your mother have some powerful stuff. I didn't want to fall into anything again."

"What kind of shit is that? Do you think I want you to knock me up, too?"

"Yolie, what is the matter with you? You are never like this."

"How would you know what I'm really like, Kaliq?"

He could feel himself losing his grip on the situation again. He didn't like it one bit. What the hell was going on?

They played two games before they agreed it was time to get cleaned up for church that evening.

Yolie was changing into the navy velvet tank dress she had brought with her. Dessa tapped on the door. Yolie told her to come in.

"That's a pretty dress you've got there, missy," Dessa praised.

"Thank you. It's past my knee so it's appropriate, right?"

"Oh, it's perfect. Let me play with that pretty hair of yours." Dessa picked up the wooden brush from the bureau. She caressed Yolie's hair with long strokes. Yolie allowed her to put it into a French roll. "I'm glad you came down with Kaliq. We've always been fond of you. How's your mother doing?"

"She's doing fine. She told me to tell you that she's praying for your mother."

"Next time she's got to come down, too," Dessa insisted. She wanted to give Yolie the same pep talk that she had given her son, but she held off. She was sure this determined young lady would eventually get what she wanted. She just wanted her to know that she approved. "No matter what happens or doesn't happen with you and Kaliq, you're always welcomed in our home."

Yolie was a little surprised by the comment but you couldn't wipe the smile off her face. She was still perplexed by the tension that had sprung up between her and Kaliq, but she was not going to let it affect her relationship with the Nichols.

The twins were attired in dress shirts and slacks. They complained, but they looked adorable. Some of the same people they had visited during the day were in attendance for the revival meeting. It wasn't a large church, but they had done a lot of work on it. Conversation died down as the choir took its place. The organist worked the instrument like he and it were one being. The choir made a joyful noise indeed. Yolie didn't know the words to this particular song, but was swept up in its message the same as the rest of the congregation.

The pastor was a statuesque man with a booming voice. He preached of love and forgiveness and what the Lord could do for you. Kaliq said a silent prayer for his grandmother and a second one asking God to help make the right decisions about the two women in his life.

The boys were amazed to witness people "catching the Holy Ghost." They questioned Dessa about what was going on, but she shushed them and said she'd explain later. Several people got up to give testimonies. Yolie was so moved by them, that she stood up herself before she had realized it.

"I'd like to give thanks for arriving here safely and for being able to see first-hand that the Lord does answer prayers."

"Amen, little sister."

"We know that's right."

Everyone knew she was speaking of Mother Zora Abernathy. Then the pastor called for the choir to dedicate a song to Nana. The room worked itself up again and all was right with the world.

CHAPTER 21

Rue was having a pretty good day. Last night had been incredible with Cari. They had christened every room in the apartment. They went out to the movies. Went shopping in the Village. They had taken care of Rue's apartment. She hadn't paid any more rent on it since she had left it. The tenants felt that they should be compensated for their lost property. The owners carried insurance, didn't they?

They went jogging in the mornings before they headed into Manhattan for work. Rue had never been this content with Petra. She was just glad to see that Cari had no hang-ups about their being together. She had committed to a new way of life and she was sticking to it. Rue worried from time to time about Meshach. She felt like Cari still loved the man, despite their years apart. Even though they had major disagreements, they seemed to feed off of it. Rue tried to reassure herself that Cari loved her more. They hadn't said the words to each other yet, but Rue felt it.

Cari took the day off to have her biannual pap smear. Rue decided that she would head into Manhattan early. She wanted to go into Macy's to find something special for Cari. Perhaps she'd make it out to be an anniversary present, gratitude for the last few months. The store was crowded, but Rue waded her way through. Her first stop was the jewelry counter.

"Can I see those earrings?" she asked the woman behind the counter. She jumped when she felt someone tap her shoulder.

"How's it going, Rue?"

Rue was shocked to see her sister's oldest son, Ian. "Oh my God. Ian, how are you? You're the last person I expected to run into!"

"Where you been keeping yourself? The family asks about you all the time," he told her.

"Yeah, I'm sure. How is Siobhan? I haven't seen your mother in so long," she asked her nephew.

"Mom is doing okay. Her and Dad divorced last year. She's still working for that investment company. Hey, I'm going to Manhattan College this fall. Just like you."

"Let's hope you finish. How are your grandparents?"

"Grandmother's doing okay, but they had to put Grandpa Ike into a nursing home last summer," Ian answered.

Rue could not imagine Ike Tenney holed up in some nursing home. Her father had been a stern, uncaring man. Rue had grown up in the Riverdale section of the Bronx, a neighborhood that claimed many well-to-do families. Her family hadn't been billionaires, however, they had lived very well. Her father was in the banking business. Her mother had always insisted upon working although Ike had never been happy about it. He had wanted his wife to stay home and raise their five daughters (of which Rue was the youngest). He had never been happy that all his children were girls. There was never anything that any of them did that made the old man satisfied. He'd even called his wife defective because she hadn't produced any sons.

"Any other big family news?" she went on.

"Just the usual stuff. Divorces, death, shit like that," Ian said, checking his Swatch.

"Deaths? Who died?"

"Aunt Erin's husband. Look, Rue, it's been good chatting with you, but I've got to get to Penn Station. Call us sometime," he instructed as he brushed her cheek with a swift kiss.

"Goodbye, Ian. It was good seeing ya."

He waved at her as he fought his way to the nearest exit.

Rue hadn't thought about her family in ages. The last time she'd been to Riverdale had been a catastrophe. It had been about six years ago. She'd gone home at her sister Siobhan's insistence. Her parents were celebrating their thirty-fifth wedding anniversary. Rue had dreaded it, but agreed to attend.

When she had finally arrived, the party had been in full swing. Most of her extended family members were there as well as her parent's business associates. Ike Tenney could be heard from every room in the house. He was a large man with a ruddy-colored face. Her mother used to say she married him because he reminded her of John Wayne. The house itself hadn't changed any and neither had her father.

She had made her rounds greeting everyone. Ike had waited until she made her way to him before acknowledging her. "Well, if it ain't Baby Rue as I live and breathe," he'd said, his breath drenched in whiskey. "You fellows remember her, don't you? She wants to be the son I never had." His colleagues tried to hide their discomfort. Rose Tenney, his wife, tried to run interference.

"Rue, honey, I'm so glad you decided to come. How have you been, dear?" her mother greeted her coolly.

"How the hell you think she's been, Rosie? I can't believe she showed up. First she embarrasses me by getting kicked out of Manhattan College, then she nails the coffin with this gay shit. Fellas, I hope none of your children cause you the grief this one has heaped on us."

To save face, Rose made a halfhearted attempt to quiet her husband. Rue couldn't contain herself.

"You cantankerous piece of shit. You could care less what I do as long as it doesn't upset your image. All of us girls tried so hard to please you. You never let us forget that you were disappointed each time the doctor said it was another girl. You could have done all of us a favor and just had your dick lopped off so we wouldn't have had to be born. Nonexistence would be preferable to being your child." Rue hissed. "Even my damn name means to extremely regret. Well, fuck you, Daddy dear."

Rose nearly choked on the martini she'd been sipping. Her father's colleagues had managed to slither away. As Rue made her way back across the huge living room, she saw the stunned faces of her sisters. Siobhan's and Erin's chins had nearly hit the floor, while Lauryl and Jody gave her a quick thumbs-up.

Rue cursed herself for not knowing better. After she'd been expelled from the college, she had taken up residence with some friends who all shared a loft. She couldn't take the constant ravings of her parents.

Her days at Manhattan College had been wild ones. The Riverdale campus was not the upstanding learning institution it made itself out to be. There were drunken brawls on a regular basis. Rue and her friends were champion drinkers. They made out openly in the quad at night. Some had even gotten busted screwing in their cars. They could care less; let security get a cheap thrill.

One night, a group of students were hanging out in the lounge area of the dormitory. They had been complaining of boredom. Someone suggested a game of truth or dare. Naturally, the festivities got out of hand. The final straw was when a guy dared Rue to throw a piece of furniture out the window. Not one to be outdone, Rue complied with the request. Unfortunately, she had narrowly missed hitting one of the Brothers of the college. Residents' Life had been notified and that was the beginning of the end.

Ike Tenney had ranted like a madman. Rose tut tutted the entire time. Rue hadn't even declared a major yet when her college career came to a crashing end. The days following had been filled with non-stop barrages from her father. That's when she took her friends up on their offer to room at the loft. She'd drifted from job to job. On a whim, she took the postal exam. She knew she'd need something steady in the very near future. It was hardly a job she dreamed of, but Rue knew it was a matter of time before they all were evicted from the loft. There had been several complaints against them.

Rue had met Petra at a bar soon after she'd started at the post office. Petra had worked at Madison Square Garden's box office. Rue also remembered the first time she'd seen Cari. She would have gone for Cari first, but she knew she was straight. Friendship was all she could've hoped for.

Rue smiled to herself as she asked the clerk to show her a pair of diamond studs. She knew Cari had been wanting a pair for her second holes. From time to time, Rue missed her sisters. They hadn't been overly close, but they shared a hatred of their father (and Mom had been no great prize either.) She didn't want to dwell on her family or Petra. Cari was her future.

"I'll take them," she instructed the clerk as she pulled out her Macy's card.

CHAPTER 22

The family was having a great time entertaining Nana Zee. The doctor had given permission for her to spend a little time on the sun porch with them. He cautioned them not to overwhelm her.

"When y'all gonna be heading back to New York?"she asked her grandson.

"As much as I'd like to stay, we'll be driving back tonight, Nana."

"I'd like to come back in the summer before I start college in the fall," Yolie said.

"I'll be in tiptop shape by then. I'll show you how to really burn in the kitchen. Goddess do all right, but she don't do better than her mama," Zora boasted.

Dessa cut her eyes at her mother. "You'd better watch out, old woman. You've got some serious competition. I ain't no slouch in the kitchen. Ask Nate."

"I've done put on so much weight since we moved back down here it ain't even funny," Nathan concurred as he rubbed his stomach.

The kids expressed their desire to go to Shoney's. They loved the all–you-can-eat salad bar. "Just like children to have no appreciation for home cooking," Dessa stated.

They bid Zora goodbye with hugs and kisses as they noticed the nurse give them the signal. "I'm so glad y'all children came to see me. It was so good being with these little ones. I hope to be around for the next baby," Nana Zee said, holding back tears.

"Don't worry, Nana. You will be," Kaliq assured her.

Yolie expressed her pleasure in meeting Zora. "I have to tell my mother that we need to plan a trip to Puerto Rico to see my grandmother soon. I feel like I have an extra one now."

"That's right, Yolara. I'm everyone's Nana Zee."

The Nichols and Yolie complied with the kids' demands and lunched at Shoney's. Afterwards, they went to Food Lion to stock up on food to make the trip back North.

"I wish I knew where my father's people stayed. I know he's from some-place in Carolina, but we do have relatives in Georgia, too," Yolie stated as she pushed the cart up the aisle.

"Well, you can ask him when y'all get back. If you do come down here again this summer, Nate and I would be glad to take you around to see them," Dessa offered.

"That's if he let's you come down again. He wasn't thrilled," Kaliq interjected.

"Oh and why is that?" Nate asked.

"Who knows? I guess he thinks I'm going to take advantage of Yolie or something," Kaliq answered, as he tossed a bag of Lays into the cart.

"He doesn't have to worry about that 'cause I'd kill you myself," Nate said, winking at Yolie.

"The confidence is staggering," Kaliq kidded.

That night Dessa offered to cook dinner...again. Yolie and Kaliq didn't tell her they were still full from Shoney's. Yolie called New York to remind her mother that they were leaving that night, but there was no one home.

Kaliq loaded their bags into the Saturn. He shook his father's hand as he approached. Nathan slipped a hundred-dollar bill into his palm. "What's this?"

"It ain't much, but I knew you wouldn't ask for any. Use it to buy some-thing for the boys," Nathan advised.

"Thanks, Daddy," Kaliq said as he hugged his father.

"How are you doing financially, son?"

"Well, it helps that the house is paid for so I don't have to worry about rent. The construction thing is cool although it's not as steady as I'd like.

I really do good with the money I make using my computer. I want to set up some kind of home-based business—maybe even set up my own web site."

"You go ahead with your bad self. And here I was worried."

Dessa, Yolie and the kids came out with the last of the bags. "You sure you don't want to take a nap or something, Kaliq? You've been up all day, you know," his mother cautioned.

"I'm all right, Ma. Yolie can take over if I get tired."

"She sure can. The way she took charge of my van was pretty impressive," Nate agreed.

"Thank you, thank you," Yolie said as she gave a bow.

"Well, y'all just be careful and call us when you get there," Dessa said.

They finally got the kids into the car despite their whining that they didn't want to go back home or to school. They cooperated when they were told that Cari would cry if they had to stay away any longer.

After another round of hugs and kisses, they were finally on their way. Yolie popped a tape in as soon as they pulled out of the driveway. It was her favorite slow jam tape. She'd made it just before she'd left home. She turned up the volume when Tamia's "So Into You" came on.

The tune was one of Kaliq's favorites, too. Yolie began to sing. She was no future Grammy winner, but he didn't want to be the one to tell her. The twins were oblivious. They had fallen off to sleep ten miles into town. By the time the tape clicked over to the side, Yolie was fading fast as well.

Kaliq gently pulled her into a better position. Her head had been resting on the window and it hadn't looked very comfortable. She moaned a little, but didn't wake. The sound reminded him of the view he'd gotten that first night at his parents' home. The memory of her body made him stir. He was glad she was asleep; he would not have wanted her to notice his arousal. He'd have a difficult time explaining that in light of their bickering.

A gentle rain had started, but it was turning into a downpour with every mile. They were entering South Carolina, when Kaliq began to feel his eyes get heavy. He was humming to another love song, but decided it might be better to play some upbeat music instead. He felt around until he came up with a tape labeled *Def Squad Favorites*. Redman would help

keep him up or so Kaliq had thought. In a split second, he had fallen asleep.
A tractor-trailer driver leaned on his horn. Kaliq jumped up and was
barely able to regain control before slamming into a guardrail.

"What's going on?"Yolie asked terrified.

Travis woke up, but they could still hear Trevor snoring. Kaliq's nerves
were so rattled he jumped out and began kicking the car. Yolie assured her
little brother that everything was all right. He didn't look convinced, but
he sat back in his seat. Yolie got out and joined Kaliq in the rain.

"Are you okay?"

"Shit, I could have killed us all," he shouted into the darkness.

"You didn't. We're fine, Kaliq. What happened?"

"I fell asleep. I should have listened to my mother. I didn't feel tired, but
I should have taken a nap anyway. Damn, how fuckin' stupid can I get?"

If it weren't for the headlights of the car, they would have been in total
darkness. The woods on the other side of the guardrail were a little too
scary for Yolie's liking. "Is there a hotel nearby?"

"How the hell do I know?" he snapped, regretting it immediately. "I'm
sorry, Yolie. I'm just freaking out here."

"I understand. Look, let's get back in the car. I'll drive until I see a hotel.
We'll spend the night and get a fresh start in the morning. How's that?"

He wasn't going to argue with that reasoning. Kaliq got in on the
passenger's side. Yolie adjusted the seat and then fastened her seat belt.
Travis had gone back to sleep. Kaliq was visibly angry as he turned off
Keith Murray mid-sentence.

Yolie had only driven about seven miles before she noticed a sign advertis-
ing a Comfort Inn. The billboard said the hotel was a mile off the next exit.

She pulled into the parking lot. Kaliq slammed the door as he got out to
inquire about a vacancy. Yolie wished she could make him feel better, but
she understood how frightened he was. Drenched, he came back and told
them that a room was available. They debated if it were a good idea to
leave their luggage in the trunk. However, as true New Yorkers, they
decided to drag their luggage in with them.

The room was pleasant. There were two double-sized beds, a television and other hotel amenities. The kids were excited because they had never spent the night in a hotel. They fought over what to watch on the television.

"Again, I'm sorry about drifting off, Yolie."

"Don't worry about it, Kaliq. I guess it's like that bumper sticker your Pops had on his van. The one about God being his co-pilot." Yolie smiled.

"Why don't we do this? I'll sleep with Travis in one bed, while you and Trevor take the other one."

"Sounds like a plan to me. I've got to take this wet shirt off." She started to pull the top over her head.

"Wait, what are you doing?"

"I have a sports bra under this. You know the kind girls work out in. If it would make you...uncomfortable..."

"That's okay. Do what makes you comfortable. I'll just go and splash some cold water on my face."

The kids had finally settled on a program. Now that they were settled into the room, Kaliq was wide awake. "Ain't that always the way?"

"So what do you want to do? The kids are not going to give up the television," Yolie said as she ran a brush through her wet hair.

Kaliq dug into his duffel bag. "I had brought this mini backgammon board with me. Dad and I used to play all the time, but with all the running around we did, I forgot to break it out. Do you know how to play?"

"No, but I do know how to play chess. If I can play that, I can learn this."

He taught her the rules of the game. She got off to a shaky start, but after a few games she was getting the hang of it. "You're not going to win any tournaments, but you're doing all right," he teased.

"Give me a break. I'm just learning how to play."

They got the kids to agree to let them switch to the news so they could get a weather report. The rain would be over by morning. As soon as the meteorologist had said his piece, the kids turned back to a kiddie channel.

Kaliq lay back on the bed. "Are you tired yet?"

"No, but I'm tired of backgammon." She yawned.

Before long they were all asleep. The boys had drifted off on one bed while Kaliq and Yolie were piled on the other. Kaliq's rolling over onto the board game woke him up. He watched Yolie's chest rise and fall as she dozed. She was indeed a beautiful girl. Maybe his family was right. He should stop denying his feelings for her. They had grown into good friends and his parents had taught him that was the basis of any good relationship. He realized that once they had arrived in Georgia, he hadn't given Jeneill much thought. He thought he had promised to call her, but he hadn't done so. That very fact spoke volumes.

Kaliq tentatively stroked Yolie's hair as she slept. The black sports bra she was wearing was driving him crazy; her lying that close to him was driving him crazy. She lazily opened her eyes. She didn't say anything. Yolie hesitantly traced his lips with her finger. Kaliq could see the plea in her eyes. He scooted up towards her so they would be face to face. He planted a gentle kiss on her mouth. Yolie could feel her insides melt. She greedily sought a deeper kiss and he willingly obliged. Their tongues explored and played with abandon. Sometimes they would miss each other's mouths in their haste. Kaliq lined his body alongside hers and Yolie was pleasantly aware of his desire. She could feel him grow beneath his jeans. She reached down to unbuckle his pants.

"No, Yolie," Kaliq stopped her. "Not like this with the boys in the room. Believe me, I want to, but I'm not going to disrespect you or them by losing control. I'm trying to get it together. I acted like a jackass the whole time we were in Wynetta. I'm just afraid of ruining everything."

Yolie seemed pleased with his answer. They continued to kiss and hold each other until their mouths grew slack with fatigue. Kaliq spooned her in an embrace. A few minutes later, Yolie could hear him snoring softly in her ear.

Before she drifted off, she imagined what Jerry Springer would say in his "final thought" segment.

"We know that we don't always choose whom we fall in love with. Perhaps that person doesn't seem like a logical choice. Love seldom is logical. However, if you find a person who is dedicated to you for all the right reasons and your being together doesn't hurt anyone, including each other, then go for it. Isn't that what life's all about? Thank you for watching. Take care of yourself and each other."

Fade to black.

CHAPTER 23

Meshach was getting a little tired of battling both the traffic and the dollar vans on Flatbush Avenue. He once again wondered why he had picked the B41. This route was just full of accidents waiting to happen. His mind wandered despite his need to stay focused. Meshach was thinking about the conversation he'd had with Egypt the night before. She had asked him what had happened between him and Olive the other night. She apparently had come back with a serious attitude she had yet to get over. Meshach was confused as to what Olive had expected to happen. He didn't mean to cause her any additional hurt, but frankly he was surprised she cared. He had also mentioned his confrontation with Rue Tenney. He hadn't meant to burden his daughter with the sordid details, but she had pointedly asked him if he were contemplating a union with Cari.

A very large Jamaican woman with a sour look on her face cleared her throat. "Mon, you want ma arm to fall off while I wait for ya to give me a damn transfer?"

He pressed the key to dispense the transfer and ignored her teeth sucking. The traffic on Livingston Street was a mess. He couldn't wait until he reached Tillary. He planned to call Cari and ask if they could have a talk. He could have used Yolie as an excuse, but he wanted to be straight-up with Cari.

Finally, he made it to his terminal. He reached behind him and pulled his cell phone from his knapsack.

"Hello," Cari answered.

"Hey, what's up? It's me," Meshach announced, relieved it wasn't Rue who had picked up.

"Hi, Burk. Yolie's not back yet. She did call and say they should be home this evening."

"That's cool, but I called to talk to you. Is there any chance we can meet up later to talk?"

"Talk about what, Burk?"

"I'd rather not get into it over the phone. I can pick you up or we could catch up to one another someplace," Meshach offered. She didn't respond right away. "Still there, Cari?"

"Are you sure you want to do that, Burk? You know what my situation is."

"Yes, I know how you livin', but I'd still like to get together. We're still friends, aren't we? At least I thought so," he said.

"We fight like cats and dogs almost every time we see each other," Cari told him with a laugh.

"It's just the fires still burning. Really, I'd like to treat you to something to eat. No strings attached."

"All right, Burk. I'll meet you at the Country Kitchen. What time do you get off?"

He gave her the details, pleased that she had chosen their old stomping grounds, so to speak. His last two trips were even less tolerable. Meshach waited impatiently on the fuel line. Every time he was in a hurry, there was always some kind of a delay pulling the bus in. Once he parked the bus, Meshach took the stairs two at a time to get to the crew window. He turned in his paperwork and raced back down to his jeep. There really was no need to drive his Explorer to work. His apartment was only a few blocks away, but he was already doing without his house. His jeep was his only comfort.

Meshach grabbed a quick shower and threw on his black jeans with a football jersey. They had agreed to meet at five-thirty. He was starting to feel a little foolish, but the thought of spending time with Cari was exciting him. It reminded him of old times.

He saw her as soon as he pulled into the parking lot. Cari was wearing her riding boots with a pair of navy corduroy shorts. She also wore a beige bulky fisherman's sweater. Her long blondish-brown hair hung down to her shoulders. Her makeup was minimal and she was radiant.

"How you doing, Burk?" she asked as she brushed his cheek with a kiss.

"I'm doing okay. Let's go inside. I'm starving," he suggested as he guided her towards the door.

The same women still worked there. Complete with built-in attitudes. Meshach ordered the barbecue ribs with collard greens. Cari had the smothered pork chops along with okra and rice. They both had a side of macaroni and cheese and shared a large potato salad. Meshach asked for an iced tea while Cari decided to have a cola.

They carried their heavy trays to a table near the window. "I haven't even started on this yet and I'm already looking at the peach cobbler," Cari told him as she sipped her soda.

"This place will add on the pounds if you're not careful. I see you've kept up with your working out."

"Hey, just trying to keep everything in place," she said as she reached for a chop. "What's the status between you and your wife? Might as well cut to the chase. I know she's part of the reason you wanted to talk to me."

Meshach had no desire to talk about Olive. "Well, we're headed for a divorce. She did surprise me by dropping by the other night. It's too late. It's over. Despite any feelings I have for you, it's not going to work between me and Olive. Egypt is grown now, practically out the house. We both need to get on with our lives."

Cari studied his face for a few moments. "Burk, I'm trying to give my relationship with Rue a shot. It's new territory for me, but love can't be wrong, right?"

"Do you love this chick for real?" He tried not to sound disgusted.

"I don't expect you to get it. I barely do. What I want to know is why are you trying to get with me again after all this time?"

"Cari, I've never stopped wanting to get with you. You broke it off with me."

"Can you blame me?" she asked, licking her fingers.

"Well, what's past is past. I want to know if there could be a future in store for us now. The girls are adults; we can be together if we want."

"Burk, you're not hearing me."

"No, you're not hearing me. I want to be with you, Cari."

She shook her head. "The only reason you're contemplating this is because you got busted, Burk. I'm sure you've never stopped caring for me. I'll always love you, too, but that doesn't mean I want to drop everything to be with you. Don't you think Rue might be a little upset about that?"

"I couldn't give a flying fuck about that butch," he hissed.

"I don't expect you to. That's my job. Even without Rue being in the picture, I ain't at your beck and call."

Meshach bowed his head. He wasn't sure what to say. He had grasped onto the small hope that Cari might be willing to give their relationship another shot. He realized that it might have been a bit arrogant to assume that she'd jump at the opportunity now that he was available.

"Damn, I screwed up. I'm sorry, baby. I've made a lot of mistakes with you and Yolie. If I could turn back the hands of time...," he managed to say before she interrupted.

"You know, Burk. I made the biggest mistake by getting involved with a married man. I was young, dumb and full of cum, as they say. The only thing I don't regret is Yolie. I have no idea what the future has in store. I never say never, but right now, I'm building something with Rue," she told him as she took his hand.

"I suppose I just have to deal with it. We can work on our relationship as far as the bickering goes. I know Yolie is eighteen and doesn't need me as much, but we don't have to lose touch."

"Please. Yolie will always need you, Burk," Cari assured him.

He tried to hide his emotions by changing the subject. "I see you ain't accustomed to all this food anymore."

"I'm just getting warmed up," she answered with a wink.

CHAPTER 24

B.P. was busy cleaning up the kitchen. He had called up Jeneill as soon as he'd hung up. Kaliq told him about what had happened. After falling asleep behind the wheel, they had decided to spend the night at a hotel. B.P. teased his cousin about finally doing Yolie.

"Hey, man. Not that it's any of your business, but nothing like that went down, all right? I just called because I know you'd probably be wondering what was up."

"You spoke to Jeneill since you been down there?" B.P. asked.

"Nah, man. With everything that was going on with Nana Zee, I didn't get a chance."

"Didn't get a chance to? You must be on some shit."

"Whatever, Dennis. I'm breaking out. This call is gonna cost me enough as it is."

The wheels began turning right away. With this new information, B.P. hoped to get next to Jeneill. It was obvious Kaliq didn't care. He was sure that Yolie and his cousin had had sex. Kaliq couldn't be that stupid.

Jeneill had been happy to hear from B.P. She was looking forward to welcoming Kaliq home "properly." She had planned a meal that was designed to impress. B.P. just thought it was a waste of time cooking up some mess that nobody liked to eat. Crepes. Quiche. Shit.

B.P. had also stocked up on some weed. If his guess were correct, Miss Artsy Tartsy would be down with a spliff for inspiration. Except for his straight-laced cousin, B.P. assumed all college kids smoked weed.

He couldn't be exactly sure when Kaliq would reach New York, so he planned to get Jeneill to spend the day with him waiting. BulletProof had never had a problem with the ladies. Good girls loved bad boys as he had found out. They saw him as an adventure or something to that effect. He didn't care what the attraction was as long as he was getting his. He had made up his mind the moment he saw Jeneill that he would get into her drawers. He could care less about being serious with any one female. There were too many fly women out there to be tied down. He had just thrown on a CD when he heard the doorbell. B.P. saw Jeneill standing on the other side of the peephole.

"What up, Jay? Come on in." He stepped aside to allow her to pass.

"How you doing, Dennis? Can you take these bags for me?" she asked as she handed him the groceries.

"Yeah, sure. Have a seat. You want something to drink or anything?" he called from the kitchen.

"Not right now, thank you." She took her coat off and draped it behind the couch. "So what time do you think Kaliq will get home?"

B.P. pretended not to hear her question. "I really appreciate you doing my hair for me, Jay."

"It's not a problem. I can do it while the food's cooking." She walked over to him and examined his head. "I brought over this new herbal shampoo I've been using. I think you'll like it, too."

B.P. coyly licked his lips as he breathed in her scent. "If it smells as good as you, it will be aw-ight."

She smiled at him and stepped over to the sink to wash her hands. "Let me get started with the food. Then we can do our thing."

B.P. secretly agreed with her. She rolled up the sleeves of her cropped sweater and began to season chicken cutlets.

"Did you bring enough so there would be leftovers? I know this is supposed to be a cozy dinner for two, but y'all can hook a nigga up." B.P. grinned.

"Oh, I didn't forget about you. Hopefully, there'll be enough for the kids, too."

"Cool. So what's going on, girl? You about done with college?" B.P. asked as he picked up a carrot to nibble.

"I've got another semester to go. I've been going out on auditions and things. I've done almost every production that the department has put on. I'm trying to write a play, too. As a matter of fact, you'd be just right for my lead character. Ever thought about that? You could be like the next Tupac."

B.P. wasn't sure if she were serious or not. "You like a thug?" he teased.

"I don't discriminate. I like everyone," Jeneill informed the brother.

B.P. could have sworn she was playing with him. Then again she probably wasn't aware of how damn sexy she was. *Your loss, cousin,* he thought to himself.

She tested the water before pulling him over to the sink. Jeneill guided his head beneath the faucet. B.P. could feel her breasts against him as she scrubbed his scalp. She was forceful, but it felt good. "Who is that you've got playing on the stereo?"

"That's my man, D'Angelo. You know, *'you're my lay-deeeeee,'*" he crooned.

"Okay, okay. I know who you're talking about now. Just please stop croaking," she jested.

"I'd like to see you do better. Sandman Sims got a hook waiting for you at the Apollo probably."

She began to sing a little of the same song. She wasn't half-bad. "I'm not going to win any Grammies, but I don't embarrass myself either." She rinsed him twice and grabbed a towel to dry his hair.

"You've got some magic fingers, girl. My shirt got wet, though," he told her as he pulled his top over his head. B.P. had a very nice "six-pack" and he saw her react to it the same way other women did—with stunned delight.

"Very nice, Dennis," she complimented. Her stare traveled up to the tattoo he had on his left breast. "Who's Angel?"

"That's my moms. She died of heart disease a year or so ago."

"Oh, I'm so sorry. It's a really nice tatt. I've got one, but I can't show it to you."

"Aw, come on. I thought we was friends," B.P. whined playfully.

"Yeah, but we ain't all like that." She laughed. "I know it's still a little early, but I could go for some wine. I brought a bottle for Kaliq…and you to try."

"Shit, if it's seven o'clock in the morning and you want to get your drink on, then get your drink on." He reached up in the cabinet for the fancy glasses his Aunt Dessa had left behind.

She went into the living room and sat the glass of wine down on the end table. "I want to oil your scalp. Come here."

Jeneill sat in the E-Z chair and B.P. sat on the floor. She parted her legs so that he could lean back against the seat. He could smell the fruity scent she wore from beneath her denim skirt. B.P. decided to test the waters. "You wanna share a blunt?"

She looked down at him. For a second, he thought he had screwed up. "I'm a guest. I can't have one to myself?"

After she had expertly braided his hair, they both sprawled on the living room floor to watch music videos on BET. They sipped wine and smoked weed.

"I think the understanding that you and Kaliq got is phat."

"What understanding is that?" Jeneill purred as she rolled onto her back. She had entered the mellow mode.

"You know how y'all got each other but still can do y'all's separate thing."

"What separate thing?" she asked as she sat up.

"You know the thing Kaliq's got with Yolie. Women fighting over a dude is tired. Who needs to be tied down? That's why I like..."

"What thing with Yolie, Dennis? Are you saying that Kaliq is talking to Yolie and me at the same time?" Jeneill practically growled.

"Man, you didn't think you were an exclusive thing, did you, Jay?" He moved in for the kill.

"Excuse me, but yes I did."

"Sure. Did he call you once while he was gone? The reason they are a day late is because they had to get they groove on. They spent the night in some hotel in Carolina last night."

Jeneill was seething. She reached for the bottle of wine and turned it up to her head. "I don't believe this shit. I had a feeling and I ignored it. I should have known that he was too pretty to be up to any damn good."

"Hey, Cuz is cool and all, but he's a man, Jay."

"What a motherfucking lowlife!" she yelled, losing her cool.

"Calm down, Jay. I sincerely thought that was how you wanted it," he said with mock sympathy.

She cut her eyes at him and slammed her back against the couch. "Women should be more like guys. Just go for yours and forget about this falling-in-love shit," Jeneill declared, her speech slurred.

"Love ain't shit," B.P. advised as he took another long drag from his joint.

Jeneill scooted across the floor and laid her body on top of B.P.'s. She brought her face close to his and slipped her tongue between his teeth. She could feel his reaction and it spurred her on. B.P. felt triumphant.

"Yo, baby. It's all good," he murmured.

"I don't care about it all being good. Just shut the fuck up."

CHAPTER 25

Yolie could feel the difference as soon as they crossed the George Washington Bridge. The stress of living in the city was almost tangible. She missed Wynetta already. She knew a big part of that was due to what had finally happened between her and Kaliq. Yolie didn't know where they were headed next, but at least everything was out in the open.

"What are you daydreaming about?" Kaliq inquired as he rubbed her thigh.

"Oh, I'll give you two guesses." She grinned.

"We've got to take things slow, Yolie. It's tempting to rush because Lord knows, it's been on my subconscious mind forever. This is gonna affect a lot of people and I don't want you to get disillusioned."

"Listen to you. Kaliq, I know it's not the traditional boy-meets-girl situation, but I don't see who's gonna have a problem with it except Miss Unbeweavable."

"Oh you don't, do you? What about your very large father?"

"I can handle Daddy. Trust me."

"Yeah, the question is can I?!"

The boys were excited to be back in New York. "I miss Grandma and Grandpa, but I can't wait to get back to my stuff," Travis told them.

"What about seeing your mother?" Kaliq chided.

"Yeah, her, too."

"Is that how y'all do me when I'm not around?" Kaliq asked, feigning disappointment.

"Pretty much," Yolie jested.

The FDR Drive was packed. "Do you want to hang out tonight, or are you too tired? I can return the car in the morning so we can spend some time together," Kaliq suggested.

"That would be nice. Maybe we can go into the city."

"Yeah, maybe we can do that," he concurred as he stroked her cheek. The twins started to giggle uncontrollably as they playfully imitated Kaliq and Yolie.

The sun was just beginning to set as they finally reached the Brooklyn Bridge. They were all grateful to be home although the streets seemed like they could care less. As they were pulling into the parking lot, Yolie spotted her parents. She leaned over to blow the horn. They turned in unison to see who it was.

"All right. Glad to see y'all made it back safely," Meshach said as he hugged his daughter and shook Kaliq's hand. "What up, little men?"

The boys offered a bashful shrug of their shoulders and ran to their mother. "Kaliq, I was so glad to hear that your grandmother is gonna recover," Cari said as she went to hug him.

"Thanks a lot. You don't know how relieved my family is. My parents send their regards."

"Yeah, that is good news, man," Meshach added. "So how did you make out with the driving?"

Kaliq, Yolie and Cari exchanged glances. Yolie spoke up first. "You'll be glad to know that your driving lessons paid off. I drive better than you, Daddy."

"Now don't go getting carried away with yourself, little girl. It's got to be in the genes." Meshach chuckled.

"Where are you guys coming from?" Yolie questioned her parents.

"We just went out to get something to eat and talk," Cari responded.

"Oh, I get it. Making secret plans for my graduation, huh."

"Uh-huh," they both chimed in.

"Mr. Burkette, I know you probably want to hang out with Yolie now that she's home, but I wondered if it was all right for me to take her into the city before I turn the car in. Neither one of us is tired and it would be nice to take advantage of having a ride for a change."

Yolie and Cari both looked at Meshach daring him to say no. "That'd be fine with me. You kids go have fun. Damn, I sounded so old just then," he complained.

"Nah, you all right, Burk. You ain't grown yet." Cari smiled.

He playfully grabbed at her and then pulled her into an embrace. Rue was sickened by the whole scene. She stood at the window, her blood pressure rising as she watched Meshach put his arms around Cari. They were all laughing—at what she had no idea. Rue was thoroughly pissed. Cari had told her that she had some business to take care of. She neglected to mention that business pertained to her ex-boyfriend.

Rue could not pull herself away from the window. She was glad to hear that Cari's family was okay after their near accident, but she was also glad to have an extra day alone with her woman. Obviously, Cari had not been enthused about spending that time with her. Rue tried to be rational. They did share a child. However, she didn't think that merited the mutual exchange of affection she was witnessing.

"Fucking shit," she muttered. She saw Meshach and Kaliq shake hands as if they were about to part. Cari gathered up the boys' luggage.

"I can help you take those upstairs, Cari?" Meshach asked.

"No, that's all right. They can each handle their own knapsacks. I'll carry the suitcase. Besides, I'm sure Rue is home by now and I don't want any static, Burk."

"If you say so. Thanks for agreeing to…Don't y'all have somewhere to be?" He turned from Cari to Yolie and Kaliq who were all ears.

"Okay already. See you later, Daddy," Yolie said as she hugged her father. He closed the car door behind her and waved as Kaliq pulled out of the parking lot.

"I know what you are going to say, Burk. Let's just leave it at that," Cari said. The boys were already lugging their baggage towards the building.

Meshach restrained her long enough to gently plant a kiss on her lips and then her forehead. She blew him a kiss as she took off after her sons.

"That bitch! It's the same shit Petra pulled. I don't believe this!" Rue raved. She could feel herself losing it. Hot, angry tears began to stream down her face. Without giving it much thought, she undid the belt she wore. She wrapped it a couple of times around her fist with the buckled end dangling. The pain and frustration she had felt during her time with Petra came over her like a tidal wave. Outside the door, she heard the elevator arrive and the boys come tearing down the hallway. She could then hear the familiar sound of Cari's keys jangling. The boys burst into the room first and immediately ran for their room. Cari turned to lock the door behind her and never saw Rue as she came up and grabbed her by the hair.

"What were you doing with him, Cari, huh?" Rue demanded as she yanked Cari towards her.

"Rue, let go of me! That hurts. Stop it!"

"I ain't stopping shit, you fucking whore. I can't trust you. I thought you were over him, bitch," Rue snarled.

"What are you talking about? Stop it, Rue, please."

"Now you want to play games? I ain't playing with you, Cari," Rue shouted into her face. Cari hadn't noticed the belt in Rue's hand until she was smacked across the face with its buckle. She tried to free herself from Rue's grip, but that seemed to anger her more.

"You're gonna scare the kids, Rue. You don't have to do this, baby."

"Those boys deserve a better mother than you, whore, and don't tell me what I don't have to do. I love you and you were with him."

"I wasn't. I swear I wasn't," Cari began but was dealt another blow.

Rue kicked Cari's legs from under her, causing her to hit the floor hard. Then she began to pummel and whip Cari as she straddled her.

The pain was immense. Cari couldn't believe what was happening. Finally, the twins came to investigate. They started to scream when they saw what was happening. Cari had been trying to ward off the blows, but now her attention was divided between Rue and her children. From the corner of her eye, she saw Trevor racing towards Rue.

"You leave my mother alone!" he hollered. Travis then tried to jump on Rue's back. As she attempted to throw him off, the belt buckle made contact with Trevor's face, making an immediate welt. Cari was about to go crazy. With the little bit of strength she had she raised her lower body in an attempt to knock Rue off balance. This only seemed to upset the woman more. Cari saw pure evil staring her down. Rue tried to wrap the leather belt around her neck. Even though he was terrified, Travis ran to the front door. He unlocked the door as quickly as he could. He began to run up and down the halls yelling for help. Trevor saw that his brother had left the apartment. He was reluctant to leave, but he knew he couldn't pull Rue off by himself. Trevor then decided to run, too. Instead, he pounded on the doors that were closest to their own and screamed out "fire."

Inside, Rue seemed to be losing steam. She heard the commotion the twins were making. At last, she got off Cari. "Don't fuck with me. I love you, but I will kill you before I let you leave me or make a fool of me," she hissed. She threw the belt down and gave Cari a final kick to the stomach. She snatched her bag from the closet's doorknob and left. In the hallway, people had finally emerged to see what was going on. Rue strode right past them as she made her way to the elevator. She decided to take the stairs instead. She could still hear the kids screaming as she took the stairs two at a time.

***

"Before we head out, I want to go check my messages. Someone might have called me about a job or something. Dennis isn't exactly reliable when it comes to messages," Kaliq said.

"Good, I need to go to the bathroom anyway. I haven't been since we made that stop on the turnpike."

Kaliq opened the door for her and helped her out. Yolie was flattered. She hooked her arm around his as they went through the gate together. Kaliq stopped to pick up the mail from the floor. He paused and sniffed. "Don't you smell something burning?"

They quickened their steps to investigate. The television was turned up to full blast. It took a few seconds for Kaliq and Yolie to adjust to the darkness of the room, but they soon got the picture. They could make out B.P. and Jeneill semi-naked. B.P. had her bent over the arm of the couch. He was delivering hard and rapid strokes that were sending Jeneill into a frenzy. The tattoo she had of the comedy and tragedy masks was a blur as her behind quivered. She was reaching behind her, trying to grasp B.P.'s buttocks. They could hardly believe it when she demanded that he go deeper. B.P. was glistening from his efforts. Yolie was almost sorry to see Kaliq head for the wall switch. It was a strangely erotic scene. The two didn't notice the flooding of light right away. B.P. was the first to turn around. He would pick that moment to "explode." Kaliq turned Yolie away from the action.

"What happened? Why did you stop?" Jeneill whined.

Kaliq could see that her eyes were bloodshot. An empty wine bottle had rolled to a stop in front of the television.

"What the hell is going on up in here?" Kaliq shouted.

"Yo, what up, cuz? Yolie?" B.P. said, searching for something to cover himself with.

"Oh, like you care! You got who you want standing right beside you. If you didn't want me, you didn't have to string me along, motherfucker," Jeneill slurred, lifting herself off the couch.

"What did you do to her, Dennis?"

"I ain't did shit to her. She was riffing because you were doing her and Yolie at the same time. She just turned to me to vent her frustrations, cuz. That's all."

Yolie looked at Kaliq with a raised eyebrow. She was trying hard not to laugh. She could see he was not amused at all.

"This is some lowdown shit, Dennis," Kaliq said, tossing his cousin the towel. "Wipe that shit off my couch and the both of you get the fuck out."

Jeneill whimpered as she searched for her skirt. Yolie headed for the kitchen to turn off the burning chicken cutlets. "I was trying, Kaliq. I thought you were, too," Jeneill told him as she buttoned her clothes.

"Jeneill, I know we need to talk, but I can't while you're high as a kite. Did he get you drunk? Did Dennis force himself on you?"

"Now, *that's* some low shit. I ain't no rapist, man. Once homegirl found out you and Yolie got it on last night…"

"How many times I got to tell you, we did *not* get anything on last night!" Kaliq shouted at his cousin. "But, you know what? I should have if I was gonna get dicked like this." He went off into the kitchen to be with Yolie.

Jeneill looked at Dennis in disgust. "You know I can't even be mad at you. I'm the dumb ass that got caught up with you and your sorry cousin. Thanks for nothing." She stormed out of the house slamming the door behind her.

B.P. shrugged. He had gotten what he had wanted. It would have been nice to get it again, but he didn't think old girl would be down with that anytime soon. He also figured his cousin wouldn't be mad forever. He'd get over it. After washing up in the downstairs bathroom, B.P. left the house, too.

"Well, wasn't that a nice welcome home," Yolie teased.

"I don't think it's funny. I wasn't honest with myself so I wound up being dishonest with Jeneill. Still, what kind of judgment do I have getting with some chick that would do my cousin at the first sign of a problem. And Dennis, I can't believe his disloyal ass."

"I'm sorry. You're right. You know I ain't crying tears over Miss Thing, but I am surprised at B.P."

"Do you still want to go out?"

"It might be a good idea to get out of here," Yolie said as she rubbed the back of his neck.

They cleaned up the mess in the kitchen and were about to leave when the phone rang.

"Hello? Yes, this is he," Kaliq answered. He listened to the story, but couldn't quite comprehend what it meant. "What do you mean you're taking her to the emergency room?" He reached out for Yolie's hand and she instinctively knew this concerned her.

"All right, we will be right there. Thank you," he said and hung up.

"What now? Your face is scaring me."

"We got to go back to your place. That was your neighbor. She says that Rue beat Cari up pretty bad. The boys are with her kids. She doesn't want to wait for an ambulance," Kaliq continued.

"Let's be out," Yolie urged as she headed for the door.

Yolie could hardly keep still in the car. By the time they reached her building, Gloria from next door was coming out with Cari leaning against her for support.

"Oh my God, Mommy!" Yolie yelled, shocked at Cari's battered face. She was holding her side as she gingerly took each step. Kaliq rushed to support her other side.

"That woman went crazy. She just jumped your mother. The boys were so brave. They tried to pull her off. One of them got a small welt on his face from the belt she used. Other than that, they are fine. My kids are watching them. Let's get Cari to Woodhull," Gloria said, filling them in.

"Yeah, let's go. There could be some internal bleeding or something. Are you sure my kids are okay?" Kaliq was worried.

"They'll be all right. I know Gloria's family. They will keep a good eye out. Please, let's go."

Cari's right eye was swollen shut. Her face was tear-stained and her body lax. "Yolie, baby. I'm sorry about all this…"

"Hush, Mommy. None of that matters right now," she told her mother as she helped to ease her into the back seat.

It seemed like the entire block was congregated on their corner. People openly pointed and stared. Cari's beautiful face was black, blue and purple in several spots. The story had spread in record time. Opinions flew and rumors were generated.

By the time B.P. got wind of it, there were four or five different renditions. He had heard that one of the twins was beaten up, as well. That was not acceptable.

***

There had been a long wait at the emergency room. Woodhull was not the best hospital, but it was the closest. Cari didn't seem to be in any mortal danger, just a lot of pain.

"Mommy, what made Rue go off like this? She isn't my favorite person, but I wouldn't have thought she was capable of physically hurting you."

Cari tried to answer through swollen lips. "She thought that I was cheating on her with your father. She had been watching all of us from the window and she saw Burk kiss me."

"This has just been a great day. First Dennis, now this," Kaliq mumbled.

"What's this about Dennis?" Cari asked.

"Nothing important. Just another example of something you wouldn't think could happen," he responded.

"I'm going to call Daddy," Yolie said.

"Don't tell your father yet, Yolie. You know how he will react," Cari pleaded. "I can't deal with any attention from him right now."

Yolie was skeptical, but she agreed to wait. She knew that her father still loved Cari very much and he would just fly off the handle, making matters worse. She'd call when they got home.

"You want something from the vending machine?" Kaliq asked Cari. She shook her head. Gloria also passed. Yolie volunteered to take a walk with him.

"It's gonna take a long time for all those bruises to heal. I hope that bitch has the good sense not to come back around. The whole block knows about this shit now. Her safety is not a guaranteed thing anymore," Yolie commented.

"That's one thing about Bed-Stuy. People will unify to kick somebody's ass," Kaliq agreed as he checked out the snack selection.

Yolie came up behind him and wrapped her arms around him. He offered her a bite of the Snickers bar he had bought. Kaliq wiped away a string of caramel that hung from her lip. She was so special. He didn't want to see her upset and worried, but it gave her a softness that was irresistible. Kaliq took her face into his hands and softly pressed her mouth with a kiss. She returned his affection. Afterwards, she heaved a small sigh and buried her face in his chest.

Egypt had been talking with her boyfriend's sister. "She just beat her down like that?"

"Yeah. Girl, Cari was jacked up. I haven't seen somebody stomped like that in a long time. I hear that one of the kids got hurt, too. Them little boys are only five years old," Helene declared.

"First of all, that's what she gets for messing with a dyke. I don't expect much from this Cari woman anyway."

"Honey, I hate to tell you, but if your father was gonna cheat, it woulda been some other woman. Now I ain't close personal friends with her, but she seem to be all right," Helene told Egypt. "It's still fucked up, but who stays together these days?"

Egypt was about to answer her when she heard the beep signaling that she had another call. She asked Helene to hold on. "Hello?"

"Hey, what's up, Egee Bird? I found that book you were talking about when I was Downtown Brooklyn yesterday. When can I bring it by?"

Egypt didn't know if her father was aware of what had happened. She also wasn't sure if she wanted to be the one to tell him if he hadn't. She gave in. "Daddy, do you know that they had to take Cari to the hospital?"

"What? What did you say? Cari's in the hospital? Why? Who told you that?"

"I just heard it from Helene; she's on the other line. I guess it would have been Woodhull."

"Baby, I've got to find out the deal," Meshach said.

"Well, from the story she got, that girlfriend of hers beat her up real bad. Yolie and some other people took her in a car. I know you got to go, so I'll catch up to you later, okay?" Egypt said to him.

"Thank you, Egee. I know you didn't have to tell me. Thank you."

"That's okay. I know she is still important to you. Besides, you should know what's going on with yo baby's mama," Egypt quipped.

He couldn't blame her for her sarcasm so he let it go. Egypt clicked back over to Helene. "Yeah, you still there? That was my father. I told him about his ex."

"He would have heard about it anyway," Helene comforted her.

"Ain't no big deal. I just hope he don't go and do something stupid."

***

Rue walked the streets for hours. She had hopped a bus until she had come across water. She was not familiar with all of Brooklyn, but this particular section seemed to be a place of peace. Whatever that was. Her head was full; it hurt. She was concerned about Cari's condition. She hadn't meant to hurt her so bad. She had gotten caught up in a rage that had surprised herself. Rue was sincerely sorry for what she had done, yet at the same time, she felt somewhat justified. What was Cari thinking? Didn't she know that Rue loved her that much?

Rue had wanted to call the house, but she realized her concern would not be welcomed. What was she going to do now? All of her things were at Cari's. She didn't have the apartment in Manhattan anymore. Rue needed to get her stuff and make other living arrangements. This was pay week. She would have to try to rent a room somewhere, probably back in the city. As she continued down a street lined with restaurants and shops, Rue decided to chance a phone call. She dug deep into her jean pocket and came up with a quarter. Her hand actually trembled as she dialed the number. It rang several times without anyone picking it up. Rue then realized that they were probably at the emergency room. She had a flashback of the time she had offered to take Petra to the E.R. She had emphatically refused.

Rue thought perhaps she could sneak back while they were out and retrieve her things. It would be something short of a miracle to get back to Bed-Stuy quickly, but she had no other choice. She wasn't sure what she would say to Cari if she ran into her. She instinctively knew Cari would not want to hear any excuses. There were none that would have been acceptable to her either.

Rue approached the first friendly face she came across and asked directions. A kindly old woman pointed out the way. Rue trudged on towards the subway.

***

"That's some dumb shit right there. How you gonna beat up a little kid, man?"

B.P. had brought his running partners up to speed on the situation as he knew it. Or as he thought he knew it. His barber was dusting the back of his neck with baby powder. "She must be straight-up crazy. Motherfuckers have been blown away for less than that. She a stranger up in here. She should have asked somebody; you know what I'm saying?"

Every brother in the shop agreed wholeheartedly. "You know Cari is a fine piece of ass. It would be messed up if she's like permanently disfigured or some shit like that," the barber added.

"Man, I'd hit that even if she had a hump on her back!"

That caused a round of applause and a few high-fives. B.P. joined in the laughter, but in the back of his mind he was still thinking about his cousin, Kaliq. He honestly didn't see what the fuss over Jeneill was. He could tell that Kaliq was genuinely angry. He wouldn't go so far to say he was sorry, yet he didn't want any bad blood between them either. If he couldn't get over it, then fuck him. B.P. wasn't about to beg anyone's forgiveness.

Long after the last customer was taken care of, the guys hung around the shop talking yang. It had been dark for a few hours then, and the barber unsuccessfully tried to disband the group. He'd decided to start cleaning up. There was a small bag of garbage he had been meaning to put out at the curb all day. On his way back into his shop, he looked over and noticed Rue crossing the street. "There go that she-man over there."

B.P. craned his neck and caught sight of Rue just as she entered the building. His blood began to boil. "Look, I'll catch you niggas later. I'm out."

Sensing that something was about to go down, a couple of his friends followed B.P. out of the shop. They lounged on a bench that was in the center of the project's small playground. B.P. lit a Newport and let it dangle between his lips. He gazed up at Cari's window and saw a light come on.

***

Rue had been relieved to find that no one was home. She wasn't up to dealing with a confrontation; she just wanted her things. Rue surveyed the

154

bedroom with regret. The nightshirt Cari liked to sleep in was crumpled at the foot of the bed. Rue brought it to her nose and breathed in the familiar dewberry smell. Rue began to worry that Cari would seek legal action just as Petra had threatened to do. She set the shirt aside and took her duffel bag from the closet. After clearing the dresser of her belongings, she went into the bathroom to collect her toothbrush. When she was done she turned out the lights again. Rue had considered leaving Cari a note, but what would she have said?

The elevator was taking a long time to reach her floor. Rue didn't like the idea of using the stairs. At night, the stairway always seemed unsafe to her. When the elevator opened she stepped aside to allow the guy with the pit bull to pass her. On the ride down, she unsuccessfully tried not to cry. She had managed to damage another relationship. She rationalized that it wasn't entirely her fault. Why couldn't they have understood the depths of her love for them? Why did she always have to be the villain? Rue wiped her eyes with the back of her hand. She quickened her step. The walk to the J train would take an eternity. Rue lifted her bag back onto her shoulder.

The sound of screeching tires caught Rue's attention. A jeep had stopped in the middle of the street. Music blared from it. Its windows were darkly tinted. Rue turned her attention away from the vehicle. She never noticed the passenger's window slide down nor did she see the barrel of the gun pointed at her. Three shots rang out in the night. Rue felt an incredible bolt of pain go through her body. She dropped her bag as she descended to the ground. Her hand touched the spot where blood was now flowing like a river. She wanted to scream out but couldn't. Rue knew that every drop brought her closer to the end of her life. She could feel her body convulse; she writhed violently in an attempt to fight death. Finally, her body came to rest. The jeep then sped off down the street. After a few moments, someone from the second floor ventured towards their window to try to find out what was going on. "Oh dear Lord. They done shot somebody in front of the building."

***

The nurse had called Cari's name at long last. She ushered her into a cubicle where a resident prepped Cari for stitches. Her brief physical exam found no broken bones or internal bleeding. After the stitching was done, the doctor advised her to take any over-the-counter pain relief medicine she preferred. Cari thanked him for his time and gingerly hopped off the table.

"What did the doctor say, Ma?" Yolie asked as she came up to her mother.

"He says nothing is broken and I can just take Tylenol or something for the pain, *mi hija*."

"Well, I'm glad to hear that. We just called my house and the boys are okay," Gloria said.

"Good. I don't want them upset anymore tonight. I know they are going to freak when they see me," Cari moaned.

"Come on. Let's get out of here," Kaliq suggested.

The four of them were so exhausted that no one said much in the car. Cari was contemplating what she should do. It would have made perfect sense to press charges, but somehow she knew that she wouldn't. No man had ever laid their hands on her; Cari could not believe what Rue had done. Foolishly, she felt sorry for the woman. What kind of demons must she possess to feel so threatened? Cari had thought she knew Rue, but obviously she didn't. She just wanted to be rid of her. Cari said a silent prayer that Rue would find help.

Kaliq pulled over to a bodega. "Name your poison. Advil, Motrin or Tylenol?"

"Tylenol, please. Extra strength."

Gloria was lightly snoring beside her in the back seat. Yolie turned around to face her mother. "I know you kicking her out, right?"

"I may be a goody-goody sometimes, but I'm not stupid. You know, I always figured that if someone loved you, they could never hit you. Still I don't doubt that Rue loved me, but I just think she's got a warped sense of what love is."

Yolie wondered to herself if Cari had suffered any head trauma. She was convinced that Rue didn't love anyone. "Well, as long as you know she is *not* going to be staying with us anymore. I know it's your house and all that, but…"

"It's our house," Cari corrected her. "I want to hear all about this budding romance you've got going on here. In the morning, though. I think I will sleep like a rock tonight."

"What is it you think is going on?" Yolie asked, barely about to hide her smile.

"Daughter, please. You are glowing like you're radioactive. All I want to know is did Kaliq wear a condom."

"Mommy!"

Kaliq jumped back into the car and they continued up the street to the Roosevelt Houses. Several police cars were parked in front of the building. A crowd had gathered, but the cops were keeping them at bay. Yellow police tape roped off a section of the sidewalk. A body, covered by a sheet, had not yet been removed.

"Hasn't there been enough drama for one night?" Kaliq groaned.

He parked the car and helped ease Cari out the back seat. An officer shone a light on them as they tried to make their way to the building's entrance. The officer looked at Cari's face. "Are you okay, ma'am?"

"Yes, I will be. I've just come from the hospital."

"Go on ahead. Just stay clear of the crime scene."

Cari felt her head began to throb again. She leaned her weary body up against Kaliq. As they were passing the yellow tape, Cari felt a chill. A blue duffel bag was sitting inside a plastic evidence bag. Cari recognized it because she had gotten the same blue bag from the Postal Service. Cari could make out the set of souvenir key rings Rue hung from the bag's shoulder strap. Kaliq felt her body go slack. "Cari, you okay?

She began to tremble as she walked back towards the officer that had spoken to her. "Has the victim been identified?" she weakly asked the officer.

"We can't release that information. Why? Do you know something about this?"

"That's my girlfriend's duffel. Her name is Rue Tenney."

The officer immediately signaled for a detective to come over.

"Ah, Mommy, no," Yolie gasped.

CHAPTER 26

Meshach woke up with a migraine. He was glad that he had put in to have the day off. Even though he couldn't remember what he had originally needed it for. It had been a really hectic night. After Egypt told him what had happened to Cari, he raced over to Bed-Stuy immediately. There was no one at the apartment. He tried the emergency room at Woodhull, but had no luck there either. As he had hopped back into his jeep, his beeper went off. The page was from Yolie. When he called her back to find out what was going on, she had informed him of Rue Tenney's murder. By the time he got back to the neighborhood, the police were battering them with questions.

There were reporters everywhere. A white woman gunned down on a Bed-Stuy street was beyond newsworthy. When the interrogation was over hours later, Cari and Yolie were advised not to leave town.

"How dare they treat you like suspects. You were at the hospital getting treated for the damage she had inflicted," Meshach fumed.

"It's because of that the police are stressing them. You know how it goes around here, Mr. Burkette. You've got to be guilty of something," Kaliq commented.

They had all fallen out in Cari's living room. Kaliq wanted to take Travis and Trevor back to his place so they could regroup without having to worry about the twins being in the way. Cari agreed. She didn't want her babies exposed to this senseless violence any more than he did. Meshach didn't miss the longing glances Kaliq and Yolie had exchanged. He would have to find out what, if anything, was going on between them.

When Cari was finally able to absorb what had gone down, she was nearly inconsolable. She felt that somehow she was to blame for Rue's death. Meshach and Yolie could not understand her logic.

"I don't know, but this doesn't seem like a random sort of thing. People get shot around here all the time, but you know it's usually some drug shit. Why would someone just shoot her for no reason?" she cried.

***

Neither had any answers for her. Cari had assumed that someone had retaliated on her behalf. That didn't make much sense either, but it was how she felt. She just as easily could have been an innocent bystander caught in a crossfire.

Meshach had spent the entire day with them. Calls and arrangements had to be made. Apparently, this woman had not been close to her family, so it had taken some investigation to find someone to notify. She hadn't listed anyone as next of kin at the post office. Cari knew she had grown up in the Riverdale section of the Bronx so she asked information if they had any listings for the name Tenney. The few numbers they had were unlisted. Rue had left a couple of things behind. Cari had broken down again when she had found a pair of diamond stud earrings with a gift card addressed to her.

Yolie had then taken over the search through Rue's things. She found an old photo of Rue and some woman seated behind a desk. The name plaque on the desk had read Siobhan Tenney-Hayworth. A framed logo hung behind them read Trinity Investments. Yolie called information herself and asked for the number to Trinity Investments. She guessed that it was probably a Manhattan-based firm. The automated operator recited the number. Yolie was a little nervous about having to talk to this woman, so Meshach volunteered to deal with it.

"This is Ms. Tenney-Hayworth. How may I help you?"

"Good afternoon. My family and I are trying to locate someone. Are you related to a Rue Tenney by any chance?"

"Who is this? What do you want?"

"I'm not sure how to say this…" Meshach stammered.

"If you're calling to tell me Rue is dead, don't bother. The police informed us this morning. I asked who is this? Are you a friend or relative of her so-called lover? The bitch that probably had my sister killed!"

Meshach had not expected that. Impulsively he hung up the phone.

"What happened, Daddy?"

"Um…they were already notified by the police. Should have figured the cops would have taken care of it."

"Yeah, but Mommy's gonna want to know about funeral arrangements and all that," Yolie said.

Meshach hadn't thought of that either. He just wanted the whole mess to go away. He confided in her what Rue's sister had said.

Night was falling again when Meshach said that he was going home. He assured them he would be back if they needed him. He was so tired that he had slept later than he had intended. True, he was on his regular day off, but he had wanted to run some errands. His feet had barely hit the floor when he heard his doorbell.

He was surprised to see Egypt on the other side of the door. "Hey, Egee. Come on in."

Egypt stepped in and took a seat at the kitchen table. "How are things over at Cari's?"

"Man, it's a mess. Someone did a drive-by and Rue was killed," he told her as he pulled a bottle of soda out of the refrigerator.

"Yeah, me and Ma were watching *New York One* and we saw the report. The police ruled out the possibility of her being an innocent bystander. Some witness claimed that a jeep had deliberately stopped and the passenger had aimed directly at her," Egypt went on, her brows knit together.

"No one had volunteered that information at the scene. That night I didn't know what the cops believed," Meshach said, pouring two glasses of Pepsi. "I just know we are not going to see an end to this for a long time. If the media doesn't make it out to be something racial, it's gonna make it seem like a lover's spat gone wrong."

Egypt paced the kitchen with her glass of soda. She hadn't touched it yet. Meshach knew something was disturbing her. He curiously looked at her. "Daddy, I had a thought. I know it's gonna sound fucked…I mean messed up, but I have to ask. Were you involved with the shooting?"

Meshach nearly choked on his drink. "I know I didn't hear you right. Come again?"

"Well, me and Mommy were thinking. We know how much you want Cari. She had just gotten beaten up by her woman. You drive a jeep and I know for a fact that you be packing when you go to Bed-Stuy," she deduced.

"Do you really think I'm capable of killing someone in cold blood, Egypt?"

"We don't know what we're capable of when a situation involves someone we love. If someone had hurt me…or Yolie, what would you do?"

Meshach couldn't argue that point, but it still bothered him that his own child thought he was a murderer. "Well, you don't have to start baking cakes with files in them. I didn't do it."

"But what if the police start to wonder about you, too? It wouldn't be the first time an innocent man went to prison."

"Gee, thanks. I feel a lot better now."

"I'm sorry, Daddy. I'm just afraid for you," Egypt whimpered.

He stood up and took his daughter into his arms. Suddenly, he was afraid for himself, too.

27

I t had taken more work to find out the arrangements for Rue's funeral. Siobhan was not forthcoming with any details when Cari had called her. Jody, Rue's youngest sister, had called the post office and left the information in case any of her co-workers had wanted to attend the services. Her family was not familiar with any of Rue's friends, so this was all they could do.

Garcia and his wife had offered to take Cari and Yolie to the funeral. Cari was extremely nervous. She didn't know what to expect from the Tenneys. She just knew she had to go and pay her last respects. She would carry the bruises for several more days, but Rue was gone forever. Cari regretted not being able to set her straight. She had loved Rue even though she had never said those words to her—another thing she regretted.

There was a large turnout. Cari recognized her friends from the job, but she didn't know any of the other people gathered outside the church. Cari knew that Rue had a big family, but all those people couldn't possibly all be related. Cari looked sharp in her black coatdress. She wore dark glasses to try and hide the damage to her face. Yolie wore a cranberry two-piece pantsuit. She wouldn't let go of her mother's arm. All the postal employees went in with Cari as a group. They found a section where they could all be seated together.

Yolie could feel her mother's body tremble as they walked up to the cherrywood-colored casket. Rue was laid out in an off-white, lace-collared dress. Cari knew she would have hated it. Her friend looked at peace. Cari wondered when she would feel that way again. She gingerly caressed Rue's hand. Her vision blurred as tears streamed down her face.

Yolie hugged her mother with one arm. She hadn't been a fan of Rue's, but she was saddened by her death. Her father had shared Egypt's concerns with her. Secretly, she wanted to slap the girl for even suggesting such a thing. Yet, at the same time, Egypt had made a good point. Meshach was still crazy about Cari. He had been upset to find out he was the reason for the beating in the first place. He didn't really have an alibi that anyone could corroborate. However, Yolie couldn't believe that Meshach would do something that would take away his freedom to be with his children.

"Are you here to make it look good?" a woman hissed at them.

Cari cleared her eyes so she could face the attack she knew was coming. "Are you Mrs. Tenney? I'm Caridad Flores…"

"I know who you are. Your picture has been splashed on every channel and newspaper. I can't believe my daughter died because of you," Rose Tenney told her.

"That's not fair," Yolie tried to intervene. Cari quieted her by touching her arm.

"I never wanted to see any harm come to Rue. We cared very much for each other," Cari said in her defense.

"Then why did she beat the shit out of you?" Siobhan had joined in.

"You people are unbelievable," Yolie said under her breath.

"No, you people are unbelievable. Rue should have never been in that neighborhood to begin with. She should have kept her tendencies to herself or at least found someone suitable," the sister went on.

Mr. Tenney joined their little exchange. "This is hardly the time or the place, ladies. The father is staring. He asked me to take charge of this display," he informed them as he shuffled his wife and daughter to their seats. He cast a long disgusted look as he went.

Yolie tried to steer her mother away as well. Cari stole one more look at Rue before she took her seat. Her friends patted her shoulders and back in sympathy. She held her head up and waited for the sermon to begin. A short blonde woman sat in the pew behind them. She tapped Cari's shoulder.

"Hello, Cari. I'm Jody. I'm sorry for what my family just did. I just want you to know that not all of us feel that way. Rue didn't keep in touch with us. Honestly, I couldn't blame her. We're not the Waltons. A few of us are keeping an open mind until her murder is solved." Jody slid back out the pew and joined the rest of the Tenneys.

Cari was feeling utterly stressed. The huge church felt more like a small box that wouldn't allow her to breathe. The priest droned on. At the end of the service, Garcia asked Cari if she were up to the internment.

"It's at some cemetery called Woodlawn. Ariana and I would be glad to take you there if you want to go."

Cari was at a loss. Instinctively she knew she would lose it if she had to watch them put her in the ground. On the other hand, she didn't want to give her family the satisfaction of not going. Cari turned to Yolie. "What do you think?"

Yolie heaved a sigh. "If it's what you want to do, Mommy, don't worry about these people."

That hadn't helped, but she knew the decision was hers. No one else from the job wanted to attend the burial. They felt they had bid Rue a respectful and proper farewell from the church. Cari felt they were right. Besides, she wanted to alleviate some of the tension of the day. It made Cari feel even more sorry for her lover.

There had been news crews stationed outside the church as the procession emerged. Flash bulbs popped as Rue's casket was being lifted into the hearse. Garcia and Yolie flanked Cari on either side as reporters shouted out questions.

"Do you have any idea who did it, Cari?"

"How are you healing, Cari?"

Ariana ran ahead of them to unlock the car so they could try to make a speedy retreat. Once in the car, Cari buried her face in Yolie's shoulder. "Goodbye, Rue."

CHAPTER 28

Kaliq had been glad to see all the excitement finally die down. The past couple of months had been hard. The police hadn't come up with any leads in Rue's murder case. The media had also stopped hounding Cari. It was a matter that would not be forgotten, but without anything concrete to go on, there wasn't much anyone could do.

Kaliq admired himself in the full-length mirror. He thought he looked pretty good in his rented tux. He had kicked himself for not thinking of asking Yolie to the prom himself. He hadn't attended his own; he hadn't thought about hers.

"You know, Kaliq. It's about that time of year. Dresses, corsages, yadda yadda. It would be really phat if you were to take me to the prom."

"I'd be glad to take you. Then we can have a celebration of our own." He snickered.

He hadn't pressed Yolie to make love to him, although, in the past several weeks it had constantly been on his mind. He didn't want their being together to be some kind of footnote to what was going down in her and Cari's lives. He's sure she wouldn't have viewed it that way, but he wasn't taking any chances. If he were completely honest with himself, he would have realized he was nervous about it. It's not every day you sleep with your sons' sister.

He had rented another car for the evening. The prom was being held in the ballroom of the Hotel Olympia. Kaliq had never heard of it, but he was told it was some new swanky hotel in midtown Manhattan. He had taken special care in cleaning the house. It was a much easier task with B.P. gone. After Kaliq had kicked Dennis out, he hadn't seen him again. His mother had called and said that he was down in Wynetta running the streets. Dennis had told them that he would be moving on to Atlanta, but he was still hanging out in Wynetta with some cousins Kaliq hardly knew. Kaliq had a strange feeling about Dennis' sudden move south. It wouldn't be the first time somebody had hidden out down South to escape some trouble they had caused in New York. Kaliq didn't voice his suspicions to anyone. He'd seen firsthand the hassle they had put Yolie's father through when it came out that he was the cause of Rue abusing Cari. There was nothing to substantiate the claim by Rue's folks that he might be responsible, so they had to let it go.

The drive through the tough Brooklyn streets he had grown up in could depress him sometimes. He knew plenty of people who couldn't get enough of the borough. Do or die, Bed-Stuy was the age-old motto. True, there were many sections that were nicer, but he wanted to get out of New York—period. Now that he was about to complete his degree, the sky could be the limit if he landed the right job. Perhaps he could talk Cari into joint custody so his kids would have the opportunity to grow up better than most of the children they went to school with. He'd love a house out in Rockland or Orange County. He'd enjoy designing it himself. Maybe if things continued to work out, Yolie would be in that house with him one day.

Kaliq ignored the whistles and cat-calls he received as he entered Yolie's building. He said "what up" to a couple of his friends that lived in the surrounding buildings as he pressed the elevator call button.

Upstairs, Yolie was putting the finishing touches on her makeup. "You know these shoes are gonna hurt like hell by the time I get to the hotel," she complained.

"Well, I told you to stretch them out by walking in them. Next time you'll listen, *mija*." Cari smiled as she brushed her daughter's gleaming hair.

"No more high school. I can't wait until it's time for my college graduation,"

Yolie exclaimed as she sprayed Estee Lauder's Pleasures on her pulse points.

"Don't rush it, Yolara. Believe me, time flies by all too fast. It seems like just yesterday your father kicked me off his bus." Cari laughed.

In the living room, Meshach was keeping Travis and Trevor busy. He had them help load film in his camera. He couldn't help feeling a little old. A short time ago he was taking pictures of Egypt on her prom night. He still realized that his daughters would never be close, but he had hopes that as they got older they would form some kind of real relationship.

"I'll get the door for you," he called out as he heard the knocker. "Hey, looking sharp there, man," Meshach said as he shook Kaliq's hand.

"Thank you very much, Mr. Burkette."

"I was just thinking how old Yolie's making me feel. You've got to call me something other than Mr. Burkette, please."

"Something like what?"

"I don't know. How about Burk? That's what Cari's always called me," he suggested.

"All right. Cool by me," Kaliq answered as he swooped Travis into the air. Trevor showed him the camera. "Don't break it. Daddy ain't got no money to pay for it."

"Speaking of money, I'd like to give you a little spending cash for tonight," Meshach said, pulling out his wallet.

"Nah, Mr. Burkette, I mean, Burk. Your money's no good here. I've got it covered."

Meshach was glad that Kaliq had stepped up like a man, but he'd slip the cash to Yolie just in case something went wrong. "You've done a good job with these boys, Kaliq. My experience has only been with girls. You know there is nowhere a man could run if he hurt one of my girls."

"Burk, ain't we cool yet?"

"I'm just making sure we stay cool, brother man."

"Okay, she's ready at last," Cari announced. "Burk, get the camera ready."

Yolie entered the living room with a flourish. She was decked out in a pale pink dress that hugged every curve. Tiny deep red roses spotted the gown in places. Her sling-back shoes were the same crimson color. Her jet-black hair shone brightly and was adorned with a silver hair clip on one side. Her makeup complemented her exotic features. The single piece of jewelry she wore was a silver antique cross that nestled in her cleavage.

Meshach thought his daughter was a vision. He didn't exactly approve of the spaghetti-strapped dress she wore, but she looked so happy he couldn't spoil a single moment for her.

Kaliq tried to hide his delight. It would not help for Meshach to see him salivating over his little girl. "You look gorgeous, Yolara. I'm glad you remembered to tell me to get a rose corsage." He smiled as he slipped the flowers around her wrist.

"Okay, let's get a picture," Cari said, ushering the two over to the couch. She gently moved the boys out the way.

"You should see what I have on under this," Yolie whispered to Kaliq.

Meshach snapped several pictures. The boys insisted on having their photograph taken, too. In the end there were pictures of everyone.

Cari threatened tears if the couple didn't hurry up and leave. Meshach cautioned Kaliq to drive safely and then hugged and kissed Yolie as they headed for the door.

"Well, she looked hot. Damn, we made a beautiful child," Cari said to Meshach.

"Well, she shouldn't look so damn hot. Who picked out that dress anyway?"

"I did. Want to make something out of it," she asked with a roll of her neck.

"Nah, back off. Why don't we send the little ones to bed and pretend it's our prom night." Meshach snickered. Cari hadn't enjoyed a good laugh in a long time. He just wanted to see her back into the groove. She had endured so much. Meshach missed their bickering and he hoped to provoke her into a lively debate. He was careful not to force himself on her. He didn't want to take advantage of the tragedy that had occurred. However, if he could manage to win her over in time...

"You are too much," Cari told him with a chuckle and a smile.

***

The party had turned out to be extremely nice (although Yolie had to comment on the deejay's lack of skill). The refreshments were delicious and plentiful. Some of Yolie's friends had wanted to hang out after the prom ended. One of the guys suggested they pool their money and rent a room. That idea was quickly vetoed. Instead they opted for real food. They decided to head to the Village. They ate at a place called Josie's Got It. They laughed and joked until the manager asked them did if they wanted breakfast next.

Yolie giggled as she limped back to the car. "These shoes are killing me for real."

Kaliq opened the car door for her. After she was seated, he took one of her feet into his hands. He glided the shoe off and massaged her foot. Then he gave the other one its turn. "Does that feel good?"

"I know what would feel better," she teased. Yolara looked at him with such longing, that he would have risked a hundred speeding tickets to get back to his house as soon as was possible.

Once they were back at his home, Kaliq felt a little foolish. He wasn't sure how to proceed. He didn't want to finish before he began. Yolie must have sensed his dilemma. She reached up to kiss his lips. The kiss was equivalent to a slow burn. Yolie took her time and relieved him of his tux. Kaliq tried to return the favor, but she had other ideas.

It seemed like hours had passed while they played with each other. The teasing was tortuous, but delectable. At last, Kaliq was allowed to peel her gown away. Yolie wore a pink strapless bra with a matching thong. Sheer thigh-high stockings gave her legs a lethal look.

Kaliq was overwhelmed by her beauty, but more than that, he was overwhelmed by love. "I'm glad you're here with me, Yolara."

"I love you, Kaliq."

He lifted her up and carried her into his bedroom. He had done the hokey rose petal thing, but Yolie was delighted. He set her down on the bed and gazed into her eyes. "I love you, too."

For Yolie, the moment was a long time coming. The emotion showed clearly on Kaliq's face. She had hoped that they could put all the events of the past few months behind them and move on. Yolie wanted her family to be happy. She knew Cari was still harboring feelings of guilt over Rue's murder. She wished that she could find a way to make things better for her. Her mother was pleased about Kaliq and herself, though.

"*Mi hija*, go for it. You and Kaliq might outlast all of us in the romance department."

And it had been very romantic indeed. Although Yolie knew it could not have been easy for Kaliq to restrain himself, he had been the perfect gentleman. Even as she looked into his face, she saw his concern.

"It's finally okay," she whispered.

The love they made was like nothing either had experienced. Yolie parted her arms and legs in welcome and Kaliq felt as if he were home. He filled her with himself. They held on to each other as if their lives depended on it. She wrapped her legs around him trying to bring him even closer. He buried his face in her hair as she nuzzled his neck.

"Yolie…I can't wait."

Neither could she and they enjoyed the release together.

CHAPTER 29

B.P. was bored out of his mind. Wynetta was not exactly the hotbed of the South. His cousins were small-time thugs. They took B.P. with them whenever they wanted to do a shoplifting job or attempt to steal a car. He marveled at their simpleness. He thought the whole thing was a waste of time. How could you mess up a car theft? B.P. wished he could go back to New York. His intentions had been to slip away while no one had any reason to suspect him. Only his boy La-Rone knew the truth. It had been his jeep they were in when B.P. gunned down Rue. That same night, they made tracks to Wynetta. La-Rone had returned to New York weeks ago. He had promised to call B.P. if anything came up that he should know about. La-Rone had only called once. He had said that the case remained unsolved. B.P. breathed a small sigh of relief, but he was in no hurry to get back. At least, then he wasn't.

"Yo, Dennis, man. What's up for today?" his cousin Antoine hollered from the porch.

"Nothing with you, motherfucker."

"You got a problem, man? You been moping around this motherfucka like you homesick or some shit."

"Y'all niggers ain't got shit going for you. How do you stand it?"

"I'm sorry this ain't big bad Brooklyn. It was good enough for you to run to, though, wasn't it? You ain't never gonna tell me what you did?"

"If I had wanted you to know I would have told you. Besides, ain't nothing to tell," B.P. insisted.

"Yeah, all right. Be that way, man."

B.P. waved his cousin off and went around to the back yard where he had a weight bench set up. He had gotten a part-time job at Wal-Mart so he could have some spending cash. He had enough saved up to go back to New York. He was seriously considering it. First, he had to make absolutely sure that the coast was clear. He did only a few bench presses before he set the weights back on their rack.

"Where you going?" Antoine asked as he saw his cousin head up the drive.

"None of your fucking business."

B.P. had to walk about half a mile to make a phone call at the 7-Eleven. Antoine didn't have a phone in his house and never remembered to charge the piece of crap cell phone he had. Every step in the blazing sun made him angrier. There was a white woman on the phone when he got there. She was noticeably nervous as she watched B.P. recline against a car to wait for her to finish. She hurriedly ended her call and headed for her car—the same one he was leaning on.

"Sorry about that." He smiled. She mumbled that it was okay and drove off. B.P. laughed.

"Dennis?"

B.P. was about to ask, "Now what?" when he turned and realized it was his Aunt Dessa. "Hey, how you, Auntie?"

Dessa stepped up to receive her nephew's hug. "We're all doing fine. Mama keeps asking about you. When I told her you were down here, she wondered why you hadn't been by."

"I know she still ain't up to par. I didn't want to wear her out."

"Boy, that's nonsense and you know it. It would make her feel good to see you. I'm telling you, you keep hanging with that Antoine and we'll be seeing you on the chain gang."

"All right, Auntie. You right. Matter of fact, I'll go by her house today. I might be going back up North soon. I don't know how y'all stand it down here."

"Well, we grew up down here. If you gave it half a chance, instead of running with…"

"Auntie, I don't mean to cut you off, but I've got to make this phone call before I head to work. If you talk to Nana, tell her I'll be by." He hastily kissed Dessa and turned to the phone.

"You ain't fooling me, Dennis. I know you don't care about nobody but yourself. Just make sure you see Mama before you go wherever." She patted him on the shoulder and then stepped into the 7-Eleven.

He waited until she was inside before he picked up the receiver. He told the operator he wanted to make a collect call. He could hear La-Rone accept the charges on the other end.

"Yo, what up, nigga? Ain't heard from you in a while," La-Rone answered.

"Man, I'm about to go crazy down here. I've got to come back home, for real. "

"Well, come on then. I told you they ain't solving that case. I don't even think they still trying."

"Oh, I'm sure somebody's trying. That bitch's people got money."

"Well, if they suspected you, they would have been on your trail a long time ago. Besides, I could use your help with a little situation myself."

Here it comes, B.P. thought. *Payback time.* He knew he owed La-Rone big time and it was just like the brother to want something in return. "What's going down?"

"I ain't gonna talk about it over the phone. So when you coming back?"

"Oh yeah, but it's all right to discuss all my business. I don't know. I got to get my shit together first. Maybe next week," B.P. said.

"Cool. Let me know when I can pick you up. You flying?"

"I ain't got that kind of money, motherfucker."

"You ain't had *no* kind of action down there?"

"Negro, pleez."

"Well, give me a holler when you back in the Big Apple. This call is costing me. Peace."

La-Rone had hung up before he could say anything. Suddenly, a week was too long to wait. B.P. had an idea. He might be headed home sooner than he had thought.

CHAPTER 30

The summer was gearing up to be an extremely hot one. Cari wished that she could be hanging out at the beach instead of slaving over a barcoding machine. She had missed two weeks of work while waiting for her face to heal. It still depressed her when she thought about Rue. Meshach urged her not to dwell on it, but that was impossible. Cari had to hand it to him. He turned out to be her rock. She resisted it at first. Even now, she wasn't thrilled about a reconciliation. Friendship was fine with her.

Some of the guys at work had started hitting on her again. Cari joked around with them, but she made it clear that she wasn't interested. One guy asked rather flippantly if she was turned off men for good. She gave him a smart answer in return, but she wondered the same thing herself sometimes. Had Rue just been a fluke or was she really attracted to women after all? It hurt her head to think about it.

"Cari, I'm going to take a bathroom break," Pam announced.

"Go ahead, honey. I've got it covered." As soon as Pam stepped away, Cari's pager began to vibrate. She recognized the number as Meshach's. Cari was pleased and annoyed at the same time. She was sure it wasn't an emergency; he hadn't added the 911 code.

Cari and Pam were dragging their post cons onto the line for dispatch when she got another page.

"Damn, why doesn't he leave me alone for a little while?" Cari mumbled as she saw Meshach's number again.

"Is that Burk? Why don't you give the man some so he can get off your back?" Pam kidded.

"Yeah, then I'll never get rid of him!"

"Your shit's that good, girl?"

"Pam, you know you need to stop!"

"Are you still grieving over Rue? I know it was a horrible experience, but you've got to let it go. Maybe Burk can help."

"I don't want that kind of help from him. We had what we had and it's over. I don't want to go back there with him. If something were to develop down the line, then I'd be better prepared for it. Honestly, I'm not sure a man is what I want—let alone Burk."

They headed off to the ladies locker room. The other girls wanted to hang out, but Cari declined. She promised them that she would next time. As she waved goodbye, an Explorer pulled up to the curb.

"Damn, girl. Is your beeper broke?"

"Did something happen with one of the kids?" Cari asked, immediately worried.

"Nah, baby, I'm sorry. I didn't mean to scare you. I was trying to call you to let you know that I would pick you up."

Cari didn't want him to see how disappointed she was. "You didn't have to come down here, Burk." She opened the door and stepped up into the truck.

"I know, but I figured since we were both going to be off tomorrow we could hang out—maybe go down to the South Street Seaport."

"Ah, Burk…"

"Oh, come on. Don't be such a fuddy-duddy."

She gave in. "Fine, let's go."

"What's the matter with you?"

"Nothing. Just tired."

"We can just relax and enjoy the night," he said as he reached over to massage her neck.

"Maybe we can stop somewhere and have a couple of drinks," Cari told him.

"If that's what you want, okay." He started up the jeep and headed for FDR Drive. When they got to the Seaport, they saw a lot of other people had had the same idea. There was a small band playing contemporary jazz near the water. Meshach took her hand as they started to stroll.

"So how's the job?" Cari asked, trying to make conversation.

"The wheels on the bus go 'round and 'round. I'm gonna try to do some extra overtime next pick, though. I want to get a new place. Buy a condo or something. Maybe I can convince a certain lady to come with me."

Cari decided to ignore the remark. "There's a bar. I'm thirsty as I don't know what." She pulled him towards the bar.

They sat at one of the tables the place had set up out front. Meshach ordered a beer and Cari asked for a Whiskey Sour.

"Don't think I didn't notice how you changed the subject," Meshach told her, taking out a cigarette.

"Those things will kill you," she answered, sipping her drink.

"You're doing it again. I'll be a divorced man soon, Cari. There's nothing to stand in our way now."

"Yeah, especially since Rue is dead, huh."

"Whoa, where did that come from? Listen, Olive and I have decided to sell the house and split the profits. With that money I can get us a new place and pay for Yolie's and Egypt's college tuitions. I don't know how long all of that will take, but like I said, I'm gonna sign up for a lot of overtime."

Cari looked off into the distance. New York City at night was awesome. The skyscrapers reached towards the heavens—their lights making the evening electric. She was off into her own world when she felt Meshach's hand on her arm. "Burk, please don't make any long-term plans that involve me. I don't know what's gonna happen in the near future. Don't pressure me."

"I didn't think that was what I was doing. But if you don't want to talk about it yet, I can respect that," he assured her as he blew his smoke away from her face.

"Thank you." She signaled the waiter and ordered another Whiskey Sour. She could tell that Meshach was angry even though he tried to act like he wasn't. Cari was trying to get into the music that the band was playing when she heard someone call her name.

"Hi, Cari. How are you?"

It took Cari a moment to place the young woman's face. "Oh hey, how are you? Meshach, this is Astrid. She is a trainer at the gym I used to go to."

"Nice to meet you," she said. "Where have you been? I haven't seen you at the gym in at least a year."

"You know how that goes. You get a membership and then you stop going. I work out at home or go jogging. I should start going back, though."

Meshach felt as if he were being set aside. He could sense that Cari wasn't feeling him tonight. He couldn't understand why. He was patient and understanding with her. Meshach offered to be there whenever she needed. He didn't get what the deal was.

The two women went on and on about working out. Finally Astrid said, "Well, I hope you were serious about coming back."

"I will definitely drop by one day next week. It was nice seeing you, Astrid."

"Yeah, nice to meet you," Meshach said, glad that this cute little black girl was about to go on her way.

Cari raised her hand to signal the waiter again.

"Hold up. Are you *trying* to get drunk?" Meschach wanted to know. She waved the waiter away as he headed towards them.

"So what do you want to do now?" Cari asked.

"I guess you want to go home."

"To be honest, I do, Burk." The waiter looked pissed as he made his way back to the table as Cari waved him over again.

"Will that be all?" He handed them the check and disappeared again.

Back at the jeep, Meshach opened the door for Cari and slammed it behind her. He felt he deserved better than what he was getting. He knew he had messed up in the past, but he truly thought they were beyond that. They had been through so much lately.

After a fairly quiet ride home, Cari was glad to pull into the parking lot. She jumped out and headed towards the building. Meshach held her arm. "Why won't you let me take you out these projects?"

"Burk, it's not up to you to take me anywhere. I know you care and I do appreciate it. I care about you, too; you know that. Just let it be."

He shook his head defeated. Meshach pulled her into his arms and hugged her hard.

CHAPTER 31

B.P. had bid Wal-Mart a fond farewell. He had told Antoine that he was going back to New York. And then he took care of the last detail.

Nana Zee's house looked the same as it always had. Nate had done a good job of keeping the place up. His aunt and uncle had offered to move Nana in with them into their home, but she wouldn't hear any of it. B.P. could remember all the summers he, Kaliq and his sisters had spent there. They would run around the place helping feed the hogs and chickens. They played in the dirt yard out front making a mess. Kaliq had caused him to get stung by a wasp one time. B.P. recalled crying like a girl. He had to smile.

The wooden door was open, but the screen door was latched. "Nana! Nana, you in there?"

He could hear her bedroom slippers as they shuffled towards the door. Her glasses hung from a chain around her neck. She put them on, but it still took her a moment to focus. "Dennis? Oh Lord, it is you! Come on in here, boy," Nana Zee said as she unhooked the latch.

B.P. gave his grandmother a big hug. She even smelled the same. Nana loved the smell of baby powder and lotion and that's usually what she used. "How you doing, pretty lady?"

"Oh, you ain't getting off that easy. What took you so long to come and see your Nana, Dennis?"

"Oh, Nana, you know how it is."

"No, I'm sorry but I don't. Let's go back here to the kitchen. I was soaking some clothes." He followed her to the back of the small house. All their school pictures were hung proudly on the walls. B.P. had to laugh at his first-grade photo. His front teeth were missing.

"Grab that rub board for me, Dennis."

"You ain't got a washing machine, Nana?"

"Yeah, but I ain't got a big load to do. Anyway, tell me how you like living down here."

"It's all right, Nana, but you know I got a job offer back in New York. They say they gonna give the position to someone else if I don't get back there in the next couple of days. I was wondering if I could borrow some money to fly back so I don't miss this opportunity."

Nana Zee wrinkled her brows. "You wouldn't be trying to pull a fast one on me now, would you, Dennis? Don't be like that Antoine. I love Toine, but he can be trifling."

B.P. felt a small twinge of guilt. "Nah, really, Nana. I need to get back to Brooklyn. Hey, why don't you come with me?" He knew she would never agree to that nor would his aunt let her travel.

"Child, I ain't been up there since my beloved Angel passed. You know I ain't never really cared for that place. Besides, Dessa would never let me out of the state of Georgia."

He helped her hang some things on the clothesline she had in the backyard. Nana Zee chattered on about everything. He could tell that she was really glad to see him. He regretted now that he hadn't come when they thought she was going to die. At the same time, he had not wanted to go through the pain he had experienced when his mother had left him. That's how he felt; that she had abandoned him. B.P. had loved his mother deeply. No other woman would *ever* mean as much to him. He felt like crying when he saw the picture of her on Nana's mantel. Next to it laid the program from her funeral. He had to get out of there. "Well, Nana, if you can get me the cash…"

Nana knitted her brow again, but she shuffled off to the bedroom and her hope chest. She returned with three hundred dollars. "You don't have to pay me back, baby. I can't take it with me."

"Nah, Nana. I'm gonna send you even more than this. Thank you. You know you my favorite girl, right? If I can't have Mama, I'm glad I still got you." B.P. hugged his grandmother again.

"Well, you have a safe trip and don't forget to call me to let me know you got there safe," she instructed him. He breathed in that smell of baby powder as if it were the last time he'd have the chance.

"Love you, old girl."

"Who you callin' old? Love you, too, baby."

It was a long walk back to Antoine's. B.P. tried to convince himself he was doing the right thing.

CHAPTER 32

Yolara had the music blasting. She was putting together another mixed tape. She had CDs scattered all over Kaliq's living-room floor. While she worked her magic, Kaliq was sketching at his computer desk. Yolie had finished one side of the tape and was playing it back. She went and straddled Kaliq in his chair.

"Want to catch a movie later?"

He set his sketchpad aside. "Yeah, that sounds good. What do you want me to cook tonight?"

"I'm not picky. You decide." She kissed him lightly on his lips. "I'm going to be doing another party next week. Want to come?"

"Where is it gonna be?"

"In Park Slope. Idalia's throwing a birthday party for her new guy. It's a surprise. He'll be surprised all right. They are having it at his house."

"That's cool. Make that money, girl. School's starting soon."

"I wasn't going to charge her anything; she's my godmother. But she said the same thing—school's starting soon. I'm going to be nervous as hell," she told him, reaching for a banana from the desk.

"Don't worry. You're going to bust all your classes out. At least, I'll get to show you around City for a semester before I graduate."

"That's gonna be phat. Then again you just might get tired of me. I'm over here all the time. Can you deal with seeing me on campus, too?" Yolie teased.

"Girl, I could never get enough of you," Kaliq reminded her. He could feel himself getting excited.

"Down, boy."

"Why? Can you think of anything better to do?" He dug his hands into her hair and pulled her face toward his. Within seconds, they were making frantic love on the living-room floor.

They jumped into the shower together afterwards. Kaliq and Yolie lathered each other. Kaliq loved washing her long hair. He'd shampoo and rinse it. He enjoyed brushing the long strands. Yolie's body had blossomed. He liked to think it was all the sex they had. Kaliq would joke about it with her. They were happier than he'd ever thought they could be.

The two had decided to save a few bucks by having dinner at home before heading off to the movies. They threw a couple of steaks into the oven and stir-fried some vegetables. Yolie used the rest of the bananas to make a pudding, Kaliq's favorite dessert. By the time they finished dinner, they had to run to catch the last show.

When it was over, Yolie went back to Kaliq's without a second thought. They climbed into his large four-poster bed and talked for hours. It was about three a.m. when the phone rang. He groped around the nightstand for the phone. "Hello?"

"Hello, Kaliq?"

"Cari?"

"Yeah, is Yolara there?"

Kaliq felt a little embarrassed as he nudged Yolie awake. "It's Cari."

She rolled over and took the phone from him. "Is everything okay, Mommy?"

"I could ask you the same thing, Yolara. Do you plan on coming home any time this century?"

"I'm sorry I didn't call."

"You should be, *mi hija*. This isn't like you at all. Would you please come home tomorrow? I have to talk to you."

"Okay, Mommy. I'll see you in the morning. Goodnight."

"Goodnight, Yolie."

She replaced the phone on its hook. Kaliq wrapped his arms around her. "This is going to be a problem, isn't it? I didn't mean to keep you away from home; it just happened that way."

"I know. I'll explain it all to Mommy in the morning. I know she'll get it."

"Don't be so sure. You're her only daughter. I'm a past mistake. She may have been happy for us in the beginning, but it could be that she's starting to look at it different now."

"We'll see." Yolie mumbled something that Kaliq couldn't figure out and was softly snoring in a matter of seconds.

"I think we're both gonna need some sleep."

CHAPTER 33

B.P. paced the airport lounge impatiently. La-Rone was late. The flight had arrived early in the morning, but he had called La-Rone before he had left Georgia. It was a short trip and B.P. was glad. He really hated flying.

"Yo, Bullet!"

Everyone waiting in the lounge turned to see who this loud man was talking to.

"Yo, what up, dog? It's about time you showed up, nigga."

"Yeah, yeah. Just be glad I picked your punk ass up at all. Come on."

They made their way through the parking lot. La-Rone fumbled for the keys to his jeep. "You didn't get rid of this shit?" B.P. asked, surprised to see the vehicle.

"You gonna buy me another one?"

They threw his bags in the back. "So what is this thing you didn't want to tell me over the phone?"

La-Rone rubbed his hands together as if the tale were going to be a juicy one. "You know Rahmel from 50 Stuyvesant?"

"Yeah. He's a piece of shit. I ain't never liked that kid. What about him?"

"Man, I've got to take him out. Baby Sis says that nigga raped her. They was on a date and shit and the motherfucker didn't understand the meaning of no. So you know what that means."

B.P. wasn't thrilled to hear the news. He knew that he owed La-Rone for helping him off Rue. On the other hand, he was not eager to get mixed up in another murder. Of course, he couldn't let his boy know that.

"All right. So what's the plan?"

***

The block had not changed a single bit while he was gone. B.P. and La-Rone headed over to the barbershop. He complained how he couldn't find anyone to give him a decent hair cut in Wynetta. It was B.P.'s turn to hop in the chair when he looked up to find Kaliq entering the shop. "Yo, cuz. What's happening, baby?"

Kaliq walked over to slap his cousin's hand. He had been angry with B.P. for a couple of weeks after the Jeneill incident. But he pretty much had put it out of his mind when B.P. went down South. He still had his suspicions as to why his cousin had felt the need to leave town when he had. Kaliq never voiced his opinion to anyone.

"Hey, Dennis. When did you get back, man?"

"Got back today. Nana said to tell you, what's up."

Kaliq had to laugh. "So where you staying?"

"I'm gonna be hanging at my boy's crib."

La-Rone and Kaliq greeted each other with nods. "That's cool. Stop by the house one day."

"How's Yolie? And Cari?"

"They're hanging in there. You'll be glad to know that me and Yolie are together now." Kaliq grinned.

"Shit. Y'all was together back then!"

They talked until the barber had finished them both. "I'll check you later, Dennis. Got to go pick up the kids." They shared a quick manly embrace and then Kaliq crossed the street to Yolie's building.

The streets were crowded with kids. Someone had opened a fire hydrant so the children could get some relief from the heat. They sprayed cars as they passed by. Kaliq thought it might be a good idea to take Yolie and the boys out to Reis Beach.

The elevator was out of order again. He braced himself to climb the six flights of stairs to their apartment. Cari opened the door for him. Kaliq gave her a kiss on her forehead. "Morning." Travis and Trevor left the television and their bowls of Lucky Charms behind when they heard their father's voice.

"Good morning, Kaliq," Cari greeted. She looked a little fatigued to him. "I was just having a little talk with Miss Thing here. I know she's of age and I trust *you* without doubt, but I'm not feeling what's going on here."

"Mommy thinks that we might be getting in over our heads; that we're not ready to live together," Yolie added.

"And that's practically what you two are doing. Yolara doesn't come home for days at a time. At first, I didn't say anything, but I don't want you guys to crash and burn like I've done."

"I can see where you'd be concerned, Cari, but Yolie has always been like family to me even before we got together…"

"I know. And when I stopped to think about that, I realize this whole thing is almost like incest."

"Ah, come on. Don't you think that is a stretch?"

"It's not all that farfetched. I don't know. I just want you to step lightly. Do you know what I mean, Kaliq?"

"Yes, I think I know what you mean. But, you know, Cari, I want Yolie with me all the time. I'd love it if she could move in with me. I'd love it if the boys could, too. I have our collective family's best interest at heart. I don't see Yolie's and my relationship as something to take lightly."

Both Yolie and Cari were a little surprised by Kaliq's comments. Yolie was thrilled that he was standing up for them. Cari read an underlying threat to her losing custody of her babies.

"Why don't we just chill out for a little bit. All this is still new, but it's not going away. Mommy, I'll be more considerate about calling home. Can we still take Travis and Trevor out?"

Cari felt that her daughter was missing the point, but she didn't want to press things. She told them to go out and have a good time. There were hugs and kisses, yet Cari felt a little unsettled. After she closed the door behind them, she thought to herself that they were all in for a bumpy ride.

CHAPTER 34

Meshach had to shout to be heard. The crew room at Flatbush Depot was jumping. Games of pool, ping-pong and Spades were in full swing. Dozens of conversations were going on at once. The line to pick up paychecks went clear down the hall. Meshach just hoped the money truck wasn't late again.

"Hey, Burk. You think you could do a mutual swap with me this week? I got to handle some business," Sommers asked.

"I don't know, man, I'll let you know."

"I need to know now, guy…"

"Hey, you wanna back off," Meshach answered testily.

"You ain't the only one with problems, motherfucker."

Meshach slapped Sommers on the back. "Yo, I'm sorry, Vic. Got a lot of shit on my mind."

"I can relate. My sister's kid, Rahmel, got shot up last night. He ain't dead, but he might as well be. People on the block are saying that bastard La-Rone and his boy BulletProof did it. Someone just told me that La-Rone was braggin' how they did that butch chick a few months ago, too."

"What?"

"Yeah, they ain't got the good sense to keep their mouths shut." Sommers pushed Meshach up to the window. "You want your check or not?"

Meshach absentmindedly signed for his check. His mind was reeling. If BulletProof was behind the drive-by, did that mean Kaliq had something to do with it? Did he order the hit because Rue had beat Cari down? Meshach wasn't sure what to make of it, but he knew he didn't like it at all. What kind of family was his little girl getting mixed up with?

CHAPTER 35

Cari threw a towel into her gym bag. She had promised Astrid that she would start going to the gym again. Honestly, it was just what she needed. She found that she had a lot of free time on her hands. Yolie spent every minute with Kaliq. They often took the twins with them. She didn't want to put a damper on her sons' summer. Cari tried, but she wasn't always her old self. It was taking a lot to get over Rue—not only her death, but the relationship as well. Burk was not helping matters at all. The more he tried to press up on her, the more she wanted to head for the hills.

Now she had to worry about Kaliq and Yolie. They were forming the perfect little family. Cari knew Kaliq was a good man, but she felt he was stealing her children away from her. What if Yolie got pregnant? She knew that were getting it on like jack-rabbits. Cari wasn't sure if she should allow it to go on, but then she felt like a hypocrite. How could she tell her grown daughter what to do when she had shacked up with a woman herself?

Cari waited for the B54 into Ridgewood. The bus stop was crowded. She noticed a couple of guys checking her out. She knew she looked good in her mustard-colored biker-short set and black high-top Reeboks. She'd twisted her hair into a French braid. Once upon a time she would have flirted back with them.

She rode the bus to the last stop and walked the couple of blocks to the gym. Cari signed up to use a treadmill. While she waited her turn, she went to check out the weight room. She noticed Astrid spotting a young kid. The boy was struggling to lift the weights. Astrid showed him the proper way to do it. Cari had always thought Astrid was cute. She was a deep brown-skinned beauty who wore her hair very short. Her dedication to working out had paid off in a huge way. Her body was magnificent. She had both muscles and curves. Cari felt aware of Astrid in a different way than she had before.

Astrid turned around as if she could feel Cari's eyes on her. "Hi. Good to see you!"

"Well, I said I'd be back. How are you?"

"Excuse me, Will," she said to the kid. "I'm doing very well. Business is booming."

"I can see that. I need to work off some steam. Like I was telling you, I do work out at home, but it feels good to get out the house."

"I'm sure. I read about what happened. I'm sorry for your loss."

"Thank you," Cari answered, hoping to get off the subject.

"Life is hard as a lesbian. When something like that happens, it just spurs on all the negative stereotypes about us," Astrid said.

Cari was a little surprised at her comment. "Yeah, I know. Um, I'm going to see if my treadmill is free."

"Okay, I'll be here working with Will. I'm come check you out when we're done."

"Cool, catch ya later." Cari waved.

Oh God, she's a lesbian. What were the odds of that?

Cari worked out hard for a couple of hours. Astrid would stop by to see how she was doing. By the time Cari headed for the locker room, she was drenched in sweat. She sat on a bench waiting for an available shower.

"So, how are you feeling now? Sore?"

"I'm not too bad. You know those Billy Blanks tapes whip you into some serious shape."

"Yeah, I have those at home, too. Coming back tomorrow?" Astrid wondered.

"I just might."

"Well, I'll let you get to your shower," she said with a sly grin.

Cari watched as Astrid stopped off to say goodbye to a few members. Before she knew what she was doing, she rushed up the young woman. "Astrid, would you like to go out sometime?"

Astrid could sense Cari's uneasiness. "Sure, I'd like that a lot."

A couple of the older ladies raised their eyebrows. "Um, I'll give you my number before I leave, okay?"

Astrid had a pen on a string hanging around her neck. She handed the pen to Cari and stretched out her arm. "Here, give it to me now."

Cari jotted down her number. The two women exchanged goodbyes again. Cari made her way to the showers. "Lord, here we go again."

CHAPTER 36

B.P. was fuming. How could a nigga be so stupid? He had just found out how big La-Rone's mouth really was. The whole neighborhood was gossiping about what had gone down. If he had known how things were going to wind up, he would have toughed it out in Georgia. He made it a point not to be seen with La-Rone. He knew that retaliation from Rahmel's family could strike anytime. To make matters worse, La-Rone hadn't even killed him. The word was that he was hooked up to life support.

He could feel eyes on his back as he walked down the street. B.P. decided to pay Kaliq a visit. No one answered the door. He tried his keys, but they didn't work. "Damn, he must have really been burnt to change the locks."

B.P. had moved out of La-Rone's apartment. Now he was staying with one of his ex-girlfriends. He started to trudge his way back to her building.

"Wait up, Dennis."

He turned to find Yolie running to catch up to him. She gave him a hug. "Kaliq told me you was back up here. What's up? How is everything?"

"Everything is everything, little sis. When you and Kaliq gonna make it official?"

"Man, please. Don't rush me. We already starting to catch some flack, it looks like. Mommy is tripping a little bit. I can't imagine how it's gonna be when my father jumps on the bandwagon."

"People need to mind their own business. Let you live your life." B.P. offered to buy Yolie a coquito as a woman with a small cart rolled by. They slurped the coconut-flavored ice noisily.

"They'll get used to it. So are you gonna stay in New York now?"

"I don't know what I'm gonna do. Shit's just tired. Maybe I'll try the West Coast or something."

"Yeah, I can see you now. Crip or Blood?"

He sighed. "I ain't trying to join no gang. Besides, them motherfuckers are up here now, too. I just want to be somewhere different."

"Join the army and be all that you can be," Yolie joked.

"Anybody ever tell you you ain't funny?"

"Were you coming from Kaliq's house?

"Yeah, but he wasn't there."

"I was gonna go inside and wait for him. Come on," she told him.

Yolie pulled out a set of keys and opened the door. "You done moved in?" B.P. asked her.

"Well, kinda." Yolie flicked on the air conditioner and they stretched lazily on the couch. A little while later they heard the key in the door. Travis and Trevor made their usual grand entrance.

"BulletProof!" they yelled.

"Excuse me, but what is his name?" Kaliq said to his boys.

"Hey, Dennis," they corrected.

"Hey what up, man?" Kaliq greeted his cousin.

"Just chillin'. Yolie, let me in."

"Well, I figured that. You gonna hang around and eat with us?"

B.P.'s ex was not a culinary genius so he gladly accepted the offer. It felt good to be around his cousins again. Travis carried on about how Trevor acted up at the doctor's office. Kaliq and Yolie looked happy. B.P. suddenly wished he could have a setup like theirs. After dinner, they played countless games of Tekken 3. The twins complained when Kaliq told them it was time for them to take their baths. They tossed their PlayStation joysticks on the floor and stomped off to the tub.

"I'm about to get up out of here. I'll check y'all tomorrow, cuz."

"All right, Dennis, man. Stay out of trouble," Kaliq warned his cousin jokingly.

"See what the kids are doing. I'm gonna set the garbage out," Yolie said as she followed B.P. out the door.

"We gotta check out a flick or something next time," B.P. said.

A navy Acura came screeching around the corner. In his gut, B.P. knew they were seconds away from something going wrong. He could see someone hanging from the passenger-side window. "Next time, mind your business, motherfucker!"

Inside the house, Kaliq nearly jumped out of his skin as he heard the familiar ring of bullets. B.P. moved with lightning speed to shield Yolara from the barrage. They hit the ground and he prayed they lived. The pain that exploded in his back was unbearable. Yolie's screams let him know that he was not dead yet. From the ground he could see people running in all directions. Kaliq came bursting through the door.

"Yolie! Yolie!"

She was still screaming as she cradled B.P. "Call 911, hurry."

***

It had taken a lifetime for the ambulance to arrive. B.P. lapsed in and out of consciousness. He had begged them not to let him die. Kaliq, Yolie and the kids had piled into a cab and followed the ambulance to the hospital. They waited for word in the crowded emergency room.

"I can't believe we are here again," Kaliq marveled.

"I can't wait to get out of this neighborhood. It is getting too damn scary. What did Dennis do?"

"I have no idea, but I'm going to find out. Whatever shit he got himself involved in almost got you killed. I'm not having it. He should have stayed his ass down South. I don't want to see my cousin die, but he is getting out of hand."

Kaliq heard his name called over the P.A. system. He went to the nurse's station where a doctor waited for him. She told him that Dennis had come through the emergency surgery with little complication. However, she informed him that they could not remove the bullet lodged in his spine. Kaliq thanked the doctor and asked when he could see him. He was told that he would be unconscious for a while.

"What did the doctor say?" Yolie asked anxiously.

He explained the situation. "He will probably never walk again. The doctor didn't say that, but I have the feeling that is how this will play itself out."

They left word that if Dennis were to wake up they would be at home. The nurse said they would not be able to call them; they would have to check back on their own. Kaliq hailed another cab and they headed for home. Yolie rested her head on his shoulder. "I thank God that I didn't lose you," Kaliq told her as he stroked her hair.

"I thank Him, too."

CHAPTER 37

Cari was nervous as she dressed for her date with Astrid. She wasn't even sure if she should call it a date. Astrid had called and asked if Cari were free that night. She apologized for the spur-of-the-moment invitation, but she had just gotten her hands on some Liberty tickets and wondered if she'd like to go. Cari didn't really follow the WNBA, but she did want to get out of the house.

She threw on a pair of black capri pants and a white tank. A pair of strappy flat sandals completed her look. It was a warm evening so she tied her hair into a bun. She came across the diamond studs Rue had bought her as she searched her jewelry box. Cari fingered the earrings for a moment and then opted for a pair of silver hoops. She grabbed her Coach knapsack and headed for the door.

There were very few people in the subway car. The butterflies in her stomach hadn't calmed down. Naturally, Meshach had called that after-noon. "What you doing tonight?" he had asked.

"Just getting together with a friend," she had responded, not wanting to elaborate.

"Really? Anybody I know?"

"You're so obvious, Burk. No, you don't know her. You've seen her once."

"Somebody from the post office?"

"Goodbye, Burk."

"Why are you being like that? I can't ask you a question?"

"Well, you've asked me several questions and I don't feel that I have to answer them. I didn't want to go there, but I have to say something. Burk, you are expecting something I'm not looking to give you."

"You sure know how to hurt a guy. Damn, Cari. Are you still holding a grudge over me and Olive?"

Cari tried not to laugh. "Life ain't all about you, hon. Talk to you tomorrow."

She transferred to the train that would take her to Madison Square Garden. Astrid had asked her to wait for her in front of Barnes and Noble. Cari anxiously searched the crowd until she saw Astrid jogging across Seventh Avenue.

"Have you been waiting long?"

"No. Only a few minutes. How are you?' Cari greeted her.

"Feeling good. Let's go inside," Astrid answered as she locked arms with Cari.

She stopped at a couple of stands to pick up some souvenirs. "I really should wait until after the game. Guys will be selling this stuff cheaper on the street. Would you like something from the refreshment stand before we go look for our seats?"

Cari knew she would enjoy the evening. Astrid was a very charming girl. She wore a jazzy pink back-out blouse with denim cutoffs. Her skippies were stark white with pink laces. She wore her hair short like the actress Nia Long. The girl had it going on.

They tried to make conversation between cheering for the ladies of the New York Liberty. It felt good to Cari. She had no idea where things would lead, but this moment was right.

After they lost the game, Astrid was able to get all kinds of souvenirs dirt-cheap. "Are you hungry?"

"Not really. Those hot dogs did me in. If you want something let's find somewhere to go," Cari answered.

"I think there is BBQ's somewhere in the forties. I'm craving ribs and corn bread."

"You keep that figure by eating ribs and corn bread?" Cari laughed.

"No, but it's that time of the month and I have to make myself feel better."

They walked the rest of the way. BBQ's was crowded as usual, but they were seated reasonably quickly.

"So are you having fun?" Astrid asked.

"Yes, thanks for thinking about me."

"Oh, Cari, I've been thinking about you a lot."

"I'm flattered," Cari said almost shyly.

"Will flattery get me anywhere? I'm just teasing. I know it must be kinda weird for you. I'm just letting you know I am very interested and totally available."

Cari hadn't expected Astrid to be so straightforward. "Well, let's see how it goes. But I will tell you that I've been thinking about you, too."

Astrid raised her glass of ginger ale. "I do believe that calls for a toast."

CHAPTER 38

Yolie rose sleepily from the bed. "Damn, Mommy is gonna kill me!" She shook Kaliq awake. "I've got to get going. I had promised Mommy that I would come home."

"Man, I hope she doesn't start bugging out over it. I was just so tired from dealing with Dennis' situation," he said as he tried to pull her back onto the bed.

She kissed him and pulled her arm back. "Listen, I was thinking that we wouldn't have to tell her about this."

"You're kidding, right? She probably knows already. You know how it is around here."

"Yeah, you're probably right. But just in case…"

"Okay, she won't hear it from me. She'll wonder why we didn't mention it, though."

"There has just been too much to deal with lately. I don't want to add more to her plate. Besides, I'm fine."

"I know that's true, but I think your father is really the one you don't want to have to deal with," Kaliq suggested.

"You know me so well." She gathered her things and headed for the door. "I'll tell Mommy you're bringing the boys back this evening."

"I want to walk you," Kaliq said.

"No, the kids are still asleep. I'll be fine. I love you."

"Love you, too."

Yolie rushed out the door and up the street. She wondered why she was hurrying. If she were in trouble, a few minutes wouldn't make a big difference. Yolie saw Egypt and her friend Helene as she neared her building.

"Hey, Egee," Yolie said to her sister.

Egypt seemed to cringe a little as Yolie used her nickname. "How are you, Yolara?"

"Hanging in there. All ready for Atlanta?"

"Yeah, just about," she answered. Helene smiled at Yolie. "You two know each other, don't you?"

"Yeah, sorta kinda. What's up, Helene?"

"Ain't nothing. I see your life is a never-ending roller-coaster ride. I heard about what happened last night," Helene commented.

"Now what?" Egypt asked exasperatedly.

"Your sister almost got killed last night."

"What the hell is she talking about, Yolara?"

Yolie really did not look forward to having to explain the events to Egypt. She knew she would tell Meshach. "Someone took a couple of shots at BulletProof while I was talking to him outside Kaliq's house."

"Damn, is he dead?" she asked her sister.

"No, thankfully. Chances are he will never walk again."

"Well, I hate to say it, but he asked for it. You know he was down with La-Rone. La-Rone is the one that supposedly shot Rahmel. Rahmel is still on life support," Helene added.

"What?" Yolie asked in disbelief.

"Yeah, girl. Now we see he ain't bulletproof after all."

"Egypt, please don't mention any of this to Daddy," she pleaded.

"Now, Yolie, you know he's gonna find out about this shit."

"Maybe not; he's way over there by Flatbush Depot. I just don't want him to get upset."

"Get upset? You're his damn daughter. He has a right to get upset." Egypt had said the words before she knew it. There were times when she really chose not to think of Yolie as Meshach's daughter. Suddenly, she realized how foolish that was. "All right, I know he will hear about it sooner or later, but he won't hear about it from me."

"Thanks, E. I won't forget that. I've got to get upstairs and find out how much my mother knows."

Egypt and Helene watched Yolie run into the building. "Never a dull moment with that one."

"Yeah, little sister's a mess. Dad won't have time to worry about me; he'll have his hands full with her."

The elevator was out again and Yolie was winded by the time she reached the sixth floor. She fumbled for her keys, but Cari opened the door before she could get them out. "Thanks, Mommy," she said sheepishly.

"You know, *mija*, I'm about at my wits end with you. It's bad enough you didn't come home last night, but Gloria just told me about what happened to Kaliq's cousin and you last night. I called over there right away, but Kaliq said you had left. Then I chewed him out for not calling me to tell me. You should have known better, Yolara."

"I didn't want to worry you, Mommy. I'm okay, really. See?"

"That's besides the point. You and Kaliq have some kind of secret life over there. What else are you keeping from me? You know Burk has got to be told."

"Why? I'm fine," she asked, already knowing the answer.

"*Gracias a dios*. Come on, how would you feel if I was almost gunned down and no one told you," Cari reasoned as tears came to her eyes.

"You know if anything had happened to me or the boys, we would have called right away," Yolie said as she put her arms around her mother.

"I'm not so sure these days. I feel like Kaliq is taking all three of you away from me. The boys love spending more time over there than over here. You are gone for days at a time. Your father keeps hounding me. I'm coming unglued here."

Yolie was not used to seeing this vulnerable side of her mother. "Mommy, Kaliq would never do anything to hurt you. He cares about you."

"I need to get out of the house. Are you down for some breakfast with your old lady?" Cari tried to smile.

"Anytime," Yolara assured her with another hug.

CHAPTER 39

Meshach cursed the yard dispatcher under his breath. He had sent him to pull out a bus from the lot outside. The bus had been roasting in the sun and it took several minutes to let all the hot air out. He was doing his mandatory inspection of the bus when he heard Sommers calling his name.

"Yo, man. How is your daughter? We had just made the decision to take Rahmel off life support when we heard about that boy BulletProof."

"What the hell are you talking about?"

"Man, last night some of Rahmel's friends went after BulletProof and La-Rone. They couldn't find La-Rone's punk ass, but they got the other one while he was talking to your daughter, Yolie. She wasn't hit or anything, but I'd imagine she'd be a little shook up."

Meshach immediately went back to the depot and told them he was pulling sick. They threatened him with a violation, but he quietly explained the situation to the crew dispatcher and they worked it out.

He was so angry that he literally burnt rubber peeling away from his parking space. He was just about fed up with being left in the dark. How could Yolie and Cari be so thoughtless? Well, he was going to get to the bottom of all of it.

He made it to Bed-Stuy in record time. Meshach didn't give a second thought to the chance he was taking with his license. He cursed again when he found the elevator out of order—again. He fumed when no one answered the door. He took the stairs two at a time as he raced back downstairs. He would deal with Kaliq next.

***

Cari and Yolie had decided to have breakfast at their favorite cuchifritos spot. "It's been a long time since we've done this. I miss you, Yolie."

"I guess I didn't think that you'd feel this way; that I was causing a situation."

"You can't think of anything else but Kaliq! I know how it is, daughter dear. I haven't exactly been a winner in the romance department myself, but trust me."

"Why don't you give poor Daddy another shot? You know he would jump through hoops to drink your bath water," Yolie teased her mother.

"You got some mouth! I don't know, *mija*." Cari paused. "Since we're telling all this morning, I should mention the date I went on last night."

"Really? With whom?" she asked excitedly.

After another short pause, Cari told her. "A really nice girl I know from the gym."

Yolie was a little surprised, but she took her mother's hand. "So tell me, is she hot?"

Cari breathed a heavy sigh of relief. "Yes, she's very hot. We had a nice time. I don't know where it will lead, but I've got to see."

"Gee, that's kind of how I feel about Kaliq."

Cari smirked at her daughter. "Pass the coffee, smarty."

***

Meshach was still in a rage. He parked haphazardly in front of Kaliq's house. He banged on the door. Kaliq came to the door and opened it when he saw Yolie's father.

"What's up? Come on in," Kaliq said.

Meshach looked past him and saw the twins playing on the living-room

212

floor. "I need to talk to you and I think I had better say it out here. I don't want to scare the children."

"What do you mean scare the children? What exactly do you have to talk to me about?"

"Look, we got to get some things straight," Meshach insisted.

"Well, come into the house and we can talk about it like the grown men we are," he repeated, stepping aside to allow him to enter. Kaliq could see the steam rising off the man.

"Hi!" the boys greeted in unison.

Meshach ignored them. "Ah, little men. Why don't y'all take this stuff out back? I've got to discuss something with Mr. B.," Kaliq instructed.

The children did as they were told. "Now, do you mind telling me what's going on?" He watched as Meshach flexed his fist opened and closed.

"You know I could kill your fucking ass. I told you not to do anything to hurt my child."

Kaliq was starting to get the picture. "You heard about the shooting."

"Not from any of you people. You almost got Yolara shot to death."

"I understand how you must feel…"

"You don't understand shit."

Kaliq was starting to feel threatened. "You know I wouldn't…"

"No, I don't know shit."

"If you would stop interrupting me I could defend myself. You know how much I love Yolie. I've said it and I've proven it. Now, I wish last night hadn't happened, but I'd never let harm come to her again."

Before Kaliq realized it was coming, Meshach punched him squarely on the jaw. His face felt like it had caved in. He tried to balance himself and didn't see the second punch coming. He staggered again, but managed to charge Meshach from below. Kaliq grabbed him around the knees and brought him down. The two men were going blow for blow when Yolie and Cari came in.

"What the hell is going on?" Cari cried as she ran to help Yolie pull them apart.

"Motherfucker!" Meshach shouted.

"He's gone crazy," Kaliq said, wiping the blood from his lip.

"You the damned crazy one. And you," he growled as he turned to Cari. "Why didn't you tell me about Yolie nearly getting shot?'

Cari was silent. She knew there was no reasonable response. Yolie came to her defense. "I hadn't told her either, Daddy. I was okay. I didn't want you guys to get upset for nothing."

"For nothing?" Meshach asked incredulously. "I'm about tired of this little shit disrupting my life. First Cari and then you. He's dangerous." He pointed to Kaliq.

"Daddy, please calm down."

"I will not. Did you know he was the one who had your little girlfriend killed? Or maybe you were the one who asked him to set it up. I don't know where your head is anymore," Meshach accused Cari.

"What are you saying?" a stunned Cari asked.

"Word on the street is that good-for-nothing cousin of his shot that Rue chick. Why would he do that if this piece of shit didn't put him up to it? You *are* going to stop seeing my kid one way or another. You can do it on your own or I can end it for you," Meshach went back and forth between Cari and Kaliq.

"Man, what the hell are you talking about? I didn't have Dennis do any such thing. You must be out your mind."

Cari walked up to Kaliq. "You would tell me if you knew something, wouldn't you?" Kaliq hesitated for a moment. "Oh God."

"Cari, I wouldn't do anything like that. Trust me."

"I used to trust you. Yolie was just trying to assure me there was nothing to worry about. Now this."

Kaliq looked to Yolie for help. "Mommy feels like I've been spending too much time over here."

"She's practically moved in," Cari said.

"More shit. I don't believe you people. Is there anything else I don't know?" Meshach barked.

"Daddy, I'm old enough to…"

"I ain't trying to hear that, Yolara."

"And why not? I'm an adult now."

"You haven't been acting like an adult. You've been behaving like a love-sick teen," Cari added.

"Mommy, you are just feeling insecure. Kaliq is not trying to take me and the boys away from you. I thought maybe you would have welcomed the time and space to figure out who and what you are," Yolie responded testily.

"And what is that all about? You disrespecting your mother now?" Meshach asked.

"Ah come on, Daddy. You talk about my relationship; what about yours? You know I just asked Mommy why she doesn't give you a shot and now I guess I see why."

"You watch your mouth, girl."

"Why should I? She shouldn't have to give you a *second* chance. You should have stepped up to the plate a long time ago," Yolie argued.

"I take care of mine," Kaliq said. "You have a hell of a nerve coming out your face about anything."

Cari plopped on the sofa not willing to stop the tears. "I can't deal with this."

Kaliq sat down beside her. "No matter what else is in dispute, you've got to believe I didn't have Rue killed."

Yolie continued to stand up to her father. "Aren't you man enough to keep her away from women? She's turned to another one already."

Meshach went to slap his daughter across the mouth. He stopped himself and stepped back. "I'm sorry, baby…"

Yolie joined her mother and Kaliq on the sofa. "You didn't have to say that, *mija*."

"I'm sorry. I'm just burnt. Family is not supposed to carry on this way."

"What is she talking about? You've 'turned to another one?'" Cari didn't answer him. "Damn, Cari, not again."

No one said anything more for a long while. Each was lost in his or her own train of thought—brooding over the hurtful things that had been said.

The boys broke the silence as they burst back into the room. "Mommy!"

They jumped onto her lap and hugged her neck. Cari tried to sniff back the tears so they wouldn't see that she had been crying.

"I'm outta here. The kids don't need to be as screwed up as we are," Meshach commented as he headed for the door. He was a little hurt that no one had tried to stop him.

Yolie buried her head in Kaliq's lap. She felt drained. "How did we get here?"

CHAPTER 40

Yolie felt a little out of sorts. She hadn't heard from her father all week. They hadn't spoken since the confrontation at Kaliq's. Kaliq had finally gotten Cari to believe without a doubt that he hadn't been involved with the shooting. He had denied knowing if Bullet Proof was involved. Later, he admitted to Yolie he had wondered if the drive-by was connected to B.P.'s sudden move down South. At the time he had been ashamed of the suspicion.

Yolie had apologized to her mother for her own behavior. After a day or so, everything seemed to be pretty much okay—except for Meshach. She had called and left a couple of messages on his machine. He hadn't returned them. Yesterday she had stopped by his apartment, but he wasn't there either. She had made up her mind to go find him.

She still remembered how to get to the house Meshach had lived in with his married family. It was a pretty little house that looked more or less like the ones lined up on either side of it. His jeep was not in the driveway; Yolie hadn't really expected to see it there anyhow. The bell couldn't be heard from the outside so she wasn't sure if it was working. She was about to try again when an attractive black woman opened the door.

"Yes, can I help you?"

"Hi. I was looking for Egypt. Is she at home?"

"Yeah, she's upstairs packing. I'm her mother, Olive. Which one of her friends are you?"

"I'm Yolara, Mrs. Burkette."

Yolie could see a cloud come over Olive's face. For several seconds she seemed at a loss for words. "Go on up. Egypt's room is the first door at the top of the stairs," she finally said.

"Ma, who was…" Egypt was stunned to look up and find her sister standing in the doorway.

"Hi, Egypt."

"Uh, hi. What are you doing here?"

"I've been trying to get in touch with Daddy. Have you seen or heard from him?"

"As a matter of fact I haven't. Why? What happened now?"

"We had a big argument the other day and I haven't talked to him since." Yolie tried not to look around the room, but she was curious. So many times she had daydreamed about living in this very house. It wasn't the girly type of room she had imagined. Egypt had very modern tastes. The furniture was Italian lacquer. The bed had a brass headboard. The bedding and curtains had an afrocentric design that was very appealing.

"I expect to see him soon. I leave for Atlanta in a couple of days."

"Yeah, Daddy told me you are going to Spelman. Good luck down there."

"Thank you." Yolie turned down the cigarette Egee had offered her. "You're going to college, too, right?"

"Yeah, CCNY. I can't wait. Kaliq is gonna show me the ropes, but it would be nice to have a girlfriend to hang out with there. None of my friends are going to City."

"Don't worry; you'll be all right." Egee blew a smoke ring into the air. "I guess if you're looking for him, Daddy's not hooked up with your mother after all."

Yolie sucked her teeth. Egypt went on. "I didn't mean that as a dig. Well, maybe I did. A little. I'm sorry, Yolie, but this is kinda weird."

"Yeah, I know. We're still sisters. Can't we have a civil conversation if nothing else?"

"I used to want a little sister until I realized I wouldn't be the only child then," Egypt commented, trying to joke. "I'm making an attempt to be adult about this. It's really stupid to act up about it now." She could see the relief on Yolie's face. "What did my mother say?"

"I was afraid for her for a second," Yolie joked in return.

"Man, she must have wanted to flip her wig! You don't know. I love her to death, but she can be such a pill."

"You're lucky that you get to get out of the city," Yolie said as she read the awards that adorned her sister's walls.

"Well, I can't believe I'm gonna say this, but…you can come down with Daddy to visit one day—if you want. That's if you two patch things up."

"Oh, we will—whether he cooperates nicely or not. Thanks, Egee. Really."

"Well, I got a lot to do. I'll tell Daddy he'd better call you if I hear from him, okay?" Yolie stepped up to hug her sister. "Don't get carried away with yourself." Yolie embraced her anyhow.

She nearly walked into Olive on her way out the room. "I can see myself out. Take care."

"What was that all about?" Olive asked.

"Growing up."

CHAPTER 41

B.P. was improving a little each day. The doctors had determined that he would never walk again. Kaliq was caught between sympathy and rage. He had tried to steer his cousin in the right direction. It pained him to see B.P. connected to tubes and machines, but he was thankful that he was alive at all. Kaliq wondered what kind of life it would be. Eventually, the authorities would find out everything. B.P. had never been arrested for anything before; perhaps that would make a difference in court. Kaliq then wondered whom was he kidding. Even if he wasn't charged with both crimes by some miracle, one of the shootings was enough to send him away for a long time.

Kaliq was starting to nod off in the chair when he thought he heard his name being called. He sat up and saw B.P. was awake. "Well, it's about time."

"Yo, a nigga's tired. Getting shot wears you out," he answered groggily.

"Well, if a nigga didn't do things to get himself shot he wouldn't have to worry about it."

"Okay, all right. Yolie didn't get hurt, did she? Please tell me she didn't."

"No thanks to you. What the hell were you thinking about? I told you running with La-Rone…"

"Cuz, please. I know I fucked up."

Kaliq wasn't finished. "Okay, I know you were down with shooting Rahmel. That's obvious, too, as I'm sure it will be obvious to the cops. Rumor also has it that you were the one to off Cari's girlfriend. Is that true?"

"What you don't know can't hurt you, Kaliq."

"Dennis, I ain't going for that. Tell me, did you do it."

"I had been told that crazy bitch had beat on one of the kids as well as Cari. I couldn't let that go unpunished."

Kaliq was thrown off guard. "That's why? I guess I'm supposed to be thankful in some sort of warped way. She hadn't beaten either of the boys. They were fine. What about the Rahmel thing?"

"I didn't shoot him. I owed La-Rone for helping me out with the Rue chick. I just drove his jeep like he had done for me."

"You know they took Rahmel off life support? That makes it murder."

"Oh shit."

"Yeah, oh shit," Kaliq agreed. "What have you done to yourself?"

Both cousins tried not to cry; neither was successful.

"I know I'm never gonna stand on my own two feet again," B.P. groaned. "I can't feel nothing in my legs. I guess you think I deserve it, huh. You tried to tell me. Well, if I can't walk, I can't cause more trouble so don't worry no more."

The two sat in silence for a long moment. "You need anything?"

"Nah, man. Just…Can you come back tomorrow?"

"Most def, little cuz," Kaliq said as he kissed his forehead. "And no, I don't think you deserve this."

***

Kaliq was still upset about his visit with B.P. He walked into his house expecting Yolie to be there. He became even more upset that she wasn't. He knew he monopolized a lot of her time, but she was his woman, his family. If he couldn't be with her, what was the point? He amazed himself sometimes when it came to his love for her.

He was headed for the kitchen when the phone rang. "Hello?'

"Hi, babe. It's me."

"Where are you? I miss you."

"Well, I'm still trying to track down Daddy. I even stopped by my sister's house, but she hadn't heard from him either."

"I think he's just laying low. Nothing to worry about."

"Well, I'd like to know that for sure. He's never been out of touch for more than a couple of days."

"I can help you if you need me to."

"No, I'll see you in a little while. Love you."

"Love you, too."

Yolie didn't know where to look next. She was about to give up. No one could say she hadn't tried. She had taken the train to Flatbush, but decided on the bus for the ride back. She joined the crowd at the bus stop just as the bus was pulling up to the curb. She immediately noticed her father behind the wheel. Yolie knew he had seen her, too.

She allowed an elderly man to board ahead of her. "Hi," she said as she stepped onto the bus.

"Hi, baby. How are you?"

"How do you think I'm doing? I've been trying to call you. I even went by your old house to talk to Egypt."

He lifted an eyebrow in surprise. "You did?"

"Yeah and see, she didn't strangle me. Now if me and her can get along…"

"This isn't the place to get into it."

"Well, if you had returned my calls we could have straightened this out days ago. I'm sorry for what happened."

He looked around uneasily. "You can't side with Kaliq over me. That's not right."

"It's not about taking sides. I was angry and upset. It was a matter of time before I blew up at you. We are humans in a less than perfect situation. That doesn't mean I don't love you."

Yolie could hear the two ladies in the opposite seats clucking their tongues. "He's old enough to be her father," one commented to the other.

"Well, I'm sorry for what I almost did to you," he whispered, hoping she had gotten the drift. "You know I didn't mean that."

"No, I know I sort of goaded you. Can we go back to the way things were?"

Meshach looked over at his beautiful daughter. She was so special, his heart nearly burst with pride. Sitting there she reminded him of Cari. He knew things would never be the way he wanted with her mother. The least he could do was salvage his relationship with Yolara. "No. Things need to be better than they were. I'm still not feeling Kaliq right now, but I know he's the moon and the stars to you. For right now."

"Daddy! Don't start none won't be none." She smiled.

"Now tell me, how did things go at Egypt's?"

"I thought your wife was gonna have a coronary, but Egee surprised me. She said that I could come with you to Atlanta to visit her."

"Stop! You gonna make me crash this bus."

"I'm telling you, that's what she said."

"Well, maybe life's not all bad then."

Yolie rode with her father back and forth for the remainder of his run. They talked and managed to laugh. She went back with him to the depot. "Are you going to Kaliq's or your house?"

Yolie wasn't sure how to answer. "Home, I guess."

"I was kinda hoping you'd say Kaliq's."

"What?"

"I don't want to run into Cari."

"Oh, you big chicken," she tried to tease.

"I'm giving up on there ever being an *us*. I still want your mother and I imagine that I always will, but I can't keep waiting for something I'm sure she doesn't want."

"I hate to say it, but I don't blame you. I'm sorry about that, too."

He went around to the passenger side to open the jeep door for her. "Have you seen this new woman she's dating?"

"No, but I haven't been around much," Yolie answered with a twinge of guilt. "I don't think they are in the relationship stage. I think Mommy's just testing the waters to see if she wants to swim."

"Huh? Did that make sense what you just said?"

"Oh, just drive!"

***

Cari felt good. She, Yolie and Kaliq had straightened out a lot of things. It helped to talk about everything. Cari really did love Kaliq. She knew he would never intentionally hurt her, Yolie or the boys. The more she saw them together the more she realized it. She was a little envious, too. Cari was hopeful that Meshach had finally given up. She didn't like the fact that he hadn't called Yolie in days, but she knew her ex. He'd come around. He needed some time to gather his senses. And he would because she knew he didn't want to lose his daughter the way he had lost her.

Cari checked herself in the mirror one last time. She had to admit she looked hot. Astrid had invited her to a formal dinner party that her parents were giving. Cari had wondered if that was a good idea. Astrid had insisted and Cari finally gave in.

The pale-yellow cocktail dress was sensational. Her tan skin had darkened even more during the summer months and the effect was dazzling. She chose to wear her hair in an elegant chignon. Her slingbacks were classy. She borrowed Idalia's Prada bag for the occasion. Cari was adding the finishing touches to her lipstick. The phone rang as she glanced at her watch.

"Hello?"

"Hi. It's Astrid. I'm downstairs in the car. Are you ready?"

"Yeah, I am. I'll be right down."

Cari expected catcalls and she was not disappointed. She waved at friends and neighbors as she made her way to Astrid's car.

"My God, you are a vision, Cari. Oh, I'm feeling lucky tonight."

"Hey, you just might be," Cari said coyly. "You just might be."

CHAPTER 42

K aliq was glad that he had been able to save up enough money to finally get a used car. It was only a few years old and he had gotten a really good deal on it. Burk had taken him to his mechanic to have it checked out. They weren't father and son close, but they were getting along again. To be on the safe side, neither he nor Yolie had told him they were taking a ride upstate to visit Dennis.

It was still a sore subject so they tried not to bring it up around Meshach. Yolie insisted that they visit him, though. "It's Thanksgiving week and if he hadn't shielded me I could have been in that wheelchair instead of him. I owe him more than thanks."

Kaliq didn't want to debate that issue. Besides, he wanted to see his cousin. He had been charged as an accomplice to Rahmel's murder. The detectives had never come up with any substantial proof that it had been Dennis who had killed Rue. Someone had tipped them off looking for reward money, but nothing had ever come of it. Dennis tried to make light of it, but Kaliq knew his cousin was scared. All he could do was try to be there for him—as always.

It had been a four-hour drive up to the correctional facility. Yolie had offered to take over the wheel for the trip home, but she was wiped out. Kaliq looked at her lovingly as she slept. They had been through a great deal together. He knew with Yolara there would be few dull moments. He looked forward to all that life with her had to offer.

He was glad that Yolie was still asleep when they pulled up to his house. Kaliq didn't want her to notice her father's jeep parked across the street. "We're home, sleeping beauty," he said as he nudged her awake.

"Oh, I'm sorry, babe. I wanted to drive for you," she answered as she stretched and yawned.

"That's all right. I wasn't tired." He helped her out the car. "Yolara, you do love me, right?"

She looked at her man with obvious joy. "Now what kind of stupid question is that? Let's go inside and I'll show you how much I love you."

She fumbled with the keys. She felt along the wall for the nearest light.

"Surprise!"

Kaliq laughed as Yolie practically jumped into his arms. "What's going on?"

He took Yolie's hand and pulled her into the center of the living room. They were surrounded by her parents, his sisters and all their friends. "Yolara, I know life with me so far hasn't always been an easy thing. It is a testament to your strength that you have put up with me this long. I can only pray that you will never get tired of the ride. My mother told me we are not promised tomorrow so we have to live for today. Today is the day I want to ask you to be my partner in love and in life."

Yolie was stunned. She glanced over at her parents. Cari smiled as she wiped a tear from her eye. Astrid was beside her rubbing her shoulder. Meshach nodded his head in approval.

Kaliq knelt down on one knee. Travis handed his father a velvet ring box. Yolie gave a small gasp as she gazed down at the ring. "I would feel so blessed if you would consent to be my wife and wear my Nana's ring." He slipped the diamond and emerald ring onto her finger. Those in the room held their collective breath as they waited for her answer.

"Yes. Yes, I'll marry you," Yolie finally managed to get out.

A cheer went up. "Like we thought she would say no," her godmother Idalia joked.

Everyone hugged and kissed the couple. "Someone turn on the music."

After accepting congratulations from their guests, Yolie pulled her family to the side. "Daddy, I can hardly believe you were down with this."

"Well, baby, your mother told me that you two were gonna be together regardless of my opinion. It was a choice of either being there for you or watching from the sidelines. Your happiness is all I'm after. So you've got my blessings." Meshach finished by extending his hand to Kaliq. The two shared a firm handshake.

"Thank you, man. Cari told me that's what you had said, but I wouldn't believe it until I heard it for myself."

"Well, don't get me wrong; I hope y'all wait a while before jumping the broom. Yolie's still young. By the way, Egypt asked me to send you her best wishes."

Yolara beamed from ear to ear. "Thanks, Daddy."

"Well, I've got to make my contribution to the festivities," Cari said. "Kaliq, I've decided that we should share joint custody of the twins. You have been an exceptional father and I want you to be an equal parent in every way possible. I have to admit I didn't always feel that way. I wanted to stay *the* parent, if you know what I mean. But my boys are more important and it is to their benefit. So whenever you are ready, we can go to court."

It was Kaliq's turn to stand stunned. "Wow. That is the best present you could have given me." He wrapped his arms around his children's mother.

"Okay, enough of this hokey shit. Let me at those turntables," Meshach said.

A couple of Kaliq's boys pulled back the rug so people could dance. There was laughter and love to spare. Yolie held her hand up to the light to examine her new ring. "Yolara Flores-Burkette Nichols."

"Well, that's a mouthful, baby," Kaliq told her, leading her into a corner.

"But don't it sound good? Come here, you."

Their family and friends danced joyously to Meshach's music. Yolie and Kaliq held each other tightly in a slow drag that would last the rest of their lives.